Praise for
THE GIRL WITH NO NAME

"A total rollercoaster ride of emotions...intense, full of action, and had plenty of twists...a bloody good read!"
—Bonnie's Book Talk

"What a fantastic story and rollercoaster ride that was...It knocks the breath out of you!" —Ginger Book Geek

"Fast paced and full of punches all the way through...twisted and turned so much it left me gasping for breath."
—Stardust Book Reviews

"I could not put it down! Seriously, I was hooked from page one. Reading this was like being on an emotional rollercoaster ride!"
—Open Book Post

Praise for
VANISHING GIRLS

"Anyone who knows me gets that I really like a strong, female, kickass main character, and that's exactly what I got in Josie Quinn...The plot motors along at breakneck speed, often leaving me holding my breath. I'll be waiting impatiently for the next installment."

—Angela Marsons, #1 bestselling author
of *Silent Scream*

"Five BIG stars!!!!...This book is brilliantly paced...had me from the very first page, and I could not put this book down."
—Open Book Post

THE GIRL
WITH NO
NAME

ALSO BY LISA REGAN

Books featuring Detective Josie Quinn

Vanishing Girls
The Girl With No Name
Her Mother's Grave
Her Final Confession
The Bones She Buried

Books featuring Claire Fletcher and Detective Parks

Finding Claire Fletcher
Losing Leah Holloway

Books featuring Jocelyn Rush

Hold Still
Cold Blooded

Other books by Lisa Regan

Kill For You

THE GIRL WITH NO NAME

LISA REGAN

GRAND CENTRAL
PUBLISHING

NEW YORK   BOSTON

Copyright © 2018 by Lisa Regan
Cover design by GHOST. Cover photos by Shutterstock.
Cover copyright © 2021 by Hachette Book Group, Inc.

Grand Central Publishing
Hachette Book Group
1290 Avenue of the Americas, New York, NY 10104
grandcentralpublishing.com
twitter.com/grandcentralpub

Originally published in 2018 by Bookouture, an imprint of StoryFire Ltd.
First Grand Central Publishing mass market edition: February 2021

Grand Central Publishing is a division of Hachette Book Group, Inc. The Grand Central Publishing name and logo is a trademark of Hachette Book Group, Inc.

The publisher is not responsible for websites (or their content) that are not owned by the publisher.

The Hachette Speakers Bureau provides a wide range of authors for speaking events. To find out more, go to www.hachettespeakersbureau.com or call (866) 376-6591.

Library of Congress Control Number: 2019956959

ISBN: 978-1-5387-0122-5 (mass market)

Printed in the United States of America

CW

10 9 8 7 6 5 4 3 2 1

For my brother, Kevin Brock,
for showing me what it means to finish the fight

CHAPTER 1

NEWS 5—Akron, Ohio

October 27, 2016

Local Teen Dies in Hit and Run

A nineteen-year-old boy died tonight after being fatally struck by a hit-and-run driver in Highland Square. The teenager was found in the street just after 5 a.m. by a resident walking his dog. He was transported to Akron General Medical Center where he was later pronounced dead. His name has not been released pending notification of his family. There were no surveillance cameras near the intersection where the hit and run occurred. Police are urging anyone with information to come forward.

CHAPTER 2

MONDAY

The television blared from her living room. Josie could hear it from her bedroom on the second floor of the house, even with the door closed. As the first notes of the theme song of WYEP— the local news station—drifted up she sighed, gathered up the wedding magazines on her nightstand and headed downstairs.

Her fiancé, Luke, was sprawled on her couch, his tall, muscular frame taking up almost the entire space. A foam takeout container straddled his lap, and from it he shoveled French fries into his mouth. Both feet rested on her coffee table, almost touching the stack of mock wedding invitations she'd been trying to get him to look at for the last two weeks. His eyes were glued to the television where the twelve o'clock news broadcast nonstop coverage of the Interstate Killer's trial, which had started that morning.

"Luke, can you please turn that down a bit?"

He didn't even look at her. Josie put the stack of magazines onto the coffee table and sat down next to him, her thigh brushing his. He still didn't look away from the television. On the screen, reporter Trinity Payne stood outside the Alcott County Courthouse, the breeze lifting her dark hair as she spoke confidently into her microphone. "Opening arguments in the trial of the Interstate Killer, Aaron King, were scheduled to begin this morning. However, King reportedly fell in his cell just a few hours ago, splitting his lip on the sink. Prison officials tell us he required several stitches."

Luke snorted and popped another fry into his mouth. "Fell. I'll bet he fell."

"My money's on the guards," Josie said, trying to engage him—the King case was one of his favorite topics of conversation lately—but Luke seemed not to hear her. She looked around. "Did you get me a cheeseburger?" she asked.

No answer. From the depths of the cushions, he produced the remote control, using it to turn the volume up even louder.

"Luke?" Josie said, but he dismissed her with a wave of his hand.

Blue eyes flashing from the screen, Trinity Payne went on, "Aaron King is believed to be responsible for up to thirty murders in the state of Pennsylvania in the last four years, although investigators have only been able to link his DNA to eight of those murders, the most recent of which happened right here in Alcott County."

"Should have been my stop," Luke said under his breath.

It was a familiar refrain. A year earlier, the Interstate Killer had been caught by a state trooper who had pulled him over for a routine stop. King had been speeding along Route 80 in central Pennsylvania, down a stretch of highway that Luke usually patrolled. That night he had traded shifts with a coworker so he could go to dinner with Josie and her grandmother, Lisette, to celebrate Lisette's birthday. Luke's colleague had taken all the glory and fanfare for the capture of the serial killer who had terrorized the state for nearly four years.

"I'm glad it wasn't your stop. You could have been killed," Josie pointed out, gently squeezing his thigh. His knee jerked away from her touch.

Her hand recoiled, and she felt the familiar sting of tears behind her eyes and blinked them back. She shouldn't feel rejected—this had been going on for months now—but she did.

"Luke," Josie said, taking the remote from his hand and turning the volume down.

"Hey," he protested, sparing her a glance for the first time that day.

She forced a smile. "I thought we were going to spend some time together today. Just you and me. No work, no distractions."

"I'm right here," he said.

No, you're not, she thought. His gaze had already traveled back to the television.

She picked up a mock-up of their wedding invitation from the coffee table. "I thought we could talk about the wedding. Your sister sent these for us to look over."

"Really?" he snapped.

"Oh, well, we don't have to use any of the invitations Carrieann sent. We can probably find others online. I'll get my laptop."

"Please, Josie, not now."

Josie stared at him, her body stiffening. "Oh, okay. Well, maybe we could—"

"Look, I just wanted to relax today, okay?"

"Oh, sure, yeah," Josie agreed. "We haven't had much time to relax together lately, have we?" Her duties as Denton's chief of police took up far more time than she had ever anticipated. She lived in a constant state of guilt. She knew that most of what he was struggling with had nothing to do with her, but she couldn't shake the feeling that if she had more time for him, maybe he wouldn't be drifting away from her more and more each day.

She pushed closer to him, leaning into his side, but he shifted away from her, his fingers scrabbling along the bottom of his takeout container for the last of his fries. He tossed the empty box onto the other side of the couch and Josie raised an eyebrow. "Would you like me to throw that away for you?" she asked pointedly.

"I got you a burger," he said, as if he hadn't heard a single word she'd said in the last five minutes. "It's in the kitchen." He motioned to the television. "Shh. They're bringing him into the courthouse."

With a heavy sigh, Josie turned her gaze back to the screen. She heard Luke's barely audible groan as the sheriff's deputies led King from the car to the courthouse with a jacket over his head. "They don't want to show how bad his lip looks," Luke said.

For the benefit of the viewing public, WYEP flashed King's mug shot across the screen. King was young, only twenty-three, with pasty skin, unruly brown hair, and a scraggly, wild beard. He had a long, narrow nose that hooked slightly at the end and dark eyes that seemed to penetrate right through the camera. Every time she saw his photo, it gave her the creeps. She was glad Luke hadn't been the one to stop him; King had gone after the trooper who had made the stop with a machete, a fact that Luke overlooked each time he bemoaned his horrible luck in not having been there.

By Josie's estimation, Luke had had enough trauma to last a lifetime without adding a machete attack to the list. A year and a half earlier he'd been shot and nearly killed helping Josie solve a string of disappearances of teenage girls in her town.

But that wasn't the thing that had turned him from a loving, good-humored, passionate fiancé into the apathetic stranger before her. Four months earlier he had gone around to his friend Brady's house to watch an NHL playoff game to find that Brady had shot his wife, Eva, and himself in a murder-suicide. The Conways had lived in the small town of Bowersville, out of Josie's jurisdiction, so she hadn't seen the aftermath of the crime, but Luke hadn't been the same since. It was like Brady Conway had taken a part of Luke with him when he shot his wife and himself, and Josie wasn't sure she would ever get it back. Try as she might, she couldn't seem to reach him anymore. Each day brought a new degree of distance and a new level of sadness and uncertainty for Josie.

"A real live serial killer," Luke said. "I could have had that arrest. How many people can say they arrested a serial killer?"

Josie could. "It's not all it's cracked up to be," she said. She picked up the remote once more and turned the television off. "Luke, we have this time together today. I really thought we could—"

He sat up straight, color flooding his face. "Hey, I was watching that."

He plucked the remote out of her hand and turned the television back on, blasting the volume once more.

Josie said, "Luke, I'm trying to have a conversation with you."

His eyes remained glued to the screen. "About what?"

"Whatever you want to talk about."

His gaze swept over the coffee table and then he met her eyes. "Please, Josie, I'm tired."

She was about to reply, but he was already engrossed in the WYEP broadcast again; a million miles from her even though there were only a few inches between their bodies. Not for the first time, she wondered what had happened to him. His tenderness, his innate sense of chivalry, and his absolute normalcy were the things that had drawn her to him. She knew these bouts of coldness were not really about her. She understood that. But she wasn't sure how many more of them she could take.

She had suggested he get counseling; he clearly hadn't processed what had happened to his friends and she suspected that he blamed himself. If he had arrived a few minutes earlier, maybe he would have been able to prevent the whole thing.

Her cell phone rang into the cold silence between them and both their heads turned in the direction of the sound—she had left it on the foyer table. "I have to get that," she said quietly.

Crossing the room, she snatched the phone up and pressed it to her ear. "This is Josie." It was Lieutenant Noah Fraley, her second-in-command.

"Boss," said Noah. "We have a situation. I think you need to come and meet me right now."

She didn't ask why. She simply said, "Okay," and listened as Noah rattled off an address she knew she should recognize, but that wouldn't come to her in that moment. She hung up and grabbed her jacket from the closet.

"Josie?" Luke called from the living room.

"I have to go to work," she said.

CHAPTER 3

She hadn't realized just how tightly knotted the muscles in her shoulder blades were until she was a mile away from home and her body finally started to relax. She knew she shouldn't hide behind her work, but it was the only place she felt in control. But her relief quickly dissipated as she arrived at the address Noah had rattled off and suddenly realized why it had seemed so familiar to her.

Noah stood outside of the large Victorian, a grim, fixed look on his face and a Denton PD patrol officer with a clipboard guarding the front door by his side. "We've got a crime scene?" Josie asked.

Noah nodded.

"Have you set up a perimeter?"

"Yes. I've got someone on the back door as well. All points of entry are covered."

"Is she—is she dead?"

Josie honestly didn't know how she would feel if Noah told her that Misty Derossi was dead. It was no secret that Josie detested her; ever since she caught her late husband, Ray, sleeping with the notoriously promiscuous stripper, she'd found it difficult, but after Ray confessed he'd fallen in love with her, well, that changed everything.

"No," Noah said. "At least, not yet. EMTs already rushed her to the hospital. I've got a man following to report on her condition. A neighbor found her unconscious. An older woman who lives next door hadn't seen Misty coming or going for a few days and came to check on her. She knocked and got no answer, so she went around to the back and said she found the back door partially open. She came inside and that's when she found Misty unconscious on the living room floor. Then she called 911. Misty was beaten pretty badly. Most of the house is undisturbed but the living room is a mess. You'll see."

Josie stilled her mind for a moment, resetting herself to put her personal feelings aside and treat this like any other case. She stepped past Noah, and he followed her as she nodded to the patrol officer and watched him record her name onto the crime scene log. Just inside the front door, one of their crime scene officers had set up a small supply area.

The city of Denton was roughly twenty-five square miles, many of those miles spanning the untamed mountains of central Pennsylvania with their one-lane winding roads, dense woods, and rural residences spread far and wide. With a population edging over thirty thousand, it wasn't big enough to have a crime scene unit, but they did have a small contingent of officers who were specially trained in evidence collection and scene preservation—an Evidence Response Team, or ERT.

At the supply station, Josie and Noah donned Tyvek suits with booties, skull caps, and latex gloves. "Have you got someone canvassing the neighbors?" Josie asked. "To see if anyone saw anything?"

"Yeah," Noah replied. "I've got two officers out now."

As she followed Noah deeper into Misty's home, she saw that he was right—the exquisitely furnished and carefully arranged rooms looked untouched. Josie and Noah had walked through this house once before, almost two years earlier, when Misty had gone missing after Ray's death. The place was filled with ornate antique furniture that looked as uncomfortable as it did fancy. Apparently dancing at the local strip club was extremely lucrative.

"Like I said, almost everything is in its place," Noah said as they moved down the first-floor hall.

"You said the neighbor found the back door ajar," Josie said. "Any signs of forced entry?"

Noah shook his head. "Nope. Either Misty left her back door unlocked or she let her attacker inside."

"Broken windows?"

"None."

"Misty's car?"

"Parked around the back of the house in her garage."

Noah stopped at the entrance to a living room near the back of the house. He waved a hand, indicating she should enter first. "You ready? Watch your step."

Josie swallowed a gasp as she entered the room. The once pristine living room looked as though a tornado had torn through it; the hardwood floor was covered in glass, wood splinters, and maimed pieces of furniture; the light-blue floral pattern of the area rug was splattered in blood; a few feet away, a small wooden coffee table lay splintered in half with a clump of blond hair hanging from the jaws of the broken wood. Josie counted three large lamps on their sides around her, shards of their hand-painted glass scattered around the room. One whole area of cream-colored wall to Josie's left was caved in where someone had been thrown against it so violently the drywall had buckled. Josie took a few more careful steps into the room, a small white object next to one of the evidence markers drawing her attention. She knelt and pointed to it.

"My God," she said. "Is that a tooth?"

She heard Noah take a breath. "Yeah," he said. "Paramedics said Misty was missing one of her top front teeth."

She tore her eyes away to survey the rest of the room and counted three of her officers at work. One dusted the walls and furniture for prints while another vacuumed fibers from the round area rug in the center of the room. The third officer followed the yellow plastic evidence markers that had been placed throughout the room, taking photographs of every detail. Clad in their white suits, just like Josie and Noah, all of them took slow and careful steps, as though walking across thin ice. They glanced up at her when they felt her watching.

"Boss," said the officer with the small, handheld vacuum.

She nodded at him and he moved from the area rug to a thick, white fleece blanket discarded on the floor. He pointed to it and the photographer picked her way over and snapped several pictures of it. Then the blanket was flattened and vacuumed for any hairs or fibers remaining on it. A bloody handprint marred its clean white surface—Misty's handprint, judging by the size of it.

Then something else caught Josie's gaze and she pointed to the item beside the couch.

"Noah, what the hell is that?"

CHAPTER 4

The infant bouncer chair was a soft gray with green-and-yellow pastel polka dots. It lay on its side and the mobile that normally hung from the U-shaped bar over the seat had been snapped off, its soft zoo animals sad and scattered across the floor. Beside the bouncer lay a small stuffed elephant and a crumpled green blanket just big enough to swaddle a newborn.

"There was a baby? She had a baby? Is it—?"

"The baby's not here," Noah said quickly.

That didn't quell the awful feeling of anxiety blooming in Josie's stomach.

"I didn't even know she was pregnant."

Noah nodded. "The neighbor said that Misty was due any day. Based on what we found in the upstairs bathroom, we believe she delivered the baby here at home. But there's no sign of it. We found a dog locked in the basement, barking up a storm. The neighbor said she'd care for it until things get sorted out."

"When did she deliver?"

"We don't know, but I think it was in the last day or two. The neighbor says she saw Misty four days ago and she was nearly due."

"You think she was alone when she delivered?"

"I don't think so. Come upstairs."

Josie followed Noah up the steps and he led her past a room that Misty had obviously prepared as a nursery. Josie glanced in; the walls were yellow with animals dancing across them;

the dresser, changing table, and crib all looked newly bought. If Misty had really given birth in the last twenty-four to forty-eight hours, she wouldn't have had a chance to use any of it.

Noah led her past the nursery to the master bedroom, and the first thing that hit Josie was the smell: stale sweat, a strange sweet smell that she couldn't place, and the faint coppery scent she knew to be blood. The room was a mess. The massive bed, couched in an ornately carved mahogany bed frame, was littered with crumpled towels and sheets, the bedspread tangled in a heap on the floor. Wadded towels, washcloths, and sheets made a trail into an adjoining bathroom, almost all of them covered in dried blood.

"We've processed this room already, so you can move freely," Noah told her.

Josie went to the master bathroom. "She had her baby here."

"Yeah," Noah said.

Josie didn't know much about childbirth, but she knew Misty must have had help.

"Where's her phone?" Josie asked.

"We haven't found it."

"Did the elderly neighbor see anyone coming or going? You interviewed the neighbors closest to her first thing, right?"

"I did. That was before I sent our guys out to canvass the entire street. I personally talked to the neighbors on either side of Misty's house."

"Did they see anyone? Perhaps carrying a baby? Any unusual vehicles?"

"No one saw anything," Noah said.

"We need to issue an Amber Alert for the baby immediately."

"Based on what?"

"This meets the criteria. Amber Alerts are to let the community know when a child under eighteen is missing or has been abducted and is in imminent danger. If a newborn baby is not here and it's not with its mother, then we need to treat this like an abduction. I'm not taking any risks, not with a newborn baby."

"Boss, we don't even know the sex."

"Then you need to find out. Someone should be talking to her ob-gyn. What about her best friend? The one who called us when she went missing last time?"

"I already have a call out to her," Noah told her. "I found an appointment card on the fridge for a local ob-gyn and sent Gretchen over to their office to see what she could find out."

"Good," Josie said.

Gretchen Palmer was the department's appointed detective. Josie had hired her shortly after she became chief of police and needed a detective to replace her. Gretchen was approaching forty and had worked as a detective in Philadelphia most of her career. She was seasoned and no-nonsense and a real asset to her team.

Noah frowned. "We have no photo, no vehicle, no witnesses."

"I know. It's not a lot to go on," Josie said. "Let's at least try to find out the sex as quickly as we can before we put out the alert. What about the father?"

"According to the neighbor, Misty wouldn't talk about him to anyone."

"So, it's possible that this is domestic, and the father has the baby," Josie said. "We need to find out who he is. We also need to work out who helped her deliver, and whether she was even planning a home birth."

"Boss? Lieutenant Fraley?" a voice from downstairs called. She recognized it as the officer standing sentry outside of the house. "Someone here to talk to you."

CHAPTER 5

Out on Misty's wrap-around porch, a woman in her mid-twenties paced, hugging herself tightly. She was dressed in dark-blue jeans that were rolled at the bottom and cuffed neatly above a pair of strappy sandals. On top, she wore a black sweater over a white T-shirt. Her skin had the deep orange hue of a spray-on tan, clashing with the jet-black hair that flowed down her back in waves. When she saw Josie and Noah she raced over to them, opening her arms as though she were about to embrace one or both of them, then pulled up short, wrapping her arms back around herself again instead.

"Can I help you?" Noah asked, pulling off his disposable head covering.

For a moment, the woman's eyes were drawn to Noah's thick brown locks. Josie had to admit, they looked even more expertly tousled after the removal of the cap than they had before he put it on.

"Ma'am?" Josie said.

She smiled uncertainly, her eyes darting briefly toward Josie. "My name is Brittney. Lieutenant Fraley called me. I'm Misty's best friend. Is she...is she okay?"

Noah pulled off his latex gloves and extended a hand, which Brittney shook. "That's me," he said. "Miss Derossi is alive but badly injured. She's at the hospital now. We don't have word on her condition yet, but a neighbor found her unconscious."

One of Brittney's hands flew to her mouth. "Oh my God. Is the baby okay?"

Noah looked at Josie. "Brittney," Josie said. "The baby is missing."

Brittney gasped. "What? What do you mean missing? She had the baby?"

"Do you know if Misty was going to have a boy or a girl?" Josie asked.

"A boy. Oh my God, where is he?"

Josie ignored the question, asking her own instead. "When is the last time you spoke to or saw Misty?"

Brittney touched a hand to her chest. "I don't know. Maybe four, five days ago? I travel for work, so I've been out of town. I told her I'd be back for her due date. I texted her a couple of times yesterday and the day before, but she didn't respond. I didn't think anything of it. Sometimes if she is tired or feeling really shitty, she'll take forever to return a text."

"When was her due date?" Josie asked.

"Tomorrow. I just got back today."

"What do you do?" Noah asked.

"I'm a sales rep for a pharmaceutical company. Wait—so, when did she have the baby?"

"Sometime in the last twenty-four to forty-eight hours by the look of her bathroom."

The color drained from Brittney's face. "Her bathroom?"

"She gave birth at home," Josie said. "Brittney, do you know—did she have a midwife lined up?"

Brittney resumed pacing before them. "No. No, she didn't. She was going to go to the hospital. I don't understand. She didn't call me. Who was here?"

"We were hoping you could help us with that," Noah said.

"Brittney," Josie said. "Did Misty tell you who the baby's father is?"

"No, it was a big secret. She wouldn't even tell me. No one knew. She said maybe she would tell me after the baby was born."

"Why would she keep it a secret?"

Brittney shrugged. "I don't know. I told her whoever it was, it wasn't a big deal—I mean, not to me. She was super sensitive about the whole thing. You know, she had an ectopic pregnancy when she was, like, twenty and it almost destroyed her insides. I was surprised she could even get pregnant, 'cause the doctors had told her she couldn't. When it happened it was like this big miracle. So, I was joking with her that I really wanted to know what man finally knocked her up, but she wouldn't say. She just said that there were some things she needed to get in order before she started telling people."

"Like what?" Josie asked.

"I don't know. It was weird, you know? She wouldn't even tell *me*. We've been friends since kindergarten. I pushed her a lot at first, but then it got to the point where every time I brought it up she'd get really upset, so I stopped."

Josie frowned. "Is it possible that her pregnancy was a result of a non-consensual encounter?"

Brittney stopped pacing and stared at Josie. "What? You mean like, rape?"

"Yes. Would she have told you?"

"I don't know. I mean she had some problems now and then with customers where she worked—you know she worked at Foxy Tails, right?"

"Yes," Noah said.

"Well, the guys there always got totally obsessed with her. I mean she was really good at her job. These dudes would come in night after night to watch her dance. She had a lot of regulars who would pay extra for private dances."

"She had relationships with several of those men, didn't she?" Josie asked pointedly, ignoring the look Noah shot her.

Brittney nodded. "Misty liked to play the field. I mean, there was one guy she was really serious about. Ray Quinn. He was a cop. Oh—" Brittney broke off and smiled awkwardly at them. "I guess you already knew that."

It occurred to Josie that Brittney had no idea who she was.

The two had never met, but Josie had been on television a lot in the last eighteen months in her capacity as chief of police. Just one of the things she loathed about her new position. Of course, with Josie's long dark hair beneath the cap she'd donned before entering the crime scene, Brittney probably didn't recognize her.

Josie said, "We knew Ray."

She felt Noah's eyes burning a hole through her profile but didn't look at him.

Brittney said, "Yeah, well, she was pretty serious about him. They were going to get married. She really wanted to settle down and always used to say that he was the kind of guy you would want to start a family with. He was, like, the love of her life. The one, you know?"

Josie felt a tiny stab just under her diaphragm. For a split second, the air was trapped in her throat and she couldn't get it out. She did know. She knew exactly because Ray had been the love of Josie's life. Her "one." Misty had been a blip on his romantic radar. They'd only dated for about a year after Josie and Ray's marriage broke up and Ray had never signed the divorce papers. Had refused to sign them, in fact. Not only that, but Josie knew by Misty's own admission that she had also been sleeping with Ray's best friend during that time.

Before Josie could point out that fact, Noah said, "Did she date anyone after Ray's death?"

Brittney shook her head. "Not that I know of—I mean, not seriously."

Josie put a hand on her hip. "We need to know who she was sleeping with after Ray passed."

Brittney stared at Josie, two circles of pink rising in her orange cheeks. "Oh, well, I can tell you a few of them..."

"A few of them?" Noah said, not quietly enough.

"Well, yeah, she...there were...Misty didn't have a serious boyfriend besides Ray, but she always had men, you know?"

"What do you mean, she had men?" Josie said.

Brittney shrugged. "Well, there were a lot of men interested in her. She likes the attention. Some of them she kind of felt bad for so, you know, she would have her flings. A lot of guys got obsessed with her, but she was never serious about them. You have to understand that Misty didn't consider a relationship to be monogamous unless she was married. That's why she planned to stop working and seeing everyone else after she married Ray."

"But she slept with married men," Josie said. "Is there a possibility that the father of the baby is married and that's why she thought people would judge her?"

Another shrug. "Well, I guess so, but I think she still would have told me. I mean I knew about most of the married guys she slept with so it's not like it would have been a big surprise if one of them was the father. She probably still would have told me."

Noah looked upward and Josie could see he was making calculations in his head. "She would have gotten pregnant sometime in December—probably the first week or two—can you think back to then? Do you remember her ever acting strangely? Or being upset, or withdrawn?"

Brittney touched her chin thoughtfully. "No. If anything, she seemed happy during that time. I remember thinking it was weird, you know, because it was near the holidays. The first Christmas without Ray and all? I thought she would be really depressed. I mean, I didn't really see her because I was away training for my job, but we texted and talked on the phone. I remember feeling relieved that she wasn't, like, suicidal. I mean I remember in high school she was ra—"

Brittney stopped abruptly.

"She was assaulted when you were in high school?" Josie coaxed.

Brittney's gaze dropped to the ground. "I shouldn't say anything. It's not my place to—she never wanted to talk about it. She told me, but that was it. She was a mess, though. For months after that."

"Did she report it?" Josie asked.

"No, no. It was a guy she was seeing, and she said that it would be his word against hers. She just didn't think anyone would take her seriously. She stopped seeing him after that, obviously. But she was messed up for a long time after. She didn't seem that way when she got pregnant. She was really happy about it."

"But she wouldn't talk about the father," Noah said. It wasn't a question.

Brittney shrugged. "I think she would have eventually, once she sorted out whatever needed sorting."

"We'll need those names," Josie told her. "Of the men she was seeing—everyone she saw since Ray's death, even guys she was seeing before Ray died."

Noah pulled out a notebook and wrote down the names as Brittney rattled them off. Some of them Josie recognized. "Get somebody to run down all of their alibis for the last forty-eight hours," Josie told Noah.

He nodded and looked back at Brittney. "Anyone else? Anything else you can think of that might be important? You mentioned the customers at Foxy Tails. Could one of them have been fixated enough on Misty to attack her?"

"I don't know. Anything's possible. I mean she's had some stalkers over the years for sure. None that have ever gotten violent, though. You should talk to her boss, Butch. He would know better than me."

"Of course," Noah said.

"One last thing," Josie said. "You said Misty knew she was having a boy. Did she have a name picked out?"

Brittney smiled. "Yeah. Victor Raymond. Cute, right?"

CHAPTER 6

Josie watched from the porch as Brittney pulled away in her old model Toyota Camry, heading to the hospital to sit by Misty's bedside. The name was bothering her. The Raymond part hurt, of course, but she had only ever known one Victor in her lifetime, and he'd been evil to the core. In fact, Victor Quinn had routinely beaten his wife while his young son hid under the kitchen table or behind the couch. Ray used to tell her that the amount of blood and guts he saw on the job couldn't hold a candle to what he'd seen in his own home before the age of thirteen.

Had Misty really named her baby after Ray's father? Not for the first time, Josie had the sense that Misty had somehow appropriated her life and was mismanaging it horribly.

"Boss?"

She looked away from Brittney's taillights to see Noah staring at her with a furrowed brow. Josie sighed. "Yes?"

"You want to ask for that Amber Alert now?"

"Yes. Immediately."

"You think it will do any good? With so little information?" he asked.

"There is always a chance that if we issue the alert, someone will notice a friend or family member who suddenly has a newborn child with them and call us. We can't take any chances with this. The Amber Alert is top priority. When we're done here, we'll head over to Foxy Tails and talk to the boss. Do you have Misty's cell phone number?"

Noah flipped through a few pages in his notepad and showed it to her. She keyed it into her own phone and called it, but was sent directly to voicemail. "Call the station, have someone there write up some warrants," Josie told Noah. "We'll find out where the phone last pinged, see if we can triangulate its location. Although, if I just stole someone's baby, I wouldn't be carrying around their phone."

"You're assuming we're dealing with someone smart," Noah said.

"Listen, I want someone going through Misty's personal effects. See if there is anything useful. Let's try not to damage anything, though. If the department has to pay to replace any of her furniture, it's going to get expensive."

As Noah nodded and started walking back toward the entrance of the house, a black Chevrolet Cruze pulled into Misty's driveway and Detective Gretchen Palmer hopped out, raising a hand in greeting as she approached. She was dressed in what Josie had come to think of as her uniform: black slacks with a white Denton PD polo shirt under a black leather jacket that had seen better days. It was a man's leather jacket and had been worn and scuffed over many years. Josie was certain there was a story there, but it wasn't her place to ask.

"Boss," Gretchen said, addressing Josie as she reached the top of the porch steps, her notebook already out. She pulled a pair of reading glasses from the inside of her jacket, slipped them on and ran a hand through her short, brown, spiked hair as she read off her findings. "Met with the ob-gyn. Derossi wasn't planning a home birth. Due date was tomorrow—she was having a boy—and they were going to induce her next week if she didn't go into labor on her own. In fact, she had an appointment she missed yesterday. She came to them about two months into her pregnancy. Everything was picture perfect. No complications. Baby healthy as can be. She never mentioned the father, and there was nothing on her chart. While I was there, I popped down to the emergency room. Miss Derossi's skull is fractured and there's some bleeding on the brain. They'll likely need to do surgery. She also has a missing tooth, a fractured wrist, and severe bruising on her forearms and on her throat. Looks like someone tried to choke her and she fought back pretty hard so our bad guy hit her over the head to knock her out and make his escape."

"Jesus," Josie said. "We have to find the baby. What else have you got?"

Gretchen flipped a page in her notebook. "They think the head injury was sustained within the last few hours. The docs also said she probably gave birth yesterday; she's still bleeding a lot and there's some tearing. Whoever was with her didn't sew her up. They'll do that at the hospital now, and they've already called for an ob-gyn consult."

Josie grimaced. "Is that typical? Do midwives usually stitch women up if they . . . tear during home births?"

Gretchen looked at her over top of her reading glasses. "Most midwives would, so long as the tear wasn't too complicated or deep."

"So, we can safely assume that whoever was here with her yesterday and helped her deliver her baby most likely wasn't professionally trained and didn't have Misty's safe recovery as a priority. If it was the same person, they let an entire day go by and then took her baby by force."

"Strange, isn't it?"

"Because why would you need to take the baby by force after all that? Why not just wait till the mom was asleep and sneak off with him?" Josie said, thinking aloud.

"You think there was another person."

"Yes. There was someone who helped her deliver the baby and someone else who took the baby. I don't think they are one and the same."

"Is it possible this person took the midwife with him?"

Josie shook her head. "I don't know. We're assuming it was a midwife. Maybe it wasn't. Maybe the person who helped her deliver was working with the person who took the baby—or maybe they're in trouble too. We don't have enough evidence to make an educated guess either way. But just to be safe, better check on all the trained midwives in Denton. There can't be that many."

Gretchen made a notation on her pad.

"Anything else?" Josie asked.

"Yeah: There were no issues with any of the testing done during Misty's pregnancy. From a cursory exam of Misty herself, she doesn't appear to have had a complicated birth. So, we should be looking for a healthy baby. As long as whoever took him takes care of him, he should be okay."

Josie shook her head. This was about as far from okay as it got.

CHAPTER 7

The search of Misty's home turned up little more, aside from an ornate antique desk with several locked drawers on each side, but no sign of a key. Noah suggested breaking into it but by the looks of it, having it fixed when Misty had recovered would cost more than the department's monthly gas budget. Instead, Josie had one of her officers call a locksmith to see if it could be opened with minimal damage. One of Josie's primary responsibilities as chief was keeping the department afloat financially. She no longer had the luxury of jumping into a case with the sole purpose of solving it; every decision had to be weighed against the department's budget constraints.

One of Josie's senior officers managed to find his way into Misty's laptop, but even that held little in the way of helpful information or leads on a suspect. They could see the sites she visited frequently—her banking site and email, which were useless without a password, Amazon, Babies "R" Us and a site called "Your Pregnancy Week by Week"—but none of that told them anything that would help locate her baby.

Josie hoped they'd get something from the prints taken at Misty's house, although that would take time as well, as they had to use the services of the state police for all fingerprint searches. It often took a few days, but Josie thought she might be able to convince them to expedite it, especially with such a fragile life at stake.

Josie felt a small thrill working alongside her officers at the crime scene, like she was just a detective again, not stuck behind a desk facing a mountain of paperwork. God, she missed this.

She was pulled away from her thoughts by the sudden buzzing, ringing and vibrating of cell phones all around her. The state police must have accepted the Amber Alert, thought Josie with relief. They were in charge of reviewing all Amber Alert requests and then issuing them once accepted. Now all Josie's team could do was wait.

She and Noah stepped outside, peeling off their suits. They had done all they could at Misty's house, gleaned as much information as they could without the kind of testing you could only expect from a lab. "I'll head over to Foxy Tails with you," she said.

Noah froze and stared at her. "You sure?"

The last time she'd been to the club had been the night that she caught Ray locked in a passionate embrace with Misty. It was common knowledge on the force, and Josie didn't want to set foot in the place ever again, but the buzz of being back in the field and the thought of Luke's cold reception waiting for her at home were enough to persuade her otherwise. Besides, Ray was long gone, and Misty's baby was missing. Her own feelings about Misty had to be put aside. She had a job to do.

"Yes," she said. "I'm sure."

"Boss," one of the patrol officers called. Noah had started calling her boss immediately after she took the position of chief. It was kind of a joke, but now it was what everyone called her. Anything was better than chief. No one would ever replace her predecessor.

Josie and Noah turned to look toward the street where the patrol officer was pointing. Beneath a slowly darkening evening sky, a black stretch limousine sat curbside.

"Well," Noah said. "That's not something you see every day."

One of the tinted windows toward the back of the limo rolled down, and Mayor Tara Charleston's face peeked out. Her brow was severely arched. "Chief Quinn," she called. "A word?"

Josie looked at Noah. He shrugged. With a sigh, she pulled off her Tyvek booties and made her way to the limousine. The door opened as she approached, and she climbed in, pulling it closed behind her. The mayor was alone in the back, enveloped in one of its long, taupe leather seats wearing a deep-blue evening gown with pearls to match, her dark hair swept back in an elegant French twist.

"Oh shit," Josie said.

She tried to pat down her own hair, which had reacted to the static electricity from her cap. She probably looked like she'd stuck her finger in a socket.

Tara frowned at her. "You forgot, didn't you?"

"The benefit. Tara, I'm really sorry," Josie said.

"Did you even buy a dress?" Tara asked.

"Of course I did. I—" She broke off, thinking about the slinky black dress that hung on the back of her bathroom door, of how she had agonized for months over what kind of dress the city's first-ever female chief of police should wear to her first charity benefit—a benefit thrown by the mayor to fund the women's center she'd always wanted to build. Josie hated hoity-toity, fancy, dress-up events—she hadn't even enjoyed her prom—but she thought the women's center the mayor was proposing was sorely needed in their city. It would be a tremendous resource for the women of Denton. Plus, she was chief now. Apparently, these were the types of things chiefs of police got behind and attended. She wondered absently if Luke was waiting at her house in his tuxedo, or if he'd even remembered at all.

"Chief Quinn, you know how important this benefit is to me. I've worked for months to put this together. Do you have any idea how hard it was for me to get Eric Dunn and Peter Rowland in the same room? The promises I had to make? Even a small donation from just one of them could make the difference between building this women's center and scrapping the whole project."

"I know," Josie said. "I'm sorry."

Peter Rowland was a billionaire who had grown up in Denton. He had gone on to make a fortune developing state-of-the-art security and surveillance systems which he sold the world over to various companies, especially casinos. He lived in New York City, but Josie knew he still kept a home in Denton. Eric Dunn was a casino mogul who had been trying for months to close a deal to build a casino on some unused land just inside Denton's city limits. Josie knew from her previous conversations with Tara that Rowland was interested in negotiating a contract with Dunn to have his security system installed at Dunn's casino in Denton and any other casino Dunn opened in the future. Personally, Josie thought opening a casino in Denton was a horrible idea, but she understood that Tara was only interested in Dunn's money. That was what politicians did: they used people. Josie hadn't been able to figure out Tara's angle in inviting her—damn near insisting that Josie come to the benefit—but she was a little relieved to have gotten out of it.

"I did buy a dress," she assured Tara. "I had every intention of attending." She motioned toward the outside, where Misty's huge Victorian sat now dark and silent, the officers packing up their crime scene kit and evidence. "But we've got a serious situation here."

"I know," Tara said. She opened her clutch purse and pulled out a cell phone, which she waved at Josie. "I got the Amber Alert and made a call to the station and found out where you all were. This is her house, isn't it?"

For a moment, Josie simply stared at her. The way Tara said the word "her" was the same way Josie had said it since she'd found out about Ray's affair. The way any woman would when referring to their husband's mistress, like something dirty in their mouths that they couldn't wait to spit out.

Tara dropped her phone back into her clutch and looked out the window. "I knew she lived in this neighborhood, but I've never been here before."

"We are talking about Misty Derossi, right?" Josie asked.

Tara nodded, her gaze lingering on Misty's house while Josie waited for her to speak again. When she did, her voice was low. "My husband had an affair with her."

"I'm sorry to hear that," Josie said, not as shocked as she should have been. She couldn't help but wonder if Misty had been sleeping with Tara's husband while she was engaged to Ray. It wasn't impossible.

Tara met Josie's eyes. "He thinks he is the father of her baby."

Josie said nothing.

"I'm not so sure."

"Why do you think he isn't?"

Again, Tara's gaze flitted away from Josie. She sounded exhausted. "Not many people know this, but my husband and I can't have children. It's me, not him. We always said we would adopt, or at least foster children or something like that, but then life just got in the way. We both had our careers...I found out about his affair in November of last year."

"Misty would have become pregnant sometime in the first two weeks of December," Josie pointed out.

"Right. Well, my husband claims they...saw each other one more time after things broke off. Late November, early December. I told him the timing doesn't necessarily add up, but he refused to believe me. Honestly, I think he wants it to be his baby. He had these grand plans for raising it, co-parenting with her while still being married to me." Here, Tara laughed harshly and rolled her eyes. "Men can be such idiots sometimes. Anyway, he finally confronted her. Imagine his surprise when he found out he wasn't the only person she was sleeping with." Here Josie detected a small amount of satisfaction in Tara's expression.

"Did he let it go after that?" Josie asked.

"Eventually. At first, he said he'd insist on a DNA test, but over time he gave up on the idea. We've been in counseling. I'm sure you can imagine the strain the entire thing has put on our marriage."

Josie wanted very badly to ask why Tara stayed in the marriage at all, but she held her tongue. Tara was ambitious, and Josie knew that her husband, a well-respected surgeon, was good for the image she liked to project of a power couple ready, willing, and able to lead the city of Denton. The scandal would not play well if she wanted to be reelected. Nor would a divorce.

"Why are you really here?" Josie asked.

"I imagine your first line of inquiry will be into who the father of the baby is."

Josie remained silent. She wasn't sure she liked where this was going.

"I wanted to head you off at the pass. Save you some time by letting you know that my husband's name would likely appear on your list of potential fathers."

"I appreciate your candor," Josie said. "Where is your husband, by the way?"

At this, Tara smiled. "He's at the hospital. He was called in for an emergency surgery a few hours ago."

That didn't absolve Tara's husband, since they really had no idea of the precise time Misty had been attacked, but Josie understood what Tara was offering, so she said, "If your husband has an alibi, why are we having this conversation?"

"Because I was hoping that having eliminated him as a suspect, it wouldn't need to be made public record that he was sleeping with Misty Derossi."

"You understand that my department will have to verify his alibi, don't you?"

"Yes, of course. I'm only asking for some...discretion."

"I can be discreet as long as there's nothing criminal going on."

Tara bristled. She had expected total compliance, but Josie wasn't going to give it to her. There was a baby missing, and Josie was going to find him no matter what stones she had to kick over—and no matter whose feathers she ruffled.

Slowly, Tara reached into her clutch and pulled out a

compact, which she flipped open, checking her eyeliner. "You know, we've never really discussed it, but you're still considered an interim chief."

"What exactly are you saying?"

Tara continued to look into the small mirror, running a fingernail beneath one of her eyelids. "I'm saying, my first choice for chief of police of this city probably wouldn't be someone with a history like yours. All that business last year and then the excessive force allegation."

"That's all it ever was," Josie pointed out. "An allegation. Made by a junkie who overdosed two months after I took this position. You know that."

Tara snapped the compact shut, her eyes burning into Josie's. "And *you* know that you have kept your position as chief because I have allowed you to do so. What I should have done after Chief Harris died was find a candidate with the right experience and an impeccable record."

Josie nearly blurted out the words, "Then fire me" but stopped herself. She'd never wanted to be chief, and missed the kind of hands-on police work her staff got to do, but she didn't need a war with the mayor right now. She needed to find Misty's baby. Instead, she said, "My staff are loyal to me. They know me and trust me—in no small part because I was Chief Harris's choice to take over. I was his choice because I was clean, and I got the job done. I will be as discreet as I can, Mayor Charleston, but if I find out your husband is implicated in anything illegal, my discretion goes out the window."

Tara glared at her. Her unspoken threat filled up the air between them, making it fizz with tension.

Josie pasted a fake smile onto her face and gripped the door handle. "Well," she said. "I'm glad we had this chat. I'll be in touch."

CHAPTER 8

"What the hell was that about?" Noah asked as he drove them over to Foxy Tails.

"You can add Mayor Charleston's husband to Misty's list of potential fathers," Josie told him.

Noah gave a low whistle. "Damn. Is there anyone she *didn't* sleep with?"

Josie hated that old double standard: a promiscuous man was virile, but a promiscuous woman was a slut. She couldn't care less how many men Misty slept with, it was her penchant for married men that made Josie's skin prickle. "You," she said, quietly, the word coming out more as a question than a statement.

He took his eyes off the road in surprise. "You're right," he said. "Well, that's one less person we have to alibi."

"Speaking of that," Josie mumbled. Pulling out her phone, she texted Gretchen and instructed her to pay the mayor's husband a visit and check his story.

Noah slowed the car. Again, he glanced at her, his brow creased with concern. "You sure you're up for this?"

Josie answered with a look that said, never ask me that again. And Noah's silence for the rest of the journey said he wouldn't.

Foxy Tails lay on the outskirts of Denton, along a winding mountain road, several miles from the center of the city yet still considered Denton. It would have been easily missed by drivers except for the giant pink neon sign at the edge of the road announcing, "Foxy Tails Live Girls." The building itself was squat and unattractive, its drab gray cinderblock walls topped with a flat black roof. A set of purple double doors added the only splash of color. It was almost dinnertime by the time Noah and Josie pulled in, and the parking lot was half full.

Inside, music pulsed, the bass drumming through Josie's body, making her feel as though she was being propelled by the beat. Topless women in thongs and high heels weaved their way through the tables scattered throughout the darkened room, delivering drinks and luring patrons from their tables to the back rooms, where Josie knew the girls gave private lap dances. A stage jutted out into the middle of the room, and a pale woman with tiny breasts and ample hips gyrated against a pole in the center of the stage. A few patrons gathered around the stage, drinks in one hand, dollar bills in the other. Other patrons hung back at the small tables, their eyes following the waitresses greedily. The place smelled of cigarettes, stale beer, and need.

Behind the bar stood a woman who looked very similar to Misty Derossi—slender, blond, and perfectly tanned. She wore a flannel crop top and cut-off denim shorts which made her look rather overdressed compared to the other women there. She smiled at Noah until she saw Josie trailing behind him.

"We're here to see Butch," Noah said, shouting to be heard as he flashed his badge.

The woman frowned and opened her mouth to speak.

"And before you say he's not here," Josie interjected, "it's about Misty."

A hand flew to the woman's mouth. "Is she okay?"

"No," Josie said flatly. "We really need to see Butch."

"The baby?"

"Missing. Can you take us to Butch now, please?"

"Oh my God, was that what the Amber Alert was about? Misty's baby?"

"Butch. Now," Josie said.

The woman looked as though she wanted to ask more questions but dared not. She glanced at Noah, who smiled politely.

Apparently, Josie's word wasn't good enough. "Just a minute," she told him.

Ten minutes later, they were being led down a long hallway with black painted walls and a threadbare hot-pink carpet. They stopped outside a black door, barely noticeable except for its gold doorknob, and the woman knocked. The door swung open and the bartender ushered Josie and Noah inside, closing the door behind them. The office was large with wood-paneled walls, drab brown carpet, and a large cherrywood desk shaped like an L. Behind it sat Butch McConnell and behind him were several small flat-screen televisions live-streaming the activity in various parts of the club. Wires snaked from a small junction box fixed to the wall beneath the screens. On the front of the box, in small gold lettering, Josie could make out the words Rowland Industries.

Josie tore her eyes from the CCTV system and looked at Butch as he stood to shake both their hands. The man was massive. Easily six foot six, he wore a black crew-neck T-shirt beneath a black suit jacket. Josie could see rolls of flab fighting for position where his stomach protruded from under the jacket. He looked like a mountain made of marshmallows. Even the skin of his face drooped like a slobbering basset hound. He was likely in his forties, his combed-back hair noticeably thinning at the top as he leaned forward to motion for them to sit, which Noah did. Josie remained standing.

"What can I do for you, officers?" Butch asked with the easy solicitousness of a man expecting trouble, but hoping that with enough smarm they might be able to work something out.

"We're here about one of your dancers," Josie said. "Misty Derossi."

Butch smiled but it didn't reach his eyes. "Misty quit. Got pregnant. Been out a few months now."

"She's not out on maternity leave?" Noah asked.

Butch laughed. "We don't have maternity leave, my friend. I told her if she could keep her ass tight, she could probably have her job back when she was ready, but I can't exactly hold the position open. No way could I let her dance again if her body was all messed up from having a kid."

Charming, Josie thought. "How long did Misty work for you?"

Butch shrugged. "I don't know. Four, five years? When she started to show, I had to have a talk with her. I mean, she had a lot of guys who came around pretty regular for private dances and she wanted to stay and just do that, but I couldn't let her. Can't have a pregnant dancer waddling around. I offered to let her work behind the bar for another couple of weeks, but she just quit."

"Did Misty ever talk to you about her pregnancy?" Josie asked.

"Nah. Nothing other than to tell me about it."

"She never mentioned the father?"

Butch shook his head. "Not to me. You can talk to the other girls. Maybe she said something to them."

"You and Misty—was your relationship strictly professional?" Noah interjected.

Butch smiled knowingly. "You're asking if we had a thing? No. Not with Misty. I try not to get involved with my girls. Makes things . . . complicated. I get accused of playing favorites. It can get ugly."

"We need a list of her regular customers," Noah said.

Butch shook his head. He still hadn't asked what happened to Misty or why they were there. Josie assumed the bartender had told him what she said, but still, she would have expected him to want more details. Did he know something, or was he really just that much of a dick? "Can't do it," he said. "Can't violate my customers' privacy."

Josie stepped forward and placed a palm flat on his desk. "If you don't give us a list, we'll arrest you for obstruction of justice."

A genuine look of surprise crossed his face. Josie realized he was used to bossing women around, not being told what to do by one. "Do I need a lawyer?" he asked.

Josie put her other hand on the desk and leaned in toward him, nailing him in place with her stare. "I don't know. Do you?"

She let a moment pass. When he didn't respond, she said, "Where were you this morning?"

He looked toward Noah as if looking for a lifeline. "What?" For the first time, he looked flustered. "What the hell is going on here?"

"Just answer the question," Noah said.

"I was...I was home. Then I was here. I—"

"And what about yesterday? Where were you?" Josie continued.

"The same. I...I...no, wait, I worked out yesterday. Yesterday, before I came here, I went to the gym."

Josie strongly doubted that but didn't say anything to Butch. "What time do you come in here for work?"

"Between one and two in the afternoon," Butch said. "It's the same, every day. I stay till closing usually."

"You don't have someone under you who manages this place when you're not here?" Noah asked.

Butch shook his head. "Are you kidding me? You know what it would cost me to pay a manager?"

"You never take a vacation?" Josie said.

"Sometimes. I usually just have the senior girl take over for the week."

"Which gym do you go to?" Noah asked, pulling out his notepad and jotting down Butch's answer.

Josie pointed to the bank of screens on the wall. "How far back do you keep video?"

"Six months," he said.

"Really?" Noah asked. "Most places keep surveillance for a week, if that."

Butch shrugged. "Yeah, my old system only kept footage for seventy-two hours. I had this one installed last year, keeps everything for six months. It came in handy back in May when some guy tried to sue, saying he slipped and fell at the bar. I had the footage showing he didn't fall once while he was here."

Josie said, "We're going to need to review the footage on this CCTV for the last seventy-two hours. Actually, if you've got footage of the last couple of months Misty was working, we'd like to have a look at that as well."

"I can't do that. I mean, don't you need a warrant or something?"

Josie snapped a look at Noah, and he pulled out his phone and sent a text; Gretchen would have the warrant within the hour.

Josie ignored Butch's question. "When your bartender came in to tell you we were here, what did she say to you?"

"She said something happened with Misty, the baby was missing, and the police wanted to talk to me."

"Yet you haven't asked us what happened to her. So why don't you tell us?"

Picking up Josie's line of questioning, Noah said, "Since you're not even the least bit curious, you must know what happened to her?"

Butch heaved himself up from his seat, raising both hands in the air. "No, no, no. I see what you're doing. Something bad happened, and you want to pin it on me. I got nothing to do with anything outside of this club. I haven't seen Misty in months."

"Then why haven't you asked us?" Josie said.

"I can prove where I was," he went on. "I can prove it. I'll let you see the videos, and you'll see that I was here the last two days, almost the whole time."

"Last year, when Misty went missing, you were concerned enough to send one of your girls to her house to see if she was there, but today you have no questions at all about what happened to her? Why?" Josie asked.

She stared hard at him until he dropped his hands. "Look," he said. "I just assumed . . . I don't know. Like, someone must have beat her up pretty bad."

"You're not interested in her condition?"

Annoyance flashed in his eyes. "Look, lady, you gotta understand. Misty was an employee, okay? It's not like we were best friends. I sent one of my girls to her house last year because the other girls said I should, but I have a business to run. You know how many girls I got coming in and out of here all the time? You know how much drama each one of them brings with her? I don't got time to get personally involved with every one of 'em. I'm real sorry if things got messed up for her, but it was only a matter of time."

"What do you mean by that?" Noah asked.

With a sigh, Butch lowered himself back into his chair and rubbed a hand over his face. "What do you think it means? Like I said, all these girls like drama. Misty, she was no different. Some of my girls, they know how to shut these losers down." He waved at the bank of screens. Across several of them, Josie could see the dancers' and waitresses' naked behinds working their way around the club. "These guys. Some of 'em just come to see some tits, you know? Have a beer, relax. Some of 'em like a little private dance and that's it. They go home or back to their lives and everything's fine. But a lot of these guys, they come in here regular-like, and they start to like a particular girl. They forget they're paying for it, you know? They start to think it's more than just tits. They get, like, obsessed. Now I seen a lot of girls use that, you know, exploit it. They'll get all kinds of money and favors out of these dudes. They'll milk it for as long as they can. Then one day the guy will cross the line, and I'll have to bounce him. I don't like doing it because that's a paying customer, but I gotta maintain some rules, you know?"

"Did Misty exploit the men who fixated on her?" Josie asked.

Butch kept his eyes on Noah, as if he were the one asking all the questions. Josie didn't care; as long as he answered her questions, it shouldn't matter that he was pretending that Noah had asked them. "No," Butch said. "I mean not really. Well, maybe.

Misty would never intentionally use a guy. Men would come in, pay for a private dance and then pour their hearts out to her, and she would listen. She would remember everything they told her so the next time they came in, she'd ask, 'How's your mom?' or 'Did you get that thing with your supervisor straightened out?' I mean, she was a good dancer, but she always seemed like she was genuinely interested in her customers. The next thing you know, they think they're in love with her."

"Did any of them ever try to cross the line with Misty?" Noah asked.

"That's the thing," Butch said. "There was no line. Misty had relationships with them. She was into it. She didn't get involved with every dude who thought he was in love with her, but she did with a lot of them. Sometimes it would last months. To her it was like an adventure, you know? She liked the attention and the newness—that's what the other girls always said." He raised his voice an octave, imitating a high-pitched female voice. "'Oh, Misty, you just like the thrill of it all.' My other dancers, they don't want to be bothered once their shift is over. They don't even want to look at another man. They get dressed and go home. It's an act. You see what I'm saying? Like part of the show."

"I understand," Noah said.

"For Misty, it wasn't like that. I think she liked having all these guys competing for her attention; taking her on trips and dates, buying her flowers and taking her shopping. The rest of the girls always asked her why she would hook up with a bunch of dirty pigs, and she said the ones she picked weren't dirty pigs. She thought they were nice."

"Did she ever fall for them?" Josie asked. "These men?"

"Nah," Butch said. "She liked them, she 'appreciated' them, she always used to say. Sometimes she'd say she cared for them, but she was never in love. Not until the cop. He was the only one she was really into. Everything changed when she met him."

Butch didn't seem to notice the flash of emotion across

Josie's face. "She cut almost all of them off after she met the cop," he went on. "That was real serious."

"Her best friend said there were some issues with some of these men," Josie pointed out, quickly changing the subject.

Butch nodded. "Well, when she broke it off, some of them didn't take it so well. Sometimes I had to throw a guy out or walk her to her car for a couple of weeks. The real issue wasn't usually with the men, it was with their wives. I told her to stay away from the married ones, but she said it wasn't about marriage, it was about 'connection.' But the wives—boy, they were vicious. Crazier than any twelve dudes you'd see in this place. And you want to talk about stalkers? One of them wrecked her car one time."

"Is that right?" Josie said.

"Oh yeah," Butch said. "One time I had someone's missus in here threatening to stab her. A couple of them went after her. Look, 'connections' or not, it was just a matter of time before someone snapped and went crazy on her. I mean, I hate to say that, but it's the truth."

"Any idea who that person might be?" Noah asked.

"Nah. Like I said, she stopped working for me, like, three or four months ago. I don't know who she was messing with or what she was into."

"What about the other girls who worked with her?" Josie asked. "Would they have a better idea?"

Butch shrugged. "I guess."

"We'll need to interview them," Noah said.

"Right now?"

"Yes, right now," Josie answered.

Butch turned slowly in his chair and looked at the bank of screens. "It's really not good for my business to have a bunch of cops hanging around, talking to my girls."

"We'll use one of your private rooms," Noah said. "We'll be discreet."

Butch didn't turn back, but Josie could see him nodding his head reluctantly.

CHAPTER 9

NBC 10—Philadelphia, Pennsylvania

December 2, 2016

Teen's Death Ruled Accidental

The Philadelphia Medical Examiner's Office has ruled the death of a teenage jogger as an accidental drowning. Three weeks ago, sixteen-year-old Central High School student Mark Conlen was reported missing by his mother after he failed to return home from an afternoon jog along the Schuylkill River Trail. One week later, his body was pulled from the Schuylkill River by the Philadelphia Police Marine Unit after they received multiple reports of a body in the river.

Police believe Conlen fell while jogging, hit his head and fell into the river. The autopsy revealed no evidence of foul play or any underlying health conditions. Although Conlen was out on bail for pending felony charges involving a series of armed robberies in Center City, police do not believe he was targeted or that his death was the result of a homicide. Funeral details will be released later this week.

CHAPTER 10

Butch's girls had little to offer in the way of new leads. Josie and Noah spent an hour speaking to each of them in turn and waiting for Gretchen to show up with the warrant for the CCTV footage. All of them confirmed what both Brittney and Butch had said—Misty was private; she refused to reveal the father of the baby; she routinely dated clients; Ray had been the love of her life; and only her pregnancy had seemed to lift her out of her grief over his death.

A blast of fresh air accompanied Gretchen into the club. From the bar, Josie watched her enter and felt relief wash over her; talking about Ray was always difficult, but hearing the girls repeatedly describe him as Misty's soulmate was unbearable.

Noah emerged from the hallway that led to Butch's office, closing his notepad and shaking his head. He and Gretchen arrived at the bar at the same time.

"That was the last dancer," he said. "And she had nothing new to offer. This is a dead end."

"Well, we added at least two names to our list of Misty's ex-lovers," Josie pointed out. "We need to check the footage, though."

Gretchen held up the warrant. "Lead the way."

Ten minutes later, they were standing behind Butch while he queued up footage of the last seventy-two hours. He fast-forwarded through it, pausing to show them what time he arrived each day so they could mark it down. After that, he pulled up Misty's last two months of work. "I don't have cameras in the private rooms," Butch told them. "But I have eyes on the hall, so you can see who goes in and out and how long they're in there."

"Let's start with Misty's last night of work, then, and work our way back," Noah said. "If you can tell us which customers were regulars, that would be helpful."

Butch fast-forwarded through most of the footage as dancers led men down the hall to various doors and then back out to the main floor several minutes later. He slowed it back down when Misty's shift started, and they watched her lead her clients in and out of one of the private rooms. Josie noticed that Misty's perfect stomach showed the hint of her baby bump. She also had far fewer clients than the other girls. "I thought you said Misty brought in a lot of revenue," Josie said.

"She did. Until she started showing. It creeped a lot of dudes out. That's why I had to ask her to leave."

They worked backward through her last week of work, Butch noting two of her regular customers who were already on Noah's list of potential fathers. Mayor Charleston's husband was not among the men who appeared on camera that week. As they went further back, a police officer in full uniform appeared on the screen walking behind Misty. Butch stopped fast-forwarding and let the tape play at regular speed. He pointed to the screen. "This guy, he was here a couple of times. Not for a dance, though; he just wanted to talk to her."

Josie's breath caught in her throat. "Can you—can you rewind that?" she asked, hoping her voice didn't sound tremulous.

"No need," Butch said. "You'll have a better view of him when they come back out." He fast-forwarded again, and Josie noted that fourteen minutes and twenty-seven seconds had passed.

On screen, Misty emerged from the private room without looking back. Luke followed behind her, his state trooper hat in his hands and his eyes cast downward. At the end of the hallway, he went one way and Misty went another.

"You should talk to him," Butch said. "If you can find out who he is. Maybe he knows something. Looks like a statie."

Josie could feel Noah's gaze on her. She gritted her teeth, wishing he would look away. At least Gretchen wasn't staring as well. She motioned for Butch to keep going. "How many times did you say that trooper was here?"

Butch shrugged. "I don't know. Two? He came in a month before this for sure. You'll see him on the tapes. He stood out like a sore thumb in that uniform. We don't like uniforms in here, makes the clients jumpy."

Josie let out a breath as the video went back into super speed. She couldn't bring herself to speak. From her periphery, she saw Noah turn toward her and sensed his body stiffen. Gretchen, who seemed unaffected, asked, "And you said he never paid for a dance?"

"Nah," Butch said. "Had some business with her, he said. Normally I wouldn't allow that sort of thing. I mean, time is money, you know? She's in there with him for fifteen, twenty minutes, that's revenue lost. But I cut him some slack 'cause he was with the police."

"And you didn't ask Misty why a state trooper was coming to her place of business to speak to her?" Noah put in.

"'Course I did. She said it was a private matter."

Gretchen raised a brow. "And you let it go at that?"

"She wouldn't tell me anything else. She said it wasn't anything to do with any crime and that it wouldn't hurt the club. She said they were working something out, and once they did he wouldn't come around anymore."

Heat crept up from Josie's collar. She could barely stay still as they watched more of the tapes and Luke appeared for a second time just over a month earlier than the first time he had been there. It was the same scenario, and again they emerged without looking at each other and parted ways at the end of the hallway without a word. Josie pulled out her cell phone and looked at it. There were no texts or calls, but she made a show of punching icons and swiping and said, "Excuse me, I have to make a call."

Outside, she sucked in the cool, clean air. It had grown dark in the time they'd been inside, and beneath the dull yellow glow of the parking lot lights, moths fluttered and dived. Josie leaned against Noah's car and looked at her phone once more. A photo of her and Luke stared back at her, their faces pressed together, smiling happily at the camera. They had been so happy once. At the beginning. Even though she had been technically married to Ray, they had been carefree and crazy for each other. Then came the horror of the missing girls cases and Luke was shot. Had things started going wrong from there? She wasn't sure. Then Brady Conway put a bullet in his wife's head and turned the gun on himself, and Luke became a different person entirely.

Was he sleeping with Misty Derossi? Could she really have lost two men to this woman? Was that why he was so on edge, why he shut down at any mention of their wedding? Then another, more horrifying thought crept into her mind. Was it possible that Luke had fathered Misty's baby?

"No," Josie said aloud.

It wasn't possible. It couldn't be. She thought back to December but couldn't remember much other than they had been happy. Hadn't they?

If he wasn't having an affair with Misty, then why had he been at the strip club to see her? Why hadn't he told Josie? What business could the two of them possibly have together?

Her finger hovered over the phone icon. She should call him. But no, she wanted to look him in the face when she asked him, see the truth in his eyes.

"Boss?" Noah walked slowly up beside her, both hands jammed into his pockets, his expression pained.

Josie sighed. "Don't."

"I'm sure Luke wasn't here to . . . I mean, he doesn't seem like that kind of guy."

"Every guy is that kind of guy," she muttered.

Noah took a step closer. "No, not every guy," he said firmly.

A moment passed between them in the silence that followed. Then Noah added, "I'm just saying, I think you should give Luke the benefit of the doubt."

She shook herself and pushed herself off the car. "I have to go talk to him," she said. "Find out why he was here and what business he had with Misty. If nothing else, I need to know if anything he knows is going to help find her baby."

Noah held out his keys to her. "I'll get a ride back to the station with Gretchen. Meet you there later?"

Josie took them. "Thank you. Once you're done with the videos—"

"I'll get to work on alibis for the men on this list," he finished.

CHAPTER 11

Luke lived in an old stone farmhouse that sat seventeen miles outside of central Denton on what was considered a rural route. The original owner of the property had divided up his farm into lots and sold them off one by one. A few buyers had built houses, but Luke's closest neighbors were still a good half mile away in each direction.

Josie and Luke spent almost all of their time at her house. In fact, he had moved in with Josie for a short period while he recovered from his gunshot wounds the year before. Josie thought it might be permanent, and was just getting used to the idea when the Conway shooting happened and he retreated back to his own home. Whenever they fought he would disappear home and stay there for a few days until he cooled down. As she pulled into his long gravel driveway, she realized she hadn't been to his house in almost six months.

Her headlights cut across the front of the house, revealing his pickup truck and, just beyond that, lights glowing from the downstairs windows. Josie parked and got out, standing in the dark and listening to the sounds of crickets and cicadas chirping and humming in the fields. She felt a familiar prickle of unease, took a step toward the house and tried to figure out what had caused it. Something wasn't right. Her hand reached to her waist, patting her service weapon. She was relieved that she had remembered to bring it with her when she left her house to go meet Noah. Of course, after what had happened to her almost two years ago, she'd probably never go anywhere without it again.

She took another step toward the house and then it hit her. His porch light wasn't on. It was motion-activated and should have flicked on the moment she pulled into the driveway. Pulling her gun out of its holster, she stepped onto the porch. Glass crunched beneath her foot, and she looked down to see pieces of it glittering from a pool of blood that extended from where Josie stood to the doorway. She paused so she could listen over the sound of her pounding heart for any movement in or outside of the house. There was nothing. Keeping her gun in one hand, she used the other to dial Noah. He picked up on the third ring. "I'm at Luke's," she whispered. "There's blood on the porch. Send units now."

"Don't go in," Noah said. "Wait for back—"

But Josie had already hung up. She pocketed her phone and held her gun at chest level as she eased inside the house. If Luke was wounded or dying, she wasn't waiting fifteen or twenty minutes for backup to arrive. It had been ages since she'd cleared a building, but her instincts kicked in, and her body went onto automatic pilot. Worry for Luke's safety battled with her more practical concern of securing a crime scene. She had to be Chief Josie right now, not the future Mrs. Creighton.

She followed the streaks of blood from the door to the kitchen, where a large splatter fanned across the painted white cabinets. Pools of it collected on the tile floor. She studied the cabinets, walls, and even the ceiling for bullet holes, just to be sure, but the spatter was more consistent with a stab wound. Judging by the drag marks along the floor, the victim—please don't let it be Luke—had initially been stabbed in the kitchen, lain there for some time, and then been dragged outside onto the porch.

Luke kept his service weapon in a gun safe in his bedroom closet along with his hunting rifle and shotgun. Useless to him if he had been taken by surprise, but he would have had ample warning if any unexpected guests wound their way up his driveway. Unless they were waiting for him when he arrived home, which would explain the broken porch light. He always locked his door, but his house was easy enough to break into through one of the windows at the side.

Holding her gun at the ready and still listening for any noises in the house, she moved stealthily through the rest of the first floor. With every room she entered, she expected to find him bleeding out on the floor, but he wasn't there. There was no blood on the stairs, but she made her way to the second floor anyway, using her sleeve to flip on the lights in each room as she went. The spare bedroom was empty, as was the bedroom he used as his home gym. She cleared the bathroom and moved on to the master bedroom, which was empty as well. In his closet, his gun safe was locked up tightly.

As she panned the room for a second time, her eyes locked on the nightstand to the right of the bed. Her side of the bed. Not that she ever slept here anymore. The lamp was the same, but there was a dog-eared paperback novel she had never seen before next to a half-full bottle of water.

"Son of a bitch," she muttered to herself, sagging against the doorframe.

The house was clear. Luke was missing. Judging by the blood in his kitchen, wherever he was, he hadn't gone there willingly. It had to be connected to what had happened at Misty's house that day; it was too much of a coincidence that Misty and Luke had been meeting in secret together and now, months later, both were in serious trouble. What the hell had Luke gotten into?

Only a few hours ago, she thought she had known everything there was to know about him. She had never pegged him for the kind of guy who kept secrets. What you saw was what you got with Luke. Maybe she had been so busy worrying about him finding out about the skeletons in her closet that it had never occurred to her that he might have some of his own. The biggest secret he had ever kept from her was that he used to be engaged to a woman who worked for the state police crime lab. Now she wondered if that was the only he thing he had hid from her. Who had been sleeping in his bed—next to him? How had she been so blind? She shook her head, trying to shake off that last question. It didn't matter at the moment. Her relationship issues had to wait. Right now, she had her second missing persons case of the day, and it was the man she loved.

She tried to still her panicked thoughts as she walked back to the kitchen. Carefully avoiding the blood, she holstered her gun and pulled out her cell phone. She dialed Luke. From the living room came the muffled sound of Blake Shelton's "Mine Would Be You" coming from his phone. She remembered the first time he had played the song for her; it was just about the most romantic song she'd ever heard, and the sound of it now caused a small ache to bloom in her chest. She found the phone on his coffee table, tossed haphazardly among the other items: his car keys, the television remote, a stack of mail. She wanted to scroll through it to see if there were messages or calls to or from Misty—or any other numbers she didn't recognize—but she was standing in a crime scene. She would have to wait for her evidence response team to come and process the house first.

She walked back to the kitchen and stared at the bloodstains, trying to calculate whether a person could lose that much blood and still be alive. Her phone vibrated with a text from Noah. He was five minutes out. That was good. She didn't want to be alone much longer.

A clatter out back startled her, and she ran to the back door and looked outside to see a figure running into the darkness toward the barn at the edge of Luke's property.

The back door banged behind her as she raced outside.

CHAPTER 12

At the bottom of the back steps, Josie leapt over a pile of gardening implements scattered across the ground and gave chase. Lucky for her, the moon was full and bright on this side of the house and within seconds, her eyes adjusted. Over the grass her feet flew, barely touching ground. She shouted, "Stop, police!" but the figure didn't slow. As Josie got closer, she could see that it was a woman. Her long golden hair flashed every now and again in the moonlight. She was slight, and her feet were bare. Josie gained on her quickly, tackling her to the ground.

They rolled together through the grass before coming to rest. Quickly, Josie pushed the woman onto her stomach and straddled her. "I said stop," Josie huffed. She held the woman's hands behind her back and realized she had no zip ties or handcuffs. She hadn't run down a suspect in well over a year and it showed.

Beneath her, the woman lay still, but Josie could feel her chest heaving as she tried to catch her breath. "What's your name?" Josie asked.

The woman said nothing. "I said, what's your name?"

Another moment of silence slipped by as Josie patted the woman down. No weapons. Josie gave a frustrated sigh. "Fine. Don't tell me. You're under arrest."

"I…I don't know," came the woman's raspy voice.

"What?"

"I don't remember."

"You don't remember your name?"

"I don't remember anything. I just, I woke up here. I don't know where I am. I heard someone in the house. T-t-there was blood. I ran."

Josie stared at the back of the woman's head for a moment, wondering if she was genuine. "What are you saying?"

"I don't know. Please. I'm really scared."

Josie stood and pulled the woman upright by one of her arms. She was small—in her mid-twenties, Josie estimated—with a heart-shaped face. She wore a pair of sweatpants and a T-shirt that Josie recognized as belonging to Luke. Josie hoped the moonlight didn't give away the agonizing flash of hurt in her eyes.

"Woke up where?" she asked.

The woman pointed to the house. "There," she said.

"I checked the house," Josie said. "You weren't in it."

"I was out back. It was dark. I don't...I don't understand what's happening."

"How did you know there was blood in the house if you were outside?"

In the moonlight, Josie could see the woman's brow furrow over a pair of wide, dark eyes. "What?"

Josie repeated her question.

"I...I was going to try the door, and I looked inside and saw blood. I thought I saw someone moving in the kitchen, so I ran."

Josie stared at her. From the back door, she would have been able to see a good deal of the blood spatter. Still, that didn't explain why she was barefoot and wearing Luke's clothes.

"You were in the house," Josie said. "Who are you? What are you doing here?"

"I don't know. I swear to you, I don't know. I don't remember. I have no idea where I am or whose house that even is." The woman's eyes pleaded for understanding.

"What about Misty Derossi? Do you remember her?"

"Who?"

The woman wasn't giving her anything. Wordlessly, Josie

turned her around and pushed her back toward the house as sirens sounded in the distance.

"What's happening?" the woman asked, her voice small and swallowed by the sound of the sirens. "Can you tell me what's going on? Where am I? Is someone hurt?"

Josie ignored her. As they reached the house, the sirens cut out, but the red-and-blue flashing lights of emergency vehicles lit up the night. Josie trudged the woman around the house to the front where Noah was just emerging from her Ford Escape. She pushed the woman toward him, and he caught her expertly. "Cuff her," Josie said.

Dutifully, he cuffed her and put her in the back of a cruiser as Josie paced back and forth in front of Luke's house. A few of her officers approached, and she gave them instructions for securing and processing the scene. They set to work, and Josie kept pacing until Noah walked over. "What the hell happened?" he asked.

She told him what she had found. "I don't know whose blood that is, so you'll have to get it typed as soon as possible. It doesn't take that long. You should be able to do it tonight. Luke is A-negative. I have no idea who that woman is, and she claims she doesn't remember who she is or how she got here. Run her prints. See if you find anything. Get her to the hospital and have her checked out. Get a scan of her head or something. Do not let her out of custody. She is our only link to Luke right now. Someone else was here. I don't know if it was her, or Misty or someone else. Apparently, he was 'that type of guy.'"

Josie stopped talking to suck in a deep breath, just as Noah took her elbow and steered her toward the Escape.

"What are you doing?" she asked.

"Get in," he said.

"Excuse me?"

Josie stared at him. "Boss," he said, deferring to her authority but maintaining his firm tone. "Get in the car."

She walked over to the passenger's side and climbed inside.

Noah got in beside her, but he didn't start the engine. "This is getting too personal now," he said.

Josie bristled. "I'm fine. I am. I—"

"Luke is your fiancé. He is missing. There's blood in his home and you found a strange woman fleeing the scene. Tell me again how fine you are."

Josie glared at him as she pushed the hysteria mounting inside her down—deep, deep down. "I am your superior," she reminded him.

"Are you really telling me that you have no personal feelings about this situation whatsoever?"

"My husband died in my arms almost two years ago in the middle of a case. I handled my shit, and I've handled it every day since then. Whatever your concerns are, you better stow them and get back in line. We've got work to do."

She got out of the car without another word.

CHAPTER 13

The mystery woman had no identification on her, and Josie's team found nothing in the house that connected to her. Josie waited impatiently while Gretchen took a crack at questioning her in the back of the cruiser. Josie and Noah stood on the porch, watching the two women speak. "I should have had you do it," Josie mumbled. "She might have responded better to a man."

"Boss," Noah said. "If she's lost her memory, she's lost her memory. Could be concussion, trauma, amnesia even?"

"She doesn't have amnesia," Josie said. "She's faking."

"What makes you say that?"

"I just know."

"You sure it's not the fact that she's wearing Luke's T-shirt?"

He didn't miss a thing, damn him. Josie shot him an icy look, but he was already walking away from her, pretending to confer with the officer standing guard at Luke's front door. Then he disappeared into the house.

Josie put her hands on her hips and blew out a stream of air. She watched Gretchen get out of the back of the cruiser, scribble some notes in her notebook, and make her way toward Josie. "I got nothing, boss," Gretchen said. "She's sticking to her story."

"You think it's a story?" Josie asked.

"Don't know. She knows the year, the month, the president. She can add and subtract. I gave her some random pop culture questions, which she answered correctly, but she claims she doesn't remember who she is, where she came from or where she is now. No signs of physical injury. I mean I know people can have that fugue state amnesia where a traumatic event causes them to lose their memory, but something's just not right."

"I agree," Josie said.

Gretchen looked back to the cruiser where Jane Doe sat in the backseat staring straight ahead. "I'll get her to the hospital. Have her checked out and then get her back to the station for an interview."

They both looked over at her now as she lifted her cuffed hands and tucked her hair behind her ears, one after the other, before relaxing back into the seat. "She's too calm," Josie said.

Gretchen said, "Shock?"

"No," Josie said. "I've seen people in shock. When I knocked her down, she was breathing heavily, but that was from the exertion of running away from me. Her heart wasn't pounding; she wasn't shaking, she didn't cry. Even now, look at her. If I woke up in a crime scene with no memory of who I was or how I had come to be there, I'd be pretty fucking upset."

"Problem is, how do we prove she's faking?"

"I don't know," Josie said. "But the first step is getting a doctor to confirm there's not a damn thing wrong with her."

Noah came back out, holding up Luke's phone. "This has been dusted. You want to have a look?"

Josie tried not to snatch it too enthusiastically from his hand. Quickly, under the watchful eyes of Noah and Gretchen, she scrolled through his calls and text messages. "Nothing," she muttered.

There were calls and texts to her, to his sister and parents, to three coworkers whose names she recognized, including Brady Conway. They'd been texting back and forth the night Luke went over there to watch a game and found the carnage. She hadn't realized that Luke had kept the message thread. She wondered how often he looked at it, trying to reconcile the normalcy of the texts with what he found when he arrived at Brady's house. She handed the phone back to Noah, but he motioned for her to keep it. "We don't need it. It's got nothing useful on it. Hold on to it and you can give it back to him when we find him."

Noah. Always the optimist.

Josie didn't miss the look that passed between Noah and Gretchen. Then Noah cleared his throat. "Uh, boss…"

He trailed off. Josie looked from him to Gretchen and back. "What?" she snapped.

Gretchen said, "Usually, when we're investigating a crime, we start with the people closest to the victim."

"And that would be me," Josie said, understanding their discomfort.

"We know Luke is your fiancé but if you, uh, know anything, it would be helpful," Noah said.

Josie sighed. "I don't know anything. I don't know what he was into or what was going on with him that would have ended this way. I didn't even know he was going to Foxy Tails to see Misty. He's been cold and distant since the Conway shooting. I thought it was just because of the shooting. Whatever he was involved in, he didn't tell me anything."

"You walked through the house," Gretchen said. "Was anything missing? Disturbed?"

In other words, was it a home invasion? A robbery? "No," Josie said. "Not that I could see."

The only thing unusual about the house was that someone had been sleeping in Luke's bed. People didn't drive miles out into the farmland to rob someone who had nothing of real value. Luke had some guns but the safe had been undisturbed, and he didn't keep large sums of money lying around. His prized possession was a small fishing boat he kept in his barn, but that was hardly worth stealing. No, whoever had been there hadn't been there to steal. They'd been there to do harm. The blood spatter made that quite obvious.

But who had come for him? Or had they come for the Jane Doe and Luke had gotten into a struggle defending her? Why? Who the hell *was* she?

"What about his sister?" Noah asked.

Josie blinked, trying to focus on Noah. "What?"

"His sister. Would she know what was going on? If he was caught up in something?"

"I doubt it," Josie said. "She lives a few hours away and they don't see each other much. I'll give her a call. I have to call her anyway, to tell her..." She broke off, swallowing hard over the lump in her throat. "Did you call the medical examiner?"

"There's no body," Noah said. "She's not coming out unless there's a body." He held up a hand as Josie opened her mouth to speak. "But I sent her some photos of the blood spatter. She said it's unlikely that a person losing that amount of blood would survive without a transfusion."

He stopped there, but Josie heard the words in her head anyway. *I'm sorry, boss.*

CHAPTER 14

Josie leaned against her Ford Escape and pressed her cell phone to her ear. It rang three times before Carrieann Creighton picked up. "Josie?"

She plunged right in. "Carrieann, something's happened to Luke."

Josie could hear her sharp intake of breath. "Is he ... is he alive?"

"I don't know," she said honestly.

Somehow, she kept her voice calm as she explained to Carrieann what she had found when she arrived at Luke's house, stopping short of telling her about Jane Doe. Saying it out loud to his sister made it so much worse. Nearly two years ago they had comforted each other in the hospital while Luke recovered from gunshot wounds. That had felt like the worst-case scenario; Luke's insides had been shredded by sniper bullets, and he was barely clinging to life after surgery. But this—not knowing where he was, how badly he was injured, or even if he was still alive—this was so much worse.

"I'm sorry," Josie concluded.

Carrieann's voice was thick with emotion. "I'm coming there. I can be there by the morning."

Josie didn't argue with her. "Carrieann, when was the last time you spoke with Luke?"

A brief silence. Then, "I don't know, a few weeks ago? You know how Luke is over the phone. It's tough to get even a few sentences out of him. Everything is always, 'I'm fine, Josie's fine, things are fine.' He never calls me. It's always me calling him."

Josie knew this was true.

"When you talked to him, did he seem...off in any way?"

"No," Carrieann answered. "He seemed the same as always. I know you said he was pretty depressed since his friend died, but I never noticed any difference in him. Josie, why are you asking me these questions?"

"I'm trying to figure out what was going on with him. What he was...what he was involved in."

"Involved in?"

"Something was going on with him, Carrieann. I don't think this was random. We'll talk when you get here, okay?"

"I'll see you soon," Carrieann responded before hanging up.

Her next call was to Luke's station commander at the barracks to let him know what had happened. He related that Luke had been much more reserved since the Conway shooting, but he hadn't given any indication that anything else was going on. Luke's commander promised to talk to the other troopers to see if they had any useful information and to lend any assistance they could to the investigation. Josie hung up feeling even more frustrated than she had before she made the calls.

When it became apparent that there was no more that she could do at Luke's house, Josie left her team there to continue processing the scene and she drove around the city. She left her police scanner on, listening to the chatter to drown out her thoughts and be first to hear if anyone called in a response to the Amber Alert. She started out on the rural route that Luke lived on, driving miles in each direction, her vehicle moving slowly while she panned the shoulder of the road on each side. She didn't know what she expected or hoped to find, but there was nothing. She just didn't want to go home. With each hour that passed, Josie fought a creeping sense of hopelessness. She had driven down damn near every street in Denton before her eyes started to burn from exhaustion.

She could hear Noah's voice in her head. *Boss, go home. Get some rest.*

She was heading home, reluctantly, when her cell phone rang. It was Gretchen. "Boss, I just got a call from the lab. The blood type from Luke's kitchen was O-neg. So, not Luke."

The relief Josie felt was so immediate and so strong, for a moment she felt a little light-headed. Collecting herself, she said, "If it wasn't his and it wasn't Jane Doe's, then there was someone else there." She hoped the blood belonged to the person who attacked Luke; it was likely that person would have bled out by now and Luke would be free. Unless he was also dead. No, she couldn't go there. "Have the lab run a DNA test on it, and we'll submit it to the state database."

"Sure thing," Gretchen said, and Josie could hear her scribbling on her notepad.

"You still at the hospital with our mystery woman?"

"Yeah, they're waiting to take her for a CT. They had to page the neurosurgeon on call to come in for a consult. It will be a while. Boss, she's got some…scars."

"What kind?"

"On her back. Burnt tissue."

"Fresh?"

"No. I'm no expert, but based on what I've seen on the job, I'd say they're from a hair straightener or a curling iron."

Josie winced. "You're thinking domestic violence?"

"Could be. They're not huge, but there are two of them and one looks older than the other, which suggests it wasn't an accident. Just thought you'd like to know."

"Thanks." Josie sighed. "Call Hummel to relieve you. He can babysit her for the night. I need you fresh in the morning."

She thanked Gretchen and hung up, driving with more purpose toward her home. As she pulled into her driveway, she saw a light glowing from her living room window. She nearly forgot to put her car in park in her rush to get inside. Was Luke there? Had he been there all along?

But her living room was empty. She stood in the doorway staring at the neat stack of wedding invitations beside a vase filled with late-blooming wildflowers. She loved wildflowers. He must have gone out and picked them and then left them for her, something he hadn't done in ages. On an end table she found a note in Luke's handwriting: *I'm sorry. I love you. P. S. These three are my favorites.* Beside the note were three mock wedding invitations he had selected from the pile on the coffee table.

He had cleaned up after himself and left the light on for her. She bet if she went into her kitchen, all her dishes would be washed and neatly stacked in the drainboard. All the chairs would be pushed beneath the dining room table. It was one of the things about him that had always driven her crazy until after the Conway shooting, when he stopped doing it. When he stopped being himself.

She clutched the note in one hand and collapsed onto her couch, eyes shut tightly against the swell of emotion that threatened to overtake her. He had visited Misty at the strip club behind Josie's back. On more than one occasion. There had been another woman in his house. Wearing his clothes. Sleeping in his bed. And yet, after acting so coldly toward her that afternoon he had gathered flowers for Josie and picked out the wedding invitations she'd been trying to get him to look at for weeks. What the hell was going on?

She wasn't even aware of having fallen asleep until a knock on her door startled her awake. Jumping up from the couch, she looked toward the television, where the cable box beneath it announced that it was nearly seven in the morning. Daylight crept around the edges of her blinds. She wiped the sleep from her eyes and started for the front door, checking her phone as she went. It was at five percent, and she had no news from anyone on her staff. With a heavy sigh, she pulled the door open.

CHAPTER 15

TUESDAY

Carrieann Creighton stood on Josie's doorstep, towering over her, a pained look on her face. Josie took a moment to shake off her fatigue and opened her arms to her. "Carrieann. I'm so glad you're here."

Carrieann's embrace was hard and long.

"Come on in," Josie told her, ushering her into the kitchen.

"I went to Luke's first," Carrieann said, plopping into a chair at the kitchen table.

Josie set up her coffeemaker and turned it on. "I'm sorry. I can send someone back to clean up the mess."

Carrieann shook her head. "No, no. I can take care of it. I just didn't know if…if I was disturbing evidence."

"It's all been processed. You won't be disturbing anything. Although you're quite welcome to stay with me. You know that."

Carrieann smiled tightly at her. "I might. I don't know if I can stay in that house alone now. Has there been any word?"

"None," Josie replied. "My team is working on processing what evidence was there, but to be honest there aren't many leads."

"None at all?"

Josie thought of Jane Doe, her stomach churning. "Well, there was a woman there."

She gave Carrieann a run-down of her encounter with the girl with no memory as well as a description of her. Slowly, Carrieann shook her head. "Doesn't sound like anyone I know."

"You knew Luke's ex-girlfriends, didn't you?"

"Well, sure, the serious ones. It's not a long list."

"Maybe you could come down to the station today and have a look at her, see if you recognize her," Josie suggested. "That is, if we don't release her photo to the press."

"You think she's an old girlfriend?"

Josie sighed. "I don't know what to think, Carrieann. The woman had clearly been sleeping in his bed and . . . and was wearing his clothes."

Frowning, Carrieann's gaze dropped to the table. She pulled her flannel shirt more tightly around her. "It's just so unlike him. Luke's not the cheating type. I mean that. I'm not just saying that 'cause I'm his sister."

A pounding started in Josie's head. "What other explanation could there be?"

She shrugged. "I don't know, but I don't think either one of us is going to like it."

*

Three ibuprofen, two coffees, and one shower later, Josie's head didn't feel much better, but her phone had a charge on it and her mind was slightly clearer. Carrieann had retired to Josie's spare bedroom—the one she normally kept for when her grandmother Lisette slept over—and could be heard snoring all the way downstairs. In the kitchen, Josie called Noah's cell phone. "Where are you?" she asked.

"Where do you think? They just brought our girl over from the hospital."

"What did they say?"

"Neurologist says all her scans are clean. She's got some old, healed orbital fractures, but other than that she's healthy as can be."

"Orbital fractures?" Josie said. "Like the kind you get from being punched in the face?"

"Yeah, I guess. Doc said it looks like someone broke her eye sockets at some point."

"Sounds like we're dealing with some domestic violence in her history, then. What did the doctor say about her amnesia?"

"He said it's a dissociative fugue state."

"You mean she experienced something traumatic and lost her memory?" Josie asked, thinking of Gretchen's words from the night before.

She heard Noah sigh. "Basically. I talked to the doctor over the phone at length. From what he said, it fits. People in fugue states usually appear quite normal, they just can't remember their past or their identity."

"Oh, is that all?" Josie snapped. "Luke is missing, and this woman may have valuable information. Either she is purposely withholding it, or whatever she saw put her into this...fugue state. Have you printed her?"

"It was the first thing we did," Noah said. "The state police got the results back to us almost immediately. She doesn't come up in AFIS."

AFIS was the Automated Fingerprint Identification System, a national database available to law enforcement that allowed them to match fingerprints found at crime scenes with anyone whose prints were in the system.

"Did the neurologist say how to snap her out of it?"

"There's not really any way to bring her out of it. He recommended having her seen by a psychologist or a hypnotist if we're really in a hurry."

"Jesus," Josie said. "We don't have time for this. What about Misty?"

"She's still unconscious. Brain swelling. The doctors are going to operate on her today to try to relieve the pressure. We'll have to wait till after that to question her."

"Keep checking on her progress," Josie said. "I'm coming in. Keep Jane Doe in the interview room until I get there. Carrieann's here; she's going to come in later to see if she recognizes her. Send Gretchen back out to Luke's and have her search the property in the daylight. I know the team checked the barn, but I want it rechecked. I want the whole perimeter looked over one more time. There's got to be something there that can tell us either who this woman is, or who came for Luke."

"You got it," Noah said.

CHAPTER 16

At the station, Josie spent five minutes watching the mystery woman on CCTV as she sat motionless and alone in the interview room, an untouched cup of coffee on the table in front of her. Josie was beginning to wonder if she had slipped into some altered state of consciousness when finally she looked around the room, pushed her hair behind her ears and let out a long breath. Then she stretched her arms over her head and yawned. She still wore Luke's clothes, and Josie didn't like the way that made her feel.

Her office door was open, and someone had left a stack of mail on her desk. She riffled through the post, not really seeing any of it. She kept thinking about Luke, wondering if he was alive. Wondering what the hell he had done to get into this situation.

"Boss?" Noah walked in with a cup of steaming coffee in one hand and his notepad in the other. He handed the coffee to her. "Thought you might need this."

"Thank you."

She sipped it standing, watching as he held up his notepad, a list of names down the side of the page. "I've got what I think is a pretty complete list of men Misty was involved with," he said. "Going back to when she got pregnant."

"So, potential fathers," Josie said.

"Right." His brow furrowed as he studied the list. "There are seven."

Josie nearly choked on her coffee. "Seven?"

"Uh, yeah, and you might find this interesting—Brady Conway is on the list."

Josie set the coffee mug on her desk. "Luke's friend?"

"None other."

She gave a low whistle and thought back to the footage of Luke in Foxy Tails with Misty; it had been right around the time of Brady Conway's death. Was that the business that Luke had had with Misty? Was he acting as some kind of go-between between her and his friend? Brady had been married and a police officer; if he was the father of her baby, it certainly wouldn't have been an ideal situation for either one of them. Josie sent up a prayer that that was, in fact, why Luke had been at Foxy Tails twice to see Misty before Brady died. But why hadn't he told her?

"Boss?" Noah prompted.

Even if Brady was the father, that didn't explain what had happened to Misty and her baby, or Luke. And where did this girl fit in? "Just thinking," Josie told Noah. "The Conway connection is certainly interesting, but Brady's dead so his alibi checks out. We won't find Misty's baby until we find the person who was at her house yesterday."

Noah gave her a wry smile. "Yeah, well, most of these other guys alibi out. There are five with alibis for the last two days, one guy we haven't tracked down yet, and the mayor's husband."

Josie raised a brow. "The mayor's husband doesn't have an alibi?"

Noah shook his head. "His wife is his alibi. He was at the hospital yesterday and the day before, but there are long periods of time he can't account for—well, he says he was with her at home and she confirmed it."

"So, it's possible he could have attacked Misty and taken the baby, but if he has the baby, then where is he?"

Noah shrugged. "Easy to hide a baby in a mansion."

"I can't see Tara Charleston going along with that. She likes the power her status gives her. She wouldn't do anything to intentionally jeopardize it."

"Yet she's already tried to cover for him once. What if she came home, found him with the baby and didn't know what to do? So, instead of calling the police, she's got this baby."

It wasn't completely implausible. Spouses covered for each other all the time. Josie would have thought Tara was smarter than that, but then again, she'd stayed with her husband despite knowing that he might have fathered Misty's baby.

Josie said, "She'd let us have a look around, but if they're hiding a baby in the house, she'll have that bundle out of there the minute she knows we're coming."

"Shall I have a few officers respond to a burglary nearby?" Noah asked.

Josie smiled. "Maybe they can pursue the suspect onto the mayor's property."

"You got it."

"What about the prints from Misty's house? Anything?"

"Nothing yet. I asked the state police to put a rush on it, but you know it can take forty-eight hours."

"That's bullshit. They ran Jane Doe's prints last night for us," Josie said.

"Yeah, because it had to do with Luke's case."

"Call them back. Tell them the cases are connected. I'll call if you want."

Noah shook his head. "No, I can handle it."

"Thanks. Also, keep on top of the mayor's husband and see if you can locate the last potential father on the list. I'm going to try talking to Jane Doe again."

CHAPTER 17

The door to the interview room banged closed behind Josie, and the girl's head snapped up in surprise. Her big brown doe eyes widened as Josie approached. A hand snaked up and pushed more of her blond hair behind one ear. Josie pulled up a photo of Luke and placed her phone on the table. She pushed it across until it was right under the woman's nose.

Jane Doe stared at it blankly. "Who is that?"

Josie stared at her. "You tell me."

The woman looked up and, for just an instant, Josie thought she saw a flicker of something real, something not practiced. Annoyance, maybe. "I don't know him," Jane Doe said.

Josie reached across and tapped the phone screen. "This is the state trooper whose home you were fleeing last night when I found you."

Jane Doe said nothing.

"That trooper's name is Luke Creighton, but you know that already, don't you?"

"No, no, I don't remember—"

"What did you see in that house last night?"

"I told you, I don't remember."

"Why were you there?"

"I don't know, I told you. I mean, not you but the other lady detective."

Josie put a hand on her hip. "I'm aware of what you told Detective Palmer. Now I'm asking you—who took Luke?"

"Took him? What are you saying?"

The screen had gone black. Josie picked up the phone and pulled the photo up again, this time zooming in on Luke's smiling face. She pushed it in Jane Doe's face. "You obviously knew him, you're wearing his T-shirt. Why were you there last night?"

Jane Doe spread her hands, palms up, on the table, a gesture of frustration. "I don't know! I don't remember anything. I don't remember why I was there, or anyone named Luke. If I knew anything at all, I would tell you. I swear it."

"What did you see?"

"I told you. I...came to and I was outside, on the porch. It was dark. I walked up to the back door and saw blood on the walls, so I ran. I don't remember anything else."

"How did you get there?"

Jane Doe rolled her eyes. "I don't know how many times I can say it—I don't remember!"

"What's your name?"

"I don't know."

"How did you get burn marks on your back?"

Her expression changed fractionally. A slight tensing of her jaw. "What?"

"My detective tells me they found burn marks on your back when you were examined at the hospital. How did you get them?"

"I...I don't know. I mean, I don't remember."

Josie appraised her for a long, silent moment. Then she turned on her phone's camera and held it up. "Smile," she told Jane Doe.

The woman's eyes bulged. Not with feigned innocence this time but with fear. "What are you doing?" she asked.

"I'm taking your photo. We'll release it to the press. Someone out there will know who you are."

The woman jumped up, throwing her hands in front of her face just as Josie snapped a photo. It was a blur. "Stop!" she cried.

Josie suppressed a smile of satisfaction. "Why? Surely you want to know who you are and where you came from?" Again, she held up the phone. "Now hold still."

The woman held her hands in front of her face. "Please," she said. "Don't."

"Why not?"

"I...I think I might be in danger."

"Really? Why is that?"

She pulled her blond locks toward her face, turning away from Josie. "Well, I was at that house, and obviously something bad happened there. The blood—I saw the blood. I do remember that. Today you want to know who took this...this Luke guy, which means he's missing. I don't know what the hell is going on, but I'm obviously caught up in it or you wouldn't even have me here. What if you show my picture on the news and whoever took him comes after me?"

Josie narrowed her eyes. "You're in police custody."

The woman turned to face Josie again, her brown eyes peeking out over her hands. "Yeah and wasn't the guy who got kidnapped a police officer? How did that work out for him?"

Josie still held the phone aloft like a weapon.

"Please," she said. "Before you splash my face all over the television and internet, just give me another day to try to remember. I mean I haven't even slept yet. Maybe if I get some rest..."

Josie pocketed her phone and put both palms on the table, leaning toward the woman. "I will protect you," she said. "I can protect you from whatever it is that you're hiding from. If you tell me what it is right now, I can help you."

"I don't remember anything," she insisted.

"Do you understand that whatever it is you're hiding or running from could get Luke killed—if he's not dead already? I need to find him. Now."

Jane Doe remained silent, chewing her lower lip.

"What about Misty Derossi?"

"Who?"

"She's in intensive care at Denton Memorial. Someone took her newborn son yesterday. You know anything about that?"

The woman's eyes widened dramatically. Josie couldn't help but feel the shock and dismay in Jane Doe's expression was fake. "That's terrible," she said. "But no, I don't know anything about that—or her. I've never even heard of her. I'm telling you, I don't remember anything."

"Tell me what you know. I will protect you, and we'll get Luke back—if he is still alive."

A long moment passed. Josie could hear the sounds of her officers walking back and forth in the hallway outside. She kept her eyes on the woman until she looked away.

"I'm sorry," she said. "I don't remember anything. But please, just give me a day. Let me sleep. I want to help."

Josie didn't believe her for a second, and as much as she wanted to stride across the room and shake the information out of her, she couldn't. It was clear she was in danger. Which meant the safest place for her was in Josie's custody.

"You've got four hours. You can sleep down in holding. If you don't remember anything by the time I come to get you, I'm releasing your photo to the press."

"Thank you."

She would just have to find Luke on her own.

CHAPTER 18

Noah waited outside the interview room for her. "Well, that was productive." He smirked.

Josie suppressed a cutting reply, instead firing off a text to him, which immediately made his cell phone chirp. He looked at it. "I thought you didn't take her picture," he said.

Josie smiled. "She was so busy performing, she didn't even notice me taking it. Send it to WYEP. I want it on the news within the hour."

"I thought you were giving her four hours."

"We don't have four hours. Put her in holding. Make her comfortable. Get her photo out on the news and on social media. We'll say she was found at the scene of a crime, and we're trying to determine her identity."

"What if she's a domestic violence victim? What if the guy who broke her face comes to get her?"

"I can help her," Josie insisted. "I can protect her, but right now she is my only link to Luke. She knows something. She is my only chance of finding him—if he's even still alive. If she can't or won't tell me who she is, then I have to use whatever means I can to find out. I have no choice."

Noah looked as though he was going to argue with her, but then he swallowed and said, "Okay. I'll call WYEP."

"Then shoot over to Foxy Tails and show her picture around—see if anyone recognizes her."

"You think she knew Misty?" Noah asked.

"I don't know. What I do know is that Misty was beaten

to within an inch of her life yesterday, and her newborn was abducted. Hours later, we find Luke on tape visiting Misty at Foxy Tails because he had some kind of business with her. Then he goes missing after an obvious struggle, and this woman is at his house. It's all too much of a coincidence. Get that photo out immediately, will you? Let's see how Jane Doe likes being lied to."

"You got it, boss. By the way, Misty's cell phone didn't respond to the GPS or triangulation."

"So whoever took it likely destroyed it. That's a dead end. What about midwives? I still want to know if any midwives in the city have been reported missing."

"Gretchen was working on that," he said. "She hasn't found anything suspicious."

"Well, that's good. Where are we with the locksmith getting Misty's desk open? It's probably a dead end, but I'd like to know if there's anything useful in there."

"Gretchen had a locksmith out there yesterday, but there's some special tool he needed to open that particular desk. Did you know it was imported from England? It's almost two hundred years old. Anyway, the locksmith said he doesn't have the right tool, but he has a buddy a few towns away who does."

"Goddamn period furniture," Josie muttered.

"Say the word and we'll smash the lock and open it ourselves."

"No. That desk must cost thousands. I'm not paying for it. The most we're going to get from any documents in it is a better idea of who the baby's father is, and I'm pretty confident about the list of potential daddies we've already put together. Just let me know when you guys get it open, okay?"

"Of course."

Noah disappeared down the hall, already on the phone. Josie's cell phone rang, and she pulled it out to see Gretchen's name and number on the display. "What've you got?" she answered without preamble.

Gretchen's voice sounded strained. "I went over to Luke's, like you said. Had a look around the outside. The yard, the barn, the perimeter."

Josie's mouth went dry. "What did you find?" she asked. Gretchen wouldn't be calling unless she had found something significant.

"I've got a body here, boss. Out behind the barn. Buried. Looks like he's been here a while."

"So not Luke," Josie blurted out.

"I don't think so, no. I called the medical examiner. She's on her way. You want to meet us out here?"

Josie looked around. She noticed three of her officers leaned against their desks, their gazes on the television affixed to the wall. There was Trinity Payne again, covering day two of the Aaron King trial on national news. Like everyone in the country, Josie's staff was consumed with the trial. Why wouldn't they be riveted to the King coverage? There were no leads to follow in the Misty Derossi missing infant case. No leads to follow in Luke's disappearance. Jane Doe wasn't cooperating. "I'll be there in twenty," Josie said into the phone and hung up.

She called to one of the officers watching the news and told him to get an evidence response team out to Luke's house immediately. She tracked Noah down to tell him about the most recent development. He promised to catch up with her later once he got their Jane Doe situated and ran down some of the leads Josie had asked him to look into. Josie headed toward Luke's house, the seventeen miles there among the longest of her life.

*

Dr. Anya Feist was in her forties and had been the medical examiner for the city of Denton for more than ten years. She was smart, efficient, and no-nonsense. Josie had always liked her. She had always had a young, vital look to her, but the missing girls case had aged her. Josie had watched in the last eighteen months as her shoulder-length blond hair turned nearly silver and the pounds fell away from her five-foot-six frame until people started asking if she was ill. "No," she always answered. "It's just the stress of the job."

Josie found her on her hands and knees behind Luke's barn, sifting through loose dirt with gloved hands. She had already set up a rectangular grid with metal stakes and string. Gretchen stood outside of it, taking photos with one of the department cameras. Near Anya's knees, in the center of the grid, a leg covered in brown trousers peeked from the dirt, its foot wearing a mud-crusted black loafer. Josie felt a small wave of relief. Not Luke's shoes. He had one pair of oxfords, which he had paid way too much for and only wore to weddings and funerals, and these were not them.

Anya stopped sifting through the dirt and squinted up at Josie. "Chief," she said.

"Dr. Feist," Josie replied, stopping outside of the cordoned off area.

Gretchen nodded at Josie. She stopped taking photos momentarily and used the camera to motion behind her to where Luke's property ended and a small copse of woods began. "There's an incline here," she pointed out. "You have to walk up that little embankment to get into the woods. We had all that rain last week. I think it washed a lot of the dirt and mud away. Otherwise, I would never have spotted part of his shoe sticking out. Doesn't look like he was buried very deep to begin with."

Anya used the back of her wrist to push a stray lock of hair off her forehead. "I'll need to get the rest of my kit from my truck. We'll need an ambulance to transport this guy to the morgue once I've got him excavated."

"Whatever you need," Josie said. "How long do you think he's been here?"

"Don't know. Can't guess. I would have to get him on the table and get a good look at him. Judging by the condition of his clothes, though, he hasn't been here too long. If he'd been here for years, I'd expect his pants and shoes to be a little more worse for wear."

"What are we talking about?" Josie asked. "Days? Weeks?"

Anya smoothed a bit of dirt away from the bottom of the pant leg. "Four to six months. Could be less. But you know how this goes. I can't give you a solid answer until I examine the body."

"I understand. I'll go get the rest of your supplies."

"Just a minute," Anya said. She leaned over the leg, pushing the dirt gently away from the top of the thigh in small, even strokes. Her fingers searched for something along the pant leg. The man's pocket, Josie realized, as Anya cleared more dirt away and her fingertips disappeared into a seam in the fabric. "Come on," she muttered under her breath as she tugged gently on something inside his pocket. A moment later, her hand reappeared with a man's wallet pinched between her fingers. "Detective Palmer," she said.

Gretchen stepped closer, leaning over the string grid and taking several photos of the wallet. She let the camera hang from her neck and snapped on her own set of gloves before taking the wallet from Anya. Josie picked her way around to where Gretchen stood and looked over her shoulder as Gretchen opened the wallet to examine the contents. She pulled out a New Jersey driver's license and read the name aloud. "Mickey Kavolis." She held it out so Josie could snap a photo of it with her phone. Gretchen continued, "He was forty-seven and lived in Atlantic City."

The man on the driver's license looked every bit of forty-seven, and then some. His salt-and-pepper hair was thick over his ears and thin on the top of his head, receding at the temples. He had deep-set brown eyes that glared past a nose that looked as though it had been broken so many times it was permanently flattened. His olive skin was riddled with acne scars. The picture looked more like a mug shot than a driver's license photo.

Josie had no doubt that when they ran his name through their various databases, he would come up with a criminal record.

"Atlantic City?" Josie repeated. "What's he doing all the way out here?"

And why was he buried on Luke's property?

CHAPTER 19

ABC 7NY—Newark, New Jersey

January 7, 2017

Man Dies after Fall from Balcony

David Hammons, a twenty-year-old Newark man, is dead after falling from his eleventh-floor balcony. Police responded to the scene on Mt. Prospect Avenue shortly after 9 p.m. He lived alone and was alone in his apartment at the time of his fall. Police believe he had gone out to his balcony to smoke a cigarette when he fell to his death.

Hammons had recently been fired from his job at a nearby community center for allegations of child abuse. However, police did not find any indication that he killed himself.

A preliminary investigation has ruled out foul play or mechanical and structural issues as a contributing factor, according to police.

CHAPTER 20

The Denton City Morgue was located in the basement of Denton Memorial Hospital, which was an old brick building that sat on top of a hill overlooking most of the city. The patient rooms had great views, but the morgue itself was windowless and drab with a lingering odor that was half chemical and half biological decay. The walls of the long hallway had originally been white but hadn't been painted in so long that they were now a dull gray and the floor tiles had become jaundiced long ago. It was also the quietest place in the hospital—maybe even the city. Every time she came to the morgue, Josie felt like she was walking through the set of a horror movie; today she felt like the star of the show. Her mind swirled with questions. Who was Mickey Kavolis? Had Luke buried him there? Had Luke *killed* him? She tried to quiet the storm raging in her head. She needed more information. She needed to approach this like the experienced investigator she was.

Dr. Feist reigned supreme over the small corner of the building. She had one part-time assistant whom she'd hired in the wake of the missing girls case. He was in his late twenties, short and stocky with a barrel chest and a neatly trimmed goatee. Josie stood in the corner of their autopsy room as he helped Dr. Feist lift the body bag containing Mickey Kavolis from the ambulance gurney onto their stainless-steel autopsy table.

He moved around the room wordlessly, helping Dr. Feist to peel away the bag and prepare her workstation while she removed her jacket, revealing a set of light-blue scrubs, and fitted a skull cap over her silver-blond locks. At one of the sinks, she spent some time washing her hands. Glancing over at Josie, she said, "You sure you want to stay for this?"

Josie smiled. "Let's see how far I get."

She hadn't had to attend that many autopsies, but they weren't her favorite thing.

"You're welcome to sit in that chair in the corner. Don't interrupt me. Save all your questions for when I'm finished. You know the drill."

Josie sat in the chair Feist had indicated and pulled out her phone, texting Noah: *"Where are you?"*

"On my way," came his instant reply.

She had called him while Dr. Feist and the evidence response team unearthed Mickey Kavolis's body. He'd been at Foxy Tails, showing Jane Doe's photo around to the dancers. No one recognized her. Josie had asked him to run Mickey Kavolis's name and relevant information through their police database and meet her at the morgue.

Josie watched as Dr. Feist clicked on her digital recorder and started calling out her findings in a loud, clear voice. They knew his name, address, and date of birth from his driver's license. One look at the man's partially decomposed face was enough to tell them he had died from a gunshot wound to the head. Josie was hoping Dr. Feist would find a bullet or some other clue that would tell them who had killed Mickey Kavolis and how his dead body ended up buried behind Luke's barn.

She knew she shouldn't make assumptions, but Luke's property was pretty remote. The chances of someone besides him burying a man there were slim to none. With each hour that passed, the feeling of doom building up inside her grew and grew. She swiped her phone to bring up the home screen so she could text Noah again, and Luke's face appeared once more in her background photo.

What the hell did you get yourself into? she asked him silently.

A light tap on the door drew Josie's attention. From the square panel of window in the upper half of the door, Noah's face peered at her. Relieved she no longer had to be alone with her anxiety and fear for Luke, she dropped her phone into her pocket and, with a nod to Dr. Feist, who had just picked up her scalpel, Josie exited the room.

Noah stepped back as she opened the door. He pressed a hand over his nose. "My God," he said. "That smell."

Josie wrinkled her nose, making sure the door to the autopsy room was securely closed. "I know," she said. "It's pretty awful. So, what do you have?"

Noah looked at the door once more and said, "Walk with me. I need some air."

They found the nearest exit, which led to an employee parking lot behind the hospital. Two dumpsters sat beside the doors, and yet the smell was more pleasant than that emanating from Mickey Kavolis's body.

Josie kept her foot in the opening of the door to keep it slightly ajar. She knew the doors would lock once they closed them, and she didn't feel like walking around the entire building to get back in. "Tell me," she said.

"Mickey Kavolis worked for Eric Dunn."

"What do you mean worked for Eric Dunn? In what capacity?"

"Private security," Noah said.

"What? Like at his casinos?"

"No, like as a bodyguard...among other things."

Josie didn't like the sound of that. "Other things, like what?"

Noah shrugged. "Hard to say. I talked to someone on Atlantic City PD. They picked up Kavolis a few times in the last three years—three assaults and one robbery."

"Jesus."

"Yeah. He always beat it. Nothing ever went to trial. Dunn's lawyer swooped in, got him out on bail, then witnesses disappeared."

Josie asked, "Did Kavolis have a record?"

"Yeah, he served twelve years for third-degree murder. Beat a guy to death when he was twenty-two."

"So he was Dunn's muscle. What the hell was he doing here? I know Dunn is in talks with the city council to get his casino built, but what was Kavolis's assignment? No one here needs to be intimidated."

"The council members who don't want the casino, maybe?" Noah suggested.

Josie's brow furrowed. "We haven't had any reports from any of them of anything criminal going on."

"Would they report it if they were being pushed around by a guy like that?"

Josie sighed. "Probably not. How did you find out he worked for Dunn?"

"Two months ago, we impounded an abandoned vehicle on one of those back roads behind the college. It was a rental picked up in Philadelphia by Kavolis, and guess whose credit card he used?"

"Eric Dunn's."

Noah nodded. "It was a corporate card registered to Dunn Hotel and Gaming, LLC."

"Mickey Kavolis hasn't been reported missing," Josie pointed out. "At least, not here."

"Not in Atlantic City either."

Josie smiled. "You already called Dunn, didn't you?"

"I called human resources and said I was calling from a private security firm where Kavolis had put in a résumé."

Josie had to restrain her guffaw. Men like Kavolis didn't use résumés. They didn't need to. Theirs was a skill set in high demand in the right circles.

Noah continued, "They said he resigned in May."

"Resigned, huh? That's one way to put it. That was four months ago. You said you picked up his rental car two months ago—that would have been back in July. When did he rent it?"

"May. The rental agency just kept charging Dunn's corporate account. They made some half-hearted attempts to contact Dunn about getting the car back but didn't get anywhere."

"And Dunn just let the charges accrue?"

"Until we called them and they had someone come out and get it from the impound, yeah."

"They paid the fees?"

Noah nodded. "No questions asked."

"Can you find out when Eric Dunn was here this year? See if Kavolis was here with him?"

"Yeah, I'll look into it."

"He's at the Eudora Hotel," Josie said. "Mayor Charleston told me he stays there every time he visits. I think he's still in town—he was her guest at the charity benefit last night."

Noah raised a brow. "Should we go have a word with him?"

"No, not yet. I need more information before we talk to him."

"What kind of information?"

"The kind that only Trinity Payne can provide."

CHAPTER 21

The Alcott County Courthouse was the centerpiece of a small town called Bellewood which sat about forty miles south of Denton. Josie sped along, white-knuckling her steering wheel to concentrate on staying on the winding mountain back roads instead of what was happening to Luke—if he was still alive. The courthouse was besieged with news vans and roving reporters covering the Aaron King trial. They milled about, faces bent to their cell phones, like well-dressed, perfectly coifed zombies. Josie found Trinity Payne leaning against a network news van with a huge satellite dish on top of it, her fingers tapping frantically at her phone screen. As Josie approached, Trinity held up one palm and, without looking at Josie, she said, "Tell him I'm going to get a quote, okay?"

"I'll tell him," Josie said. "Just as soon as you tell me who he is."

Trinity looked up, a smile lighting her face. As always, Josie was disconcerted by the resemblance between them. Almost of its own will, her right hand reached up and smoothed her black hair down over the long, jagged scar that ran from her right ear down her jawline. Trinity tossed her own shiny black locks, her blue eyes flashing. "Chief Quinn," she said. "Are you here to ask for help with your Jane Doe? I saw her on the local news. She's pretty. Where did you find her?"

"I'm not at liberty to disclose that at this time," Josie said, smiling back. "Actually, I'm here about something else. Someone else."

Trinity arched a perfectly plucked eyebrow. "Your missing fiancé, or the stripper's baby?"

"Nothing gets past you," Josie remarked. "You're not even reporting locally anymore."

"I hear things. You never know what the national audience might be interested in. So, which is it?"

"Do you have information on either one of them?"

"I'm sorry to say that I don't."

"Then it's neither. I need to know whatever you know about Eric Dunn. I know the network has had you up and down the East Coast in the last year. I saw the piece you did about the casinos in Atlantic City going belly-up. Practically all of them, except his."

Trinity pocketed her phone and put a manicured hand on her hip, appraising Josie fully. Josie already knew full well she wasn't getting what she needed without giving Trinity something in return. Trinity had been a loyal ally since the missing girls case broke, but her ambition knew no bounds now that she was on the national stage.

"You'll have to take me to lunch for that," Trinity said.

"Is that all? Lunch?"

Trinity smiled like a Cheshire cat. "I'll tell you what I know. Then you'll tell me why you want to know. If there's a story, I want it."

Josie rolled her eyes. "Come on, then."

"I want to eat at Harry's Grill."

"That's expensive."

"It will be worth it."

"You better know something I can't learn from Google."

Trinity laughed as she walked side by side with Josie. "Oh, honey, I always know more than Google."

*

Harry's Grill was housed on the first floor of an old six-story hotel that presided over Bellewood's Main Street, one of few high-end restaurants in the county. It was only a few blocks from the courthouse, and although Bellewood's population wasn't enough to support it and its exorbitant prices, the constant influx of people in and out of the county courthouse kept it in business. As the two women walked, Trinity's four-inch Jimmy Choo heels clacked against the pavement in a steady rhythm. Pulling her cell phone back out, she fired off texts in rapid fashion as they made their way to the restaurant, where they were seated within minutes by a hostess more glamourously dressed than Josie had been at her own senior prom.

Trinity put her phone on the table and narrowed her eyes at Josie. "Before I say anything, you should know that Eric Dunn is serious as a heart attack."

"What does that mean?"

"It means that people who get in his way have a tendency to disappear."

That didn't surprise Josie based on what she knew about Mickey Kavolis, but she stayed silent. The waitress arrived with water glasses, introducing herself and taking their drink orders. Trinity ordered a glass of white wine. Josie had coffee. Once alone again, Trinity leaned forward. "Is this about the casino Dunn is trying to build in Denton?"

"I wish it were," Josie said.

Trinity smiled and took a sip from her water glass. "Oh, this sounds juicy."

"You talk first."

With a shrug, Trinity placed her water glass back on the table, her index finger making lazy circles around its rim. "Eric Dunn is twenty-four. The son of a couple who come from old money. They're so rich, they didn't even have him themselves."

"What do you mean?" Josie asked.

"I mean Mr. Dunn was old as hell with a twenty-something wife who didn't want to ruin her figure, so they used a surrogate mom."

"Did the father have any other kids?"

"No. Eric is his first and only child. He'd been married a few times before that but never had any kids. Wife number four convinced him that it was now or never, and there was nothing wrong with using 'unconventional methods' to produce an heir."

"How do you know this stuff?"

"Well, I know that from a *People* magazine article from, like, two years ago, when Eric Dunn's success was front page news. But everything else I know because I prepared a story about him, and my producers wouldn't air it."

It was Josie's turn to smile. "Your producers don't air a lot of your stories."

Trinity rolled her eyes. "They won't air the ones they deem too controversial. At least, not yet. When I get more experience and credibility, I'll have carte blanche."

The waitress appeared with their drinks and took their order—soup for Josie and an appetizer and a pricey entrée with three sides for Trinity. Josie had forgotten just how much tiny Trinity could eat in one sitting.

"So, Dunn inherited his dad's empire," Josie prompted, hoping to keep Trinity on track.

Trinity shrugged. "Yes, and he's done wonders with it. He's the youngest casino mogul in the business today. When he was twenty, his father had two casinos—one in Atlantic City and one in Philadelphia. Now? They're building casinos in California, Colorado, Louisiana, Vegas. You name it. All over the country. Eric didn't go to college. Instead, he took over the family business after his father had a stroke. He's good at it. Really good at it. But he's not as . . . scrupulous as his father was."

"Is dear old dad still alive?" Josie asked.

"No. Mr. Dunn died when Eric was twenty-two. He was never the same after his stroke. He was nearing ninety anyway."

"Why do you say Eric isn't as scrupulous as his father?"

"He cuts corners; tries to build everything on the cheap, uses non-union workers, and won't pay them once the work is done.

He bribes people to get out of obtaining the necessary permits, and rumor has it that the people who won't take his bribes either disappear or have some kind of unfortunate accident."

Josie's blood ran cold. Luke had obviously gotten caught up in something involving Eric Dunn. Had Dunn made him disappear? Was she already too late? She forced down the rising emotion from within and frowned, refocusing on the conversation. "Is Dunn mobbed up?"

Trinity shook her head, taking a healthy swig of her wine. "No. I don't think so. But he runs his business with the kind of ruthlessness a mob boss would. Surrounds himself with paid thugs who will do whatever he tells them—or pays them—to do. He doesn't care who he hurts or who he screws. He has always been able to muscle his way out of tough situations. Well, until recently."

Josie took her time pouring sugar and cream into her coffee, stirring it languidly. "What happened recently?"

"They were building in Philadelphia—well, they had to knock down some existing structures. Word is that Dunn bribed a bunch of municipal workers to forgo the requisite inspections and hired a bunch of guys cheap for the demolition who didn't exactly know what they were doing. They ended up accidentally taking down two other buildings when they pressed the button."

"Oh."

"With people in them. One building had apartments over a coffee shop. Nine people were killed in that collapse. Lucky for Dunn, the other building was being exterminated for bed bugs so only three people died."

"My God."

Trinity sipped her wine and nodded. Her cheeks were rosy. "Yeah, it was really bad. I can't believe you didn't see this on the news last year. It went national."

Josie vaguely remembered seeing it on an evening news program, but she hadn't paid much attention to the particulars. Plus, the name Eric Dunn hadn't meant anything to her back then. Josie pulled her cell phone out and Googled him, wanting to put a face to the name. Most of the photos she turned up were of Dunn standing in front of a new building, cutting a ribbon with an oversized pair of scissors. He looked a bit older than twenty-four, but he had a full head of brown hair, hazel eyes that sat just too close together, and a long, straight nose that hooked ever so slightly. He was of average height and build. There was nothing remarkable about him. He looked familiar, but Josie couldn't remember ever having met him.

"I can't imagine that Dunn is worried about civil lawsuits," Josie said to Trinity. "I mean, surely he had insurance—or enough assets—to cover those."

"Of course he does," Trinity agreed. "He's been involved in these types of scandals before, but never on such a large scale. Last year definitely wasn't the first time someone died on one of his construction sites. In the past, either witnesses disappeared or recanted, or he paid the families off quietly before anything went to court. The families were happy to take their money and move on."

"But not this time?"

"This time, he may have criminal culpability. Of course, his lawyers claim he had nothing to do with the hiring of workers or anything on site. They deny all allegations of bribes. But two of the municipal workers have already killed themselves, and three of the workers operating the heavy equipment had drugs in their system. The DA is trying to pin Dunn with something that will put him away. The families won't take any of his money."

"What about the workers?"

"Oh, they've already been charged with manslaughter and a host of other things. They're going down for sure. But like I said, the DA isn't satisfied with that. This is too big for Dunn to muscle or buy his way out of."

"But surely this guy has access to the best attorneys that money can buy," Josie said.

"Sure he does. But rumor has it that there is direct evidence that he was personally involved in overseeing this demolition."

"What kind of evidence?" Josie asked as she kept scrolling through her search results. A photo of Dunn walking into one of his casinos with a blond woman on his arm caught her eye. She tapped it to enlarge, but all she could see was the back of the woman's head. Dunn had turned and waved a hand at the camera, but his date kept her gaze forward.

"Tapes—video, audio. No one is entirely sure which, but it is one or both."

"And these rumors are circulating where, exactly?"

"His organization. I talked to a lot of people. No one would go on record, but that's the story I kept getting."

Josie went back to the search page and found two more photos of Dunn with a short blond woman, but in neither of them could she see the woman's face. "Someone heard it from someone who heard it from someone…that's not reliable, and you know it."

"Yes, but where there's smoke, there's fire. Look, Eric Dunn is not a good person. The people who work for him are not good people."

"Has he ever been accused of domestic violence?" Josie asked.

"Not officially. I mean there have been rumors, but nothing ever made it into a police report."

"Does he have a girlfriend?"

Trinity arched a brow. "Why? Are you in the market? I know Luke is missing, but I would have thought you'd hold out hope for his return."

"That's not funny," Josie said.

"I'm sorry," Trinity answered. "That was in poor taste. Dunn does have a girlfriend. Her name is Kim something."

Josie pulled up the photo she had taken of their mystery witness earlier. "This her?"

"Your Jane Doe? I don't know. I never met her. I just know

he's had a girlfriend named Kim for about a year now. He was never the monogamous type; she stood out to his workers because she was around so long."

"You have no last name?"

"No. She wasn't the story. He was."

Josie went back to the Eric Dunn Google search and typed in "Eric Dunn girlfriend." The images loaded slowly. Many were with what Josie assumed were ex-girlfriends. Most were supermodels whose height exceeded Dunn's.

"Can you get me a last name?" Josie asked as Trinity's appetizer arrived.

As Trinity started digging into the steaming, crab-filled mushrooms she motioned for Josie to have some, but Josie declined with a wave of her hand. "Tell me why you're so interested in Eric Dunn?" Trinity diverted.

Josie weighed her options. Trinity had burned her before—using something Josie had said in confidence in a newscast and getting Josie put on unpaid suspension because of it, but that had been before the missing girls case, before Trinity had been accepted back onto the national news scene, her once-shattered credibility intact again. They had a tenuous trust these days. Even without telling Trinity, there was no guarantee that Mickey Kavolis's death or the location of his body would remain secret.

"We found one of Dunn's security team buried on Luke's property. Gunshot wound to the head."

Trinity's eyes widened. She nearly choked on the clump of half-chewed food in her mouth as she said, "Are you serious?"

She asked all the same questions Josie had asked her team—how they knew he worked for Dunn; where they found the rental car; whether Kavolis had been reported missing by Dunn or anyone else; what Luke's connection was to Dunn—and Josie answered them as best she could, but with as little information as possible.

Trinity used her index finger to swipe the last of the fallen cheesy crab meat from her empty plate and licked it just as their main courses arrived. Josie had little appetite, and her hand trembled as she lifted her spoon and stirred her soup.

"You think Dunn has Luke?" Trinity asked.

"You don't know Luke," Josie said. "Not really. He isn't into . . . criminal stuff."

"So, he's a state trooper. Some cops are dirty. Or don't you remember that?"

Josie bristled. "Not Luke," she said, even as her mind drifted back to his unmade bed and the nightstand on her side of the bed. "He wasn't dirty—isn't dirty. But he got into something. I don't know what, but something."

Trinity said, "For what it's worth, I'm sorry."

It was as close to nice as Trinity ever got. "Thank you," Josie said.

"What will you do?"

Josie pushed her soup away, untouched. "Bring him home."

CHAPTER 22

Josie fielded calls from Carrieann and Gretchen on her way back to the station. Carrieann didn't recognize the woman they were holding, and she was heading to Luke's house to try to clean things up. Josie couldn't bring herself to tell her over the phone that they'd found a body on the property, so she told her that her evidence team would still be working there to try to uncover any evidence that might help them find Luke. "But they'll be outside, probably out by the barn," Josie added. "So don't mind them. I'll meet you back at my place later tonight."

Gretchen called shortly after to let Josie know that she and the evidence response team had finished up at Luke's house and would be heading back to the station soon. No more bodies had been found, and no additional evidence. If Kavolis had had a cell phone, it wasn't buried with him and couldn't be found anywhere on Luke's property. The medical examiner had, however, found a .45-caliber slug in Mickey Kavolis's brain. Josie didn't know whether to be relieved or more confused—Luke didn't own any .45-caliber pistols.

Josie told her to start looking into land records in the county to see if Dunn or his company owned any real estate. If Luke was still alive—and she wasn't ready to entertain the notion that he wasn't—then Dunn's people might be holding him somewhere close. It was a long shot, but it was a lead she couldn't ignore.

As Josie stepped through the doors of the station house, her desk sergeant Dan Lamay came around the partition separating the lobby from the rest of the building. Lamay was a rotund figure nearing retirement age who very likely needed a knee replacement. Josie had kept him on at the front desk because she knew his wife was battling cancer and he had a daughter in college.

"Boss," he said. "We have some...problems."

Just then Josie noticed a flash of blue in her periphery. She turned her head just in time to see Mayor Tara Charleston advancing on her with a finger pointed at Josie's chest. She wore a smart navy-blue skirt suit and matching heels that clacked when she walked. A lot like Trinity's, Josie thought fleetingly. Tara's finger was then in her face, and her pale cheeks were red with fury. "How *dare* you!" she growled at Josie.

Josie stood her ground, folding her arms across her chest and doing her best to look bored. "I'm sorry, Mayor Charleston. Did you have an issue you would like to discuss?"

For a split second, Josie thought the woman was going to slap her. She stood her ground; she would not be intimidated by Tara Charleston, not in her own station house. Tara seemed to realize this and regained some control of herself, lowering her hands onto her hips, glaring. "First, you send your officers to my husband's place of employment to question him when I *specifically* instructed you not to. Then you sent *armed* policemen to my home on the pretense of searching for a burglar? Are you out of your mind? What are you trying to prove?"

Josie narrowed her eyes at the mayor. "First of all, you didn't instruct me to do anything. You asked me to be discreet, which I have been. You do understand that there is a baby missing, don't you? I have a responsibility to find that infant and bring him home to his mother—if she survives. Secondly, there was no pretense in sending officers to your home. We got a call from a neighbor."

"Oh, really? Which neighbor?"

"I'm not at liberty to say."

Tara's cheeks colored even more. "I am the mayor of this city," she said, her voice shaking with anger.

"And I have two missing persons cases on my hands," Josie retorted. "I don't have time for...whatever this is."

With that, she stepped around Tara and over toward Lamay, who had seen the whole exchange and was pulling a face like he had swallowed something sour. Over her shoulder, Josie heard Tara say, "You'd better watch yourself."

Josie turned back. "What exactly does that mean, Mayor Charleston?"

"You know damn well what it means."

"That you'll fire me and put someone in my position who will do whatever you tell them? Good luck with that."

Tara's finger pointed at Josie's face again. "I told you—"

Josie cut her off, advancing on her so that she had to lower her arm and take a step back or be barreled over by Josie. "And I told you that I have work to do. As long as you and your husband aren't involved in anything criminal, we have no issue with one another. Now, if you'll excuse me, I have a witness to speak with."

She left Tara standing there openmouthed and brushed past Lamay, summoning him as she went. He followed her into the suite of offices behind the lobby partition as her phone chirped, announcing a text message.

"Boss," Lamay said as he followed her up the steps to her second-floor office.

The text was from Trinity. "*Got that name for you. Eric Dunn's girlfriend is Kim Conway. That's all I could get.*"

"Conway?" Josie muttered to herself.

"Boss," Lamay said again as they reached the threshold to her office.

She was still staring at the text message. It couldn't be a coincidence, but she didn't remember Brady or his wife ever mentioning siblings. Brady had grown up in Denton, joined the state police, done a tour in Erie and then in Philadelphia before being transferred back to the Denton area. He had then moved to the smaller, quieter, more rural Bowersville. Josie knew all this because WYEP had reported it after his death: hometown boy turned domestic abuser; police officer turned murderer. Josie had gone to the funeral with Luke two weeks after the whole incident, had met Brady's weeping mother, grandmother, and several other relatives but hadn't met any sisters. She definitely hadn't met a blond woman named Kim.

"I need to talk to our Jane Doe," Josie told Lamay, finally pocketing her phone. "And next time the mayor is waiting in the lobby to attack me, drop me a text to warn me, would you?"

He grimaced. "I'm really sorry about that. She just got here a few minutes before you came. There's something else."

Josie fought the sigh that threatened to come out. "Something besides Mayor Monster lurking in the shadows?"

"Well, it's about the Jane Doe. She's gone."

CHAPTER 23

Josie stared at Lamay, uncomprehending. "What did you say?"

"I said she's gone."

Josie rushed down the flight of steps to the holding area on the ground floor of the station. It was empty. Only one officer sat at the desk, streaming coverage of the Aaron King trial on the desktop computer.

"Son of a bitch," Josie said. "What the hell happened?"

Lamay followed just behind her, struggling to keep up. "I'm sorry, boss. A United States marshal came about a half hour ago and took her. He said she was in Witsec."

"The witness protection program?"

He nodded. "He had identification. Credentials."

Since Josie had been on the force, they'd never had a United States marshal show up unannounced for a custody transfer. Of course, Lamay had been on the job for many years before Josie came along. "Sergeant Lamay, have you ever seen a U.S. marshal's credentials before?"

Lamay drew himself up a little straighter. "No, but what reason would I have to question him? He came here asking for the girl, and he had identification. It looked as real as anything I've ever seen."

Josie squeezed the bridge of her nose, a headache beginning to pound out a steady beat across her forehead. "Did he say who she was? Did he ask for her by name?"

"No, but he had a photo of her. He wouldn't tell me who she was. He said it was a very sensitive case and that with her photo on the news, he had to get her back into custody as soon as possible. He said her life was in danger."

I bet it is, she thought. "Did you call the marshal's office to confirm with them that this was an authorized custody exchange?"

"N-no, I didn't—"

"Did you have him sign the transfer forms?"

"Yes, of course," Lamay said, looking somewhat relieved. "I'll show you."

She followed him back to the lobby, texting Noah as they walked. "*I need you here now.*"

A large pile of paperwork teetered on the edge of Lamay's desk. On top of it was the custody transfer form they typically used when transferring persons in custody to another law enforcement agency. The man had filled it out and signed it, but his handwriting was completely and purposefully illegible. "Call the marshal's office," Josie instructed, surprised at the calm in her voice. Her only lead to Luke had been plucked from right beneath her nose, most likely by one of Eric Dunn's goons if not the U.S. Marshals Service. "See if they confirm this transfer. I want to see the CCTV footage. If this guy was here, he'll be on our cameras."

Noah came through the front doors, and Josie felt a sudden wash of relief come over her at the sight of him. She waved him over and together they went into the CCTV room just off the lobby in what used to be a broom closet. "What's going on?" he asked.

"The girl with no name, she's gone. I think I know who she is, but she's gone."

"How?" Noah asked.

"A man claiming to be a United States marshal came in about an hour ago and took her. Told Lamay she was in Witsec."

Noah pushed a hand through his thick mop of hair. "Holy shit," he said. "Did you get anything on the guy?"

"His signature is unreadable. I'm trying to pull him up on the video now." She sat down at the small desk and started clicking away at the computer, trying to bring up the CCTV footage of the lobby from that afternoon. "That's not all," she added, and proceeded to tell him about her meeting with Trinity.

"So, you think our girl is Kim Conway—Dunn's girlfriend? Brady Conway's sister?"

Josie nodded, her eyes never leaving the screen as she sped through the footage—the mailman, a UPS delivery driver, two women, a man Josie knew to be from the civic association, another man from the historical society and a few more women. They all spent some time at the counter speaking with Lamay before departing. A couple of them stopped to hang fliers on the community corkboard next to the front door. Cataloging them helped keep her anxiety at bay.

"Where have you been?" she asked Noah.

"At the state police barracks. I went to see if I could convince them to expedite matching the prints we took from Misty's house."

Josie kept moving through the footage, looking for a man in a suit rather than in the blue marshal's uniform. She assumed if it had actually been a U.S. marshal coming to take someone into Witsec, they would not draw attention to themselves by dressing in full uniform, and if it was someone posing as a marshal, he might not have been able to get his hands on a real uniform. A few more people zipped in and out of the lobby onscreen, dressed too shabbily to be posing as marshals. "Did they expedite the prints?"

"Uh, yeah," Noah replied. "I mean, some of them are still unknowns, but..."

By the tone of his voice, Josie knew he had found something. Her finger lifted from the mouse, pausing the footage. She turned to look up at him. "What?"

Had they found Luke's prints all over Misty's house? she wondered. Had the two been having an affair? Had he been sleeping with both their mysterious witness and Misty Derossi?

"Jane Doe's prints turned up at Misty's house. In the bed-room, master bath, kitchen, and the room where the attack took place."

"Are you sure?"

"I had them run the prints twice. She was there."

Josie turned back to the footage, her right index finger pressed against the mouse again, speeding it along. "Come on," she muttered under her breath. Beneath the desk, her leg bobbed up and down at machine-gun speed. On screen, there was a long lull in activity before another one of her officers relieved Lamay for his morning break. He returned fifteen minutes later with a cup of coffee in hand. She couldn't help but wonder what would have happened had the marshal shown up while Lamay's relief was on duty. Would that officer have questioned the marshal more thoroughly? It was a matter for another day. Right now, she had to find this guy. Her finger pressed harder against the mouse button, as though that would make the footage play more quickly. "What the hell was Jane Doe doing at Misty's house?" she asked Noah.

"Maybe they were friends?" Noah suggested.

"Do you still have the best friend's number? Brittney? Text her a photo of our girl and see if she recognizes her. I would have expected her to call if she had recognized her from the news, but you never know."

Noah perched on the edge of the desk, pulled out his phone, and sent the text.

"Got it!" Josie exclaimed.

Finally, the sped-up footage showed a burly, bald-headed man in a charcoal suit walking through the doors to the station. Josie set the video to regular speed as she and Noah watched him approach the counter and speak at length with Lamay. There were three cameras in the lobby—one overhead; one behind the front desk just above shoulder level, meant to capture people's faces; and one above the doors leading outside. The man kept his face angled so that both the camera above the doors and the one behind the front desk only caught him in profile.

"He's purposefully avoiding the camera," Josie said.

Noah leaned across her and clicked something to the left of the screen. "Did you check each camera?" He replayed the initial encounter with Lamay from all three cameras, but the man managed to avoid looking directly at all of them. "Shit," Noah said, returning to an aerial view of the lobby. "You'll never get a still from this footage. He's good."

"Too good. A real marshal would have no reason to avoid the camera," Josie said. "Shit."

She fast-forwarded through several minutes of film. More discussion between the man and Lamay. Lamay examined his proffered credentials, made a call—to holding, Josie guessed—had the man fill out the transfer form, and then Lamay made another call. For ten whole minutes, the man managed to keep his face out of the line of all three bird's-eye cameras as he perused the corkboard just inside the front doors.

Then another officer emerged from behind the partition with Jane Doe trailing behind him. Josie watched the officer motion to the man. The girl suddenly stopped walking, her entire body stiffening.

"She recognizes him," Josie said. "She knows him."

Noah squinted down at the screen. "How can you tell?"

Josie rewound the video. "Watch."

"So, she was lying about having no memory," he said.

"Did you really think she was for real?"

"I had my doubts, but mostly I thought she was genuine."

Josie rolled her eyes.

Noah's phone chirped, and he looked down at the screen. "Brittney says she's never seen the woman in the photo before."

On the computer screen, the officer left Jane Doe with the man. Josie and Noah checked the footage from all three cameras once more, but again the man was careful to keep his face in profile to the lobby's cameras. Jane Doe stood frozen in place. After a brief, tense exchange, the man grabbed her upper arm—not gently—and pulled her toward the door. She looked up toward the ceiling, craning her neck, searching until she found the dead-eye of the camera. Then she looked directly at it and mouthed two words: *Help me*.

CHAPTER 24

Josie's voice shook with rage and frustration. "I told this woman I would protect her."

"Boss, this isn't your—"

She shot up out of her seat and Noah jumped back as she pointed a finger at him. "Don't. That was not a marshal. That is either the guy who beat her badly enough to break her face, or he's taking her to that guy."

She stalked back and forth across the room, her anger like a balloon inflating inside of her, stretching her to her limits. Noah watched her pace like a caged wild animal. "She was my only connection to Luke," she said. "Now she's gone."

Noah stared at the screen where Josie had paused the footage on Jane Doe's face. "Why didn't she say something? Scream, fight? Something? She was in a police station."

"Haven't handled a lot of domestic violence cases, have you?"

He met her eyes. "What does that mean?"

Josie motioned to the screen where Jane Doe's terror-stricken eyes peered at them. "Why don't all victims of domestic violence run to the police? They're too scared. These guys have a psychological hold over their victims, and most of the time the system fails them when they do speak up."

Noah raised a brow. "She was in a police station."

"That's right. He knows where she is now. Let's say she screamed and raised hell and Lamay arrested this guy—then what? He's out on bail in a few weeks and now he's even more pissed that she went to the police."

"So it was better for her to go with him?"

Josie shook her head. The room suddenly seemed too small, the air too thick. "You don't understand what it's like to live with someone like that. Someone who hurts you. Someone who finds ways to keep hurting you even when people are trying to help you."

"You do?"

She ignored his question. That wasn't a conversation she was going to have with Noah. Not today, maybe not ever. "I need to find this woman," she said instead.

He held her gaze for a long moment, as if waiting for her to say more. When she didn't, he suggested, "Pull the external footage. Maybe we can see what kind of vehicle they left in."

Josie took a deep breath, willing herself to focus. What she wanted to do was throw everything she could get her hands on, destroy everything in her path, but none of that would help get Luke back or change the fact that she had put Jane Doe back into the hands of whoever was hurting her. She sat down to pull the footage from the exterior of the building and sent Noah to do a computer search for any and all Kim Conways in New Jersey and Pennsylvania.

They had exterior cameras all around the building. The man who took their girl had entered through the front, so Josie pulled that up first. The view extended roughly a half block in each direction and encompassed the small visitors' parking lot in front of the building. But the man didn't park out front. He entered the frame on foot and exited with one hand clamped firmly around Jane Doe's upper arm, dragging her along. They walked down the sidewalk and out of the frame.

"We can't trace his vehicle," Josie said, trying to keep the hopelessness out of her voice. "He parked out of range of the cameras. We don't even know what he was driving."

She looked around, suddenly remembering she was alone in the video room, and went out to the front desk where Lamay was hanging up the phone. He used his sleeve to wipe sweat from his brow. His face was pale, and he wouldn't look at her. "I'm sorry, boss," he mumbled. "I made a mistake. The marshal's office didn't send anyone here to pick up the Jane Doe. I can't believe I—I'm really sorry, boss."

Carefully controlling her voice, Josie said, "From now on, all transfers from us to anyone outside of the sheriff's office have to be specially approved by me. No exceptions. You call me at home if you have to. You got that, Lamay?"

He nodded.

"We'll discuss disciplinary action later. For now, I need you to send two or three units out to patrol the town looking for this guy. Notify the state police as well. They'll be eager to help since this is connected to Luke's case."

He nodded again, still unable to look at her.

Josie left him to his work and headed to her office. Noah was there already. "Where's Gretchen?" she asked.

"I put her on Kavolis since you said you needed me here. I couldn't find any record of him having been a guest at the Eudora Hotel when Dunn was here in May, but if the rooms were reserved under Dunn's name, he wouldn't be in the computer. Gretchen's going to show his driver's license photo to some of the staff and see if anyone remembers him."

"Great," Josie said. "Anything on Kim Conway?"

"There are eight Kimberly Conways in Pennsylvania but none of them are younger than thirty-eight, so not her. There are nine Kimberly Conways in New Jersey. One of them lives in Margate, which is not far from Atlantic City, and she is twenty-two."

"Criminal record?"

"No."

"Facebook account?"

"Not that I could find."

"Driver's license photo?"

Noah frowned. "I can't view New Jersey driver's license photos, only the records."

"Shit. I forgot." Josie sat in her chair. "The Conway connection is bothering me," she said.

"Is there a connection?"

"I don't know. It's too coincidental, don't you think? Luke's best friend was a Conway. Jane Doe is most likely Kim Conway—girlfriend of Eric Dunn, whose lackey we just found dead on Luke's property. Those dots aren't hard to connect."

"So, let's say the common denominator is Eric Dunn."

"No, the common denominator is Jane Doe. She was at both crime scenes."

"Okay, well, if Jane Doe is Dunn's girlfriend, why doesn't he show up and tell us that?"

"Because if she disappears with a United States marshal and we think that she's gone back into Witsec, we'll never know or even notice when he has her killed and disposes of the body."

"Why would he want to kill his own girlfriend?"

"I have no idea."

"Are you ready to pay Eric Dunn a visit?"

"Not without confirming that Jane Doe is his girlfriend. Can you get me Brady Conway's mother's phone number?"

"Of course," Noah said.

Josie was thinking of the girl's face in the camera and her silent plea for help. Guilt pricked at her. She might have lied about her amnesia, but she had tried to tell Josie that she was in trouble. The burns on her back and the old facial fractures were objective evidence, and Josie had ignored them, putting her further into harm's way by releasing her photo so quickly. What if she had waited a few hours like the girl had requested?

"Don't second-guess yourself," Noah said.

Josie gave a pained smile. "You can read my mind now?"

He smiled back at her. "I'm getting better at it," he joked. "I'm just saying—she was the only lead we had on Luke's whereabouts. You had to find out what you could about her sooner rather than later. You did the right thing by releasing her photo. How could you have known someone would be desperate enough to find her to impersonate a United States marshal?"

Josie used her fingers to roll a pen along the surface of her desk. *What if I've lost him already?* she wondered, but she didn't say this to Noah. Still, he said, "We'll find Luke. I'll go track down Mrs. Conway's number."

Noah turned to leave, and at once, Josie felt panicked. Being alone had become unbearable. So many devastating unanswered questions rolled through her mind.

"Wait," she called.

He stopped, half out the door and half in her office. "What is it?"

She beckoned him back into the room. He waited, an uncertain smile tugging at the corners of his mouth. A few seconds of silence passed between them. Long enough for Josie to hear the muffled sound of someone streaming coverage of the Aaron King case—either from their phone or from one of the desktop computers. The sound of Trinity Payne's voice floated under the door. "Today, the prosecution intends to introduce DNA evidence linking King to his last victim..."

Noah said, "Boss?"

She couldn't tell him that she didn't want to be alone. She was his superior. They had a case to work. People were missing: her fiancé, a tiny infant, and an abused woman. She motioned to the doorway. "Will you tell them to turn off that damn Aaron King coverage, please?"

"Sure thing," he said, and then he was gone.

CHAPTER 25

CBS Boston

March 27, 2017

Woman Found Dead Inside Home Filled with Carbon Monoxide

Annie Lannan, a nineteen-year-old Plymouth woman, was found dead in her home yesterday from apparent carbon monoxide poisoning. Lannan's mother returned home from working an overnight shift at a local hospital and found her daughter unresponsive in her bed.

Police and EMS arrived on the scene but were unable to revive Lannan. The fire department confirmed extremely high levels of carbon monoxide in the home at the time. Investigators are still trying to determine the cause of the carbon monoxide poisoning. However, they are urging residents to install carbon monoxide detectors in their homes.

CHAPTER 26

It only took five minutes for Noah to get Zora Conway's number.

"This has a 212 area code," Josie said when Noah handed her the number. "That's in New York, isn't it?"

"Yeah."

"I thought Brady's mother lived here."

"Evidently not," Noah said.

"You sure this is right?"

"How many Zora Conways do you think there are in New York? I remember hearing her name on the news when the shooting happened. It's right."

Wordlessly, Josie picked up the phone and dialed the number. Noah sat back down in the chair across from her desk. The phone rang four times. Just as Josie was sure she would get voicemail, a woman's reedy voice answered, "Hello?"

"Mrs. Conway?"

"Who's calling?" A note of suspicion but no confirmation that it was Zora Conway.

"This is Denton Chief of Police Josie Quinn. I'm trying to reach Zora Conway."

A long silence. Then, "I already talked to the police about my son. I told you, he was never violent. I don't know why he did what he did. I have nothing more to say."

"Oh, Mrs. Conway, I'm not calling about your son, I'm calling about your daughter."

Again, the woman fell silent. Josie forged ahead. "Your daughter, Kim," she tried.

Nothing.

"I just have some questions about her. I think she—"

"My daughter is dead," Mrs. Conway snapped. Then there was an abrupt click and, a couple of seconds later, the dial tone buzzed in Josie's ear.

She held the receiver out and stared at it, puzzled. Then she tried calling back. Four times the phone rang and rang until it went to voicemail. It was a dead end.

"What the hell was that about?" Noah asked.

"She said her daughter was dead, and then she hung up on me. Now she won't pick up."

"Now what?"

Josie thought back to the funeral. They had had it in Denton because Bowersville didn't have its own funeral parlor and the rest of the Conways were Denton locals, including their grandmother, whom Josie remembered seeing at the funeral.

"I need to go to Rockview," she said.

"To see your grandmother?" he asked, perplexed.

"No, to see Brady Conway's grandmother."

CHAPTER 27

Rockview Ridge was Denton's one and only skilled nursing facility. It sat high on a rock strewn hill on the edge of the city. Josie's grandmother Lisette Matson had been a resident there for several years now. In her mid-eighties, Lisette was still very sharp, and she made friends with any other residents lucid enough to hold a conversation. Josie suspected this included Brady Conway's grandmother, Hattie Conway.

"That's her, right there, in the blue sweater," Lisette said. She pointed to the woman Josie had met at the Conways' funeral who now sat in Rockview's cafeteria, a magazine spread on the table before her. She turned the pages slowly, leaning down close to see what was on each page through the thick glasses she wore. Like most of Rockview's residents, her hair was short and white, half-teased, half-curled and then shellacked with hairspray to keep its shape.

"Will you introduce us?" Josie asked. "I'm not sure she'll remember me."

Beside her, Lisette sighed heavily, her expression one of resignation mixed with annoyance. "You could have called me, you know, when Luke went missing. You should have called me."

"I'm sorry, Gram," Josie said.

"No, you're not."

"Yes, I am sorry. I screwed up. I should have called you right away, but I was working. I—"

Lisette raised one hand from her walker. "I know, I know.

Your work is very important. You know I understand that. Better than anyone, perhaps. But Josie, this boy is going to be my grandson-in-law. You should have told me yourself."

Josie opened her mouth to offer more apologies and some explanation, but Lisette spoke again. "We don't have to talk about it right now. I know you're upset. You don't have to go over the details with me. I'm simply saying in the future, when someone who is supposed to be a member of our family goes missing, I expect a phone call."

Without thinking, Josie suddenly leaned into her grandmother. Lisette slid a hand across Josie's shoulders and hugged her. She stroked her long black hair with one arthritic hand. "It will be okay," she whispered into Josie's ear. "Just you wait and see. You'll find him, and he'll be fine."

Josie fought the tears that threatened to come. She felt terrible for not calling Lisette immediately, but it had been too hard. Lisette was all Josie had. The only living member of her family left. Telling Lisette everything she knew about Luke's disappearance would have made it all the more real. Too real. Lisette was the only person—now that Ray was gone—who Josie was prepared to let her guard down with. She knew she'd lose her composure talking to Lisette about Luke, and she wasn't sure she'd get it back. Right now, she needed all the poise and focus she could muster. Later, when everything was over, she would deal with the thorny emotions she was barely keeping at bay.

"Thank you," she said to Lisette.

Lisette disentangled herself and cupped Josie's cheeks. She smiled. "Come now, you've got work to do."

As it turned out, Hattie Conway did remember Josie from the funerals. "We never had a female police chief before." She beamed. "I sure wouldn't forget you, and your grandmother brags about you nonstop."

Josie glanced at Lisette, who rolled her eyes as if to say that Hattie exaggerated.

"Mrs. Conway," Josie began. "I'm very sorry to bother you, but some things have been happening in the city. We've got a few missing persons now, and I think your granddaughter might be caught up in what's happening."

"My granddaughter?"

"Yes, don't you have a granddaughter?"

"My granddaughter was Eve, Brady's wife."

"Right, but didn't Brady have a sister?"

Hattie's deeply lined face puckered, as though she had eaten something bitter. "Oh, yes, he does. I mean he did. But she's not my granddaughter."

"She's not?"

Hattie shook her head vigorously. "You see, Zora married my son, Emmett. They had Brady pretty soon after they married. Emmett wanted to have more kids, so they tried...and they tried and tried, but Zora couldn't get pregnant. It took a massive toll on their marriage. My boy always wanted a big family. Lots and lots of kids. I know they fought over it something awful. He started drinking, going out to bars. A few times, she took Brady and left, went to New York City. I don't think she even had family there. I'm not sure what was there for her, but she always came back. One day, she finally announced she was pregnant. Things were good for a while. They seemed like they were getting their marriage back on track. Then we came to find out that Emmett had testicular cancer. Turns out he couldn't have gotten Zora pregnant. She said the baby was his, but he didn't believe her. He was dead by the time that baby came."

"I'm so sorry," Josie said.

Hattie's head bobbed. "It was very difficult. I knew Zora lied. She had a girl who looked nothing like Emmett. Nothing like him at all. We all knew, but she insisted on giving her the Conway name. Such a disgrace."

"The baby—did Zora name her Kim?"

"Yes, Kim, that's right. She was a troublemaker too. That's

the other reason I knew she wasn't a real Conway. She had behavior problems before she was even old enough to get into trouble. As soon as Brady graduated high school, Zora took her and moved to New York City. Probably to be with the man she had there, whoever he was."

"Is Kim still alive?"

Hattie shrugged. "As far as I know."

"Do you know if Zora and Kim had any kind of falling out?"

"Well, I'm sure they did."

"Did Zora tell you that?"

"She didn't have to. Like I said, that girl was a little demon. I guess that's what Zora got for cheating on her husband and having another man's baby."

"Did Brady ever talk about Kim? Did they have a relationship?"

"I know he kept in touch with her, tried to look after her, but most of the time she was off doing whatever floozies do. He wouldn't hear from her for months. I know he wanted to keep track of her because she was his half sister, but I told him it was a waste of time."

Josie took out her cell phone and pulled up the photo she had taken of Jane Doe, the one that was on the local news. She turned the screen toward Hattie. "Is this Kim Conway?"

Hattie took the phone from Josie's hand and brought the screen so close to her glasses they were nearly touching it. She studied it for several seconds before handing it back to Josie. "That's her, all right."

Josie put her phone away. She glanced at Lisette and then turned back to Hattie. "Mrs. Conway, how is your vision?"

Hattie laughed. "I'm sure that's her," she said. "That's Kimberly all right."

CHAPTER 28

In Rockview's lobby, Gretchen waited, leaning against the front desk in her signature leather jacket, looking more like a biker than a police detective. Josie wondered idly if she should institute some kind of dress code for her senior investigative officers. She pushed the thought aside because it didn't matter. The case was what mattered.

"What's up?" Josie asked. She passed by Gretchen and out the front doors.

Gretchen followed. "Kavolis was in Denton in May. The concierge at the Eudora wasn't any help at all, but the house-keeping staff confirmed it. Also, I can't find any evidence that Dunn or his company own any land in Alcott County. I'm sorry, boss."

The cool September air felt good on Josie's face. She stopped at her driver's side door and looked at Gretchen. "You came all the way out here to tell me that?"

Gretchen squinted against the sun. "I came out here to see how you were holding up."

"Holding up? Did Noah ask you to talk to me?"

"Lieutenant Fraley? No. I'm here of my own accord."

Josie opened her door but didn't get in. "Is there something you want to say to me?"

Gretchen hesitated, a grimace working its way onto her face. "It's just that, you know, I've been at this a long time."

"Longer than me, I'm aware of that," Josie said. "Do you have an issue with the way I run my department?"

"No, not at all. That's not what I'm getting at."

"Just say it, Detective Palmer," Josie said. "I've got work to do."

"Well, that's just it. Most departments don't let their officers work their own cases."

Josie closed her car door and took a step toward Gretchen, folding her arms across her chest. "I don't have a case."

"Your fiancé is missing."

"Yes, that's his case, not mine."

Gretchen smiled, a sardonic twist to her mouth. "You're splitting hairs there, boss."

"You think I'm not doing a very good job?"

"I didn't say that. I think the stress of having a missing loved one and running two major investigations can be a lot on a person, that's all. I'm just saying, we can handle this. You've got a lot of good people around you, and we wouldn't let you down."

Josie felt her annoyance slip a little.

"Sleep is good," Gretchen added.

"I'm fine, I really am," Josie said. "You have some experience with this?"

Something dark passed over Gretchen's face and she subconsciously tugged the lapels of her jacket tighter around her. Without answering Josie's question, she went on, "Your sister-in-law—I'm sorry, your soon-to-be sister-in-law—is in town. I met her out at Luke's house. Maybe the two of you could hang out."

Josie thought of the long, torturous hours that she and Carrieann had spent together in the waiting room of Geisinger's ICU almost two years ago. She had no desire to recreate that time in her life. She needed to keep moving. Forward movement was the only thing standing between her and an emotional breakdown.

She opened her door once more. "I have to go," she told Gretchen.

Gretchen simply nodded. "I'll be helping with the search for Jane Doe," she said.

"Kimberly Conway," Josie corrected. "I got confirmation from a family member. Could you pass that along?"

"Of course. Where are you going?"

"There's something I need to do," Josie said. She didn't give Gretchen a chance to ask what. Instead, she got into her car and quickly turned it on, pulling away and watching Gretchen shrink in her rearview mirror.

Josie was almost to Bowersville when Noah called her. "Any news?" she asked.

Noah's voice sounded strained. "There's been an accident," he said, rattling off an address. "You need to see this. We need you here now."

CHAPTER 29

It took Josie fifteen minutes to get to the scene of the accident. Her patrol officers had already cordoned the area off and a crowd of onlookers lingered on the periphery, craning their necks and taking photos of the carnage with their phones. The street was two lanes in each direction. On one side was a row of apartment buildings and on the other was a dirt shoulder marked by foliage. The street circled a densely wooded part of Denton's City Park—a green space between the college campus and Denton's Main Street, where residents walked their dogs, jogged, and held community events. Inside the park was a large playground, a gazebo, and a small pond. The closest intersecting street was a one-lane residential road several yards away.

In the middle of the northbound side of the road, a mangled Ford Bronco lay on its driver's side, glass and metal debris scattered around it. Her officers were erecting a pop-up tent around its front end, which meant there was a fatality. As Josie walked toward them, she saw blood pooling where the driver's side window kissed the blacktop. Several feet away, the front of a small red pickup truck had plowed into the passenger's side of a Toyota Corolla.

"Boss." Noah came jogging up beside her from the edge of the scene where he'd been interviewing onlookers.

A beep sounded behind them, and Josie looked back to see Anya Feist driving through the police barrier.

"Want to tell me what the hell happened here?" Josie asked Noah.

Josie watched as Dr. Feist parked next to the pop-up tent and hopped out to talk with one of the responding officers. The officer gestured toward the now covered portion of the Bronco, and the doctor marched off toward it.

Noah pointed to the apartment buildings. "A guy on his balcony said he heard a loud boom, like a gunshot. Then the Bronco lost control, hit a parked car and rolled over several times into the northbound lane. The red truck was trying to avoid the Bronco and crashed into the Corolla. Then the witness reports that a blond woman climbed out of the passenger's side of the Bronco and fled on foot into the park."

"Conway. Do you have a team out looking for her?"

"Two teams."

Josie watched Dr. Feist disappear into the tent.

"The truck and the Corolla—any fatalities?"

Noah shook his head. "No, minor injuries only."

Relief washed through her. Whatever the hell was going on with Kim Conway, Josie didn't want any innocent bystanders getting killed because of it. "Who's the driver in the Bronco? Same guy who came to get Kim at the station?"

"We assume so."

"You don't know?"

"Chief Quinn," shouted Dr. Feist.

Josie made her way into the tent, searching for the doctor. "Chief?"

It was then that Josie noticed the doctor's legs sticking out of the passenger's side of the Bronco, which now faced the top of the tent. A close look through the webbed windshield revealed the doctor's upper body dangling from the passenger's seat window, hanging down toward the driver.

"What the hell are you doing?" Josie said.

"Trying to get a good look at this guy in situ. Someone blew his damn head off."

Dr. Feist's legs kicked and flailed. Josie heard a muffled grunt as the doctor pushed her upper body up out of the cab of the vehicle. She sat on the door and held something out with a gloved hand. Josie looked to Noah, who handed her a set of latex gloves. She snapped them on and took what the doctor was handing her. Another New Jersey driver's license. This one belonging to Denny Twitch, whose photo showed a thick-necked man with a shaved head: their fake marshal.

Josie smiled at Dr. Feist. "If you could just show up at all of our crime scenes and magically produce victim IDs from now on, that would be great."

Dr. Feist smiled back and used her forearm to swipe a stray lock of hair from her forehead. "No magic to it. Always check the pockets. By the way, there's a pistol in there too. I'm just going to take some photos, and then you can have a bus bring him over to my office for a full autopsy, although I can tell you right now he was killed by a close-range gunshot to the right temporal lobe."

She leaned back inside the vehicle. Josie turned to Noah and held up the driver's license so he could take a photo of it. "I'll run a background check," he said. "And see if he works for Eric Dunn."

"Great," said Josie. "What about the vehicle?"

"It's his private vehicle," Noah answered. "Registered to him."

She took another look at the Bronco and sighed. "That's a pretty old model, isn't it?"

Noah grimaced. "Yeah, there's no GPS."

"Phone?"

"Once Dr. Feist is finished, we'll see if we can find it."

"So, no point in paying a visit to Eric Dunn quite yet. Not until we confirm that Twitch worked for him, see if we get anything from his phone. Also, we have to find Conway."

"Should I call the press?" Noah asked.

Josie shook her head. "No. Keep her off the news, would you? If Dunn's organization is so bent on finding her that they're willing to send someone to impersonate a United States marshal, then I want her and the search for her to be as off the radar as we can make it. I don't even want them to know for sure if she's missing."

"WYEP is still running her as Jane Doe," Noah pointed out.

"Then call them, tell them she has been identified and we're working on reuniting her with her family. Then stress the need for privacy. Tell them we are not releasing her name at this time. Thank the viewers and all that. Make it sound good. I don't want them getting wind that there's a story here."

"You got it," Noah said.

Josie took a slow walk around the wreckage, glass crunching underfoot. She wondered just how scared Kim Conway was that she would shoot a man in the face while he was driving the car she was in. Trinity's words echoed inside her head. *Eric Dunn is not a good person.* "Noah," she called.

He had disappeared into a patrol car to use the computer inside. He stepped out. "What's up, boss?"

"I want a K-9 unit out here looking for Conway. See if the sheriff can loan us one, would you? She may very well be injured from the accident. I don't want her out there wandering around if she needs medical attention."

He nodded and got back into the patrol car, his cell phone already pressed to his ear. Josie turned away from the wrecked Bronco and studied the tree line. She wondered how far Kim Conway would get on foot. Or would she hide until the patrols stopped searching the park for her? Josie knew she had more than enough people to search for her, that she should go back to the station or home to get some sleep like Gretchen had suggested, or even to Bowersville, where she'd originally been headed when Noah called her, but instead she walked toward the tree line and disappeared into the woods.

CHAPTER 30

Josie walked through Denton's City Park and the woods surrounding it until her feet ached and the sun dropped below the edge of the horizon. It would be another two hours before the sheriff's dog unit showed up. Several officers had fanned out across the park while patrol cars weaved throughout the city streets, searching for any sign of Kim Conway. Other officers were going door to door on the surrounding streets to see if any residents had seen or heard anything. After stumbling over a tree branch and twisting her ankle, Josie started using the flashlight app on her phone. She limped through the forested area, sweeping the beam of light across the ground, at the tree trunks, and even upward into the low branches of trees that looked particularly climbable.

Where the hell had she gone?

The snap of a branch froze Josie in place. She swung her phone around, the light dancing wildly on the tree trunks until she caught a snatch of blue police jacket in her periphery. She homed in on it only to see Noah rubbing his forehead gingerly. "Didn't even see that branch there," he muttered.

"You startled me," said Josie. "What's going on? Did you find anything?"

He drew closer and shook his head. She could see a red welt forming where the tree branch had hit him. "No, nothing."

Josie sighed, turned away from him and limped ahead, her flashlight pointed away from both of them. "Well, how about a status report, then?"

"You're limping," Noah pointed out.

"What's that got to do with anything?"

He ignored her question and gave her a run-down of where they stood with their dual investigations. "We tracked down the last potential father on the list of Misty's lovers. He's been in jail for the last three months on a drug charge so he alibis out. I'm still trying to make a connection between Denny Twitch and Eric Dunn. Word is that Dunn is still over at the Eudora. He's holding meetings this week with some council members about the plans for his casino. Gretchen's at the hospital with Dr. Feist for the autopsy. She said they've got a phone, but it's damaged so she's going to take it to that techie repair place near the college and see if they can't get something from it. Her locksmith is going to borrow the tool he needs to get Misty's desk open without damaging it. He'll pick it up tomorrow and meet Gretchen at Misty's house in the morning. Oh, and Misty came through surgery quite well, they say, but she is still heavily sedated. Her surgeon said the earliest we can talk to her is tomorrow. Also, I think you should go home and get some rest."

Josie stopped and put her hands on her hips. Her ankle throbbed. She longed for her bed so she could put it up on a bunch of pillows and pack some ice on top of it. Wine might also take the edge off. But doing that would mean stopping, and both Luke and Misty's baby—and now Kim Conway—were all missing and presumably in danger, and Josie wasn't even sure why. How could she stop? Luke needed her. Misty's tiny, defenseless, days-old baby needed her. She sucked in a deep breath and kept walking. She heard Noah's footsteps padding behind her.

"Boss."

"I can't, Noah. I just can't."

She felt him gently take hold of her elbow, stopping her from going any farther. She could see his face from the glow of the flashlight beam. So serious, so concerned. She almost laughed. "I'm fine," she lied.

"You're tired, you're limping, and I'll bet any amount of money you're starving. We'll have people working every angle throughout the night if that will help you sleep. But you'll be no good to anyone if you don't rest. Go get a pizza, go home, and talk to Carrieann. She's been alone all day."

Josie had nearly forgotten about her would-be sister-in-law. "I think we should take a look at the Conway house," she told Noah.

He raised a brow. "You think that's where Kim would go? That's a hike from here. It would take her a couple of days to get there on foot."

"I think we should check."

"I'll call over to Bowersville and ask them to send a car over."

"Okay, great. Also, see if we can get in there tomorrow. I'd like to have a look at the house, even if Conway's not there."

"Is there something you're not telling me?" Noah asked.

Josie had wanted to visit the Conway house after the shooting, but Luke wouldn't let her. There was no point, he said. She had offered to lend the Bowersville PD her Evidence Response Team the night of the shooting, but their chief had said there was no need. "Pretty obvious what happened here," he had told her. "No sense wasting manpower and money." Personally, Josie wouldn't have handled it that way, but the Conway scene was out of her jurisdiction, and she wasn't about to get into a pissing match with a small-town police chief whose shoddy work had no bearing on her own city. Still, she had never been able to shake her annoyance with the Bowersville chief's easy dismissal of the entire thing. But the more she brought it up, the angrier Luke became, telling her: "There's nothing you can do. They're dead and you going to that house won't change it. Believe me, you don't want to see it. Leave it alone!"

She had left it alone except for when he seemed most distant and closed-off, and even then she had only suggested—sometimes quite strongly—that he get counseling since he was obviously dealing with some unresolved feelings about the shooting. Now Josie had three missing persons on her hands and everything seemed to come back to Brady Conway.

"There's a connection—multiple connections—to Brady Conway," Josie explained to Noah. "Brady had had an affair with Misty, he's on the list of potential fathers. Luke was meeting with Misty weeks before the Conway shooting. Kim was Brady Conway's younger half sister—and by her grandmother's account, Brady was the only one in the family who still spoke to Kim."

"I see," Noah said.

Josie wondered now if Brady had asked Luke to look after his little sister for some reason. Was that why Kim was at Luke's house? Maybe, but that didn't explain why she had been sleeping in his bed or wearing his clothes. Maybe she'd been staying with Luke because he had been Brady's friend, but that didn't explain the intimacy. And it certainly didn't explain why Luke didn't just tell Josie.

"I think maybe Luke was hiding Kim from Eric Dunn. It's the only scenario that makes sense to me. From what Trinity said, Dunn is as ruthless as they come. He obviously has no regard for the law if he was willing to send Denny Twitch to impersonate a United States marshal in order to retrieve Kim. I mean, I know we don't have confirmation that Twitch was working for Dunn, but I think that's what we're going to find."

Noah frowned. "Even if Luke knew Kim was in danger and wanted to help his friend's little sister by hiding her, why didn't he just tell you—or anyone—what was going on?"

Because Mickey Kavolis was buried in his backyard. She didn't say this to Noah. A scenario was beginning to form in Josie's mind, but she didn't want to lay it out for Noah until she was absolutely certain. She was sure that her visit to the Conway house would confirm her theory. It still wouldn't explain why Kim's prints were found at Misty's house. Other than Brady Conway, Josie could see no connection between Kim and Misty. But she had to start somewhere.

Josie said, "I have an idea, but I'd like to see the house first."

Noah didn't argue. "I'll call over to Bowersville and talk to them about getting into the house—but in the morning, okay?"

She thought about Carrieann alone at her house. Alone with her anxiety. The same anxiety Josie had been able to keep on the edges of her consciousness by staying in a perpetual state of motion. Luke had lied to Josie—about a lot of things—and maybe even cheated on her. But Carrieann had always been good to her. Had stuck her neck out pretty damn far for her when it mattered most. She deserved better than to be pacing Josie's house alone worrying about her brother. Noah was right. A few hours of rest and some sustenance wouldn't hinder the investigation. She was chief now, and had to learn to delegate.

"Okay," she conceded. "But only for a few hours."

CHAPTER 31

Josie woke to the smell of bacon cooking. Sunlight streamed through her bedroom windows and she knew at once she had slept longer than the three hours she had intended. A lot longer. A glance at her digital alarm clock drew a lengthy groan from her body. It was nearly eight a.m. She had slept a full six hours. She lay for a moment, listening to the sounds coming from her kitchen. The clinking of dishes and silverware, the opening and closing of drawers. The gurgle of the coffeemaker. For just a second or two, in the haze of sleep, she thought it was Luke. He was back and, like he always did whenever they both had a day off, he had gotten up before her to cook breakfast. He was a talented cook, intuitive and creative. He never followed a recipe, but everything he made was delicious. Josie was far from a domestic goddess and he often had little to work with in her kitchen, but somehow, he always managed to whip up a masterpiece.

She missed him.

Her eyes snapped open and she shook off her fatigue. As the fog in her head cleared, she realized there was only one person who would be cooking in her kitchen at that moment—Carrieann. Luke was missing, she reminded herself. It had only been a couple of days, but it felt like months. She *had* been missing him for months, though, hadn't she? She had even wondered if she should end things with him as she watched him slip further and further away from her, a cold, distant façade replacing the warm, loving man she had known. Now she would take him and his coldness over not having him back in a second. With a sigh, she hefted herself out of bed. There was work to be done.

In the kitchen, Carrieann stood by the stove, pushing scrambled eggs around in a frying pan with a spatula. Bacon sizzled in a large pan beside it. She didn't look like she had slept at all; her blond hair hung down her back, lank and oily, and dark circles smudged the skin beneath her eyes. They had stayed up late talking about the leads in the case, polishing off a bottle of wine together while Carrieann did her own internet search on Eric Dunn.

Josie didn't even notice Noah sitting at the table until she was halfway to the coffeepot. She pressed a hand to her heart. "Jesus," she said. "You scared me."

He smiled and raised a steaming mug of coffee in greeting. "We thought we'd let you sleep a little longer."

Josie pushed her hands through her tangled hair, trying to tame it. Reaching down, she tugged the hem of her nightgown over her exposed thighs, wishing she had thought to throw on some sweatpants. "I wish you hadn't," she muttered.

She poured a cup of coffee and joined Noah at the table. "Any news?"

"Gretchen's got someone examining Twitch's phone. They think they can get it working again. The sheriff's dogs were out all night. They tracked Kim Conway to a treehouse in some woman's yard. There was some dried blood in there, so she definitely hid there at some point. Homeowner claims she didn't see anything. Let the deputies search her house. They didn't find anything."

Josie groaned. "A fucking treehouse. She was right there. Right under our noses."

"Well, she didn't stay there. They tracked her scent for about two miles from that house and then it disappeared."

"Which means what? She got into a car?"

"That's the most likely explanation."

"If someone picked her up, she could be anywhere by now," Josie said. She'd only been up for about ten minutes, and already there wasn't enough coffee to make this day bearable.

Noah added, "I called Bowersville PD last night. They sent a car over to the Conway house last night and again this morning. There's no sign of her there."

Josie took a long swig of coffee, wincing at the burn from the roof of her mouth to the back of her throat. Carrieann set a plate full of breakfast food in front of Josie, then Noah. She sat down with her own plate but made no move to eat. Only Noah dug in, thanking her between bites.

"I want to get into that house," Josie said, chewing absent-mindedly on a piece of bacon, surprised to find that her body was alarmingly hungry. She scooped up some scrambled eggs with her fork and pushed them down as best she could. Carrieann watched the two of them, her own food untouched in front of her.

"We can take a ride over, but we'll have to get permission from the family to get in."

Josie finished off the rest of her coffee. Her head was starting to clear. "Sometimes it's better to ask for forgiveness than permission," she said.

CHAPTER 32

They took the back roads, driving in silence over the top of a mountain and down into the small valley where the town sat, just a smattering of houses, churches, and one lonely strip mall. It was amazing to Josie that the town survived at all and that there were enough people in it to fill up the four churches that survived every natural and financial disaster that threatened to annihilate the town itself. Bowersville was so sleepy that before Brady Conway murdered his wife and killed himself, the town hadn't had a homicide in over half a century.

Josie pulled into the Conway driveway. Trees and brush separated the house from the neighbors on either side. It was possible that their visit would go unnoticed, particularly in the middle of the day, but Josie was certain tongues were already wagging after the Bowersville PD had been out twice to check the house.

They took a slow walk around the perimeter. It had been months since the shooting, but the Conway house still had shredded pieces of police crime scene tape fluttering in the wind from where it had been tied to the front porch posts. Noah tried the front door, but it was locked.

"Let's try the back," Josie said.

They took a second walk to the back of the house. Sure enough, the back door was unlocked. This didn't surprise Josie. People in Bowersville didn't typically lock their doors at all. They didn't need to. The house smelled musty with the faint scent of blood and bleach. The back door opened into the kitchen, where the cabinets stood open and empty. Cardboard boxes labeled "KITCHEN" were stacked on top of the table and counters.

"It's been months," Noah said. "Most people would have this cleaned out and sold already."

"Luke said the two families were fighting. Brady's mother hired a service to come clean and pack up the house. Eva's family was supposed to come by and take whatever they wanted, but there was some kind of disagreement, and everything stopped until they could get things ironed out."

Noah tapped one of the boxes. "Doesn't look like anything got ironed out."

"Apparently, Eva's family thought they were entitled to both the contents of the house and any profit from the sale of it and still expected Brady's mother to pay for the cleaning and packing, but Brady's mother wanted to split everything fifty-fifty."

"I imagine they'll be fighting for some time over that," Noah said.

Josie moved into the living room and Noah followed. She could see the places where someone had tried, unsuccessfully, to clean the bloodstains. A couch and two recliners had been pushed against one wall, the glass-topped coffee table flipped and placed on top of the couch. The television sat on the floor between the recliners, and the entertainment center had been moved to that side of the room, its cubbyholes filled with boxes whose labels said: "LIVING ROOM."

Noah said, "Whoever cleaned up sure didn't know much about getting bloodstains out of hardwood floors—or walls."

Josie nodded her agreement, staring at two puddle-shaped marks that dominated the center of the floor, only a few feet apart from each other where Brady and Eva must have fallen after being shot. About a foot away from the puddle stain closest to the kitchen were a series of faint reddish-brown streaks. "Look at this," she said. Noah came over and stood next to her, staring at the marks. "Jesus," he said.

Josie knelt down and ran her hand over two thick lines of

faded blood side by side. "Do these look like drag marks to you?"

Noah squinted at the area she had indicated. "I don't know," he answered. "They could be. Or maybe just streaks from when the cleaning service tried to get rid of them?"

Josie stood and stepped into the center of the room, studying the puddles again. She moved into the middle of the one closest to her, imagining that it was where Brady had stood, pointing a gun at his wife's face. "Over here," she said. "Stand in the other spot."

Noah walked over and stood in the second puddle. "Am I Brady, or Eva?"

"I don't know," Josie said. "Let's say you're Eva. I'm shooting from here." She extended a hand, her index finger pointed straight like the barrel of a gun. Her eyes searched out the faded blood spatter stains on the walls and ceiling.

"I didn't see the scene," she said. "But Luke said that Eva was shot in the face and that the back of Brady's head was missing."

"So, he shot his wife and then put the gun into his mouth and fired," Noah said. He leaned a little to his left to look around Josie at the wall behind her. Then he turned and looked at the wall behind him. "Are you thinking what I'm thinking?"

Josie lowered her arm. "If Brady shot Eva in the face at close range, the spatter would have come forward—toward him—not backward toward the wall behind Eva. Brady's self-inflicted gunshot should have been the only one that caused back spatter."

"So why were there two wall spatters?"

"Good question."

"This is why you wanted to see the house," Noah said. It wasn't a question. "You knew something was wrong."

Josie said nothing, turning instead to study the streaks on the floor again. She remembered how soaked in blood Luke had been when she retrieved him from the hospital. He had admitted to trying to revive his friend. But that wouldn't account for drag marks. Again, her frustration with the Bowersville police department rose up like acid reflux.

Had the scene been processed and analyzed properly, they would have realized that something didn't fit. Hell, even a cursory look and a couple of brain cells should have told them that something wasn't right. But it cost money to bring in an evidence response team. There were lab costs, the expense of borrowing equipment and supplies, not to mention the overtime involved in the process. Josie knew all this because she was a chief now and spent more time agonizing over her budget than she did her cases. Bowersville didn't have that kind of money. Tragic though it was, it was faster, easier, and cheaper to call the Conway shooting a murder-suicide, file it under domestic violence, and close the case quickly.

"What do you think happened?" Noah asked.

Josie didn't need to see anything more in the living room. She had a pretty good idea of what had happened there and why Luke had lied to her. It felt like a stab in her rib cage. She said, "I'm not sure, but I think both Kavolis and Kim Conway were here that night."

"You think one of those spatters belongs to Kavolis?" Noah asked.

Josie beckoned him to follow her through the rest of the house. "Well, if I'm right and Kavolis was here, then yeah, the spatter would have to be his."

"Who shot him?"

She climbed the stairs to the second floor, Noah padding along behind her. "I don't know," she answered. Could Luke have shot and killed a man and lived with it for all those months? There was only one reason Kavolis would have been there that night—to get Kim and take her back to Eric Dunn.

"What kind of gun did Brady use?" Noah asked.

The air was even more cloying in the upstairs hallway. Josie felt sweat bead along her upper lip. "His service weapon," she answered. "That was in news reports."

"So, a different gun was used to shoot Mickey Kavolis, then," Noah reasoned. "Kavolis was shot with a .45-cal but Luke doesn't own a .45-cal, right?"

"Right. Brady might have, but if there were any guns in this house I'm sure that Bowersville PD removed them."

Noah scoffed. "Yeah, 'cause they're clearly pros at evidence collection. I think Kavolis brought the .45 with him and someone shot him with his own gun. You think he came after the murder-suicide, like Luke did?"

Josie had a chilling thought. "Or maybe it wasn't a murder-suicide at all. If I'm right, only two people know the truth, and they're both missing."

They passed the bathroom and master bedroom. Both had been packed up in similar fashion to the downstairs. There were two other bedrooms which had not been packed up. One was a home office with a treadmill in it, and the other had a twin bed made up neatly with a gray blanket. A stack of books sat on the bedside table.

Noah searched the closet while Josie picked up one of the books. *What to Expect When You're Expecting.* The book beneath it was *The Girlfriend's Guide to Pregnancy.* The other three books were also pregnancy-related.

"Nothing in here but women's shoes," Noah said, emerging from the closet.

Josie handed Noah the first book in the stack. "Well," he said. "This is interesting."

"Luke told me a long time ago that Brady and Eva decided not to have children. He said they wanted to travel the world instead."

Noah stared at the book, then his gaze drifted to the other books in the pile. "Maybe they changed their minds. Maybe they were trying."

"These are in the guest bedroom, not the master bedroom."

"So, maybe the moving and packing people moved them."

"Or maybe they were Kim's," Josie suggested.

"You think Kim is pregnant?" Noah asked.

"I think she was pregnant. They did a pregnancy test at the hospital as part of her full workup. I'm sure that would have come up if it was positive."

Noah's brow furrowed. "But if she was pregnant when she was here four months ago, what the hell happened to the baby?"

Josie was about to answer when her phone rang. She looked at the screen. "It's Gretchen," she told Noah. To Gretchen she said, "What've you got?"

"We're closing in on Dunn."

"You found a connection between him and Twitch?"

"Denny Twitch used to be on his security detail. About three months ago he was let go."

"Let go?" Josie said. "That's rich."

"I know. Even more interesting, though, is that one of the unidentified set of prints we lifted from Misty Derossi's house belongs to Denny Twitch."

Josie's fingers tightened around the phone as she made her way back down the steps. Noah followed, craning his neck to try to overhear what Gretchen was telling Josie. "What?" she said. "How the hell did you get Twitch's prints run so fast?"

"Same way Noah did earlier. I ran it over to the state police barracks. They put it right through since it was related to Luke's case. There wasn't a hit before because Twitch doesn't have a record."

"Where are we with Twitch's phone?"

"I should have something back soon—at least a list of numbers."

"Well, even without the phone, I think we have enough now to pay Eric Dunn a visit. Can we find any connections between Misty and Dunn? Any chance he is the father of her baby?" Josie asked.

"I'm not so sure about that," Gretchen said haltingly.

Josie and Noah left the Conway house through the back door. The fresh air was a relief from the stale, musty scent of the closed-up house. "Why do you say that?"

"I just met with the locksmith at Misty's house. He got her desk open. There's something I think you should see."

CHAPTER 33

Josie and Noah met Gretchen at Misty's house. The top desk drawer stood open and Gretchen had spread several papers across the surface. She shifted from foot to foot as Josie looked them over.

"Misty was using a fertility clinic?" Josie said. She picked up a discharge summary from Forest Hills Fertility Clinic in Philadelphia. It was dated December of the previous year.

Over Josie's shoulder, Noah let out a low whistle. "I didn't see that coming," he said.

"Me either," Josie muttered. Her eyes scanned over the page. "*In vitro* fertilization. Why would she keep this a secret?"

Noah said, "Maybe she felt funny about using a sperm donor?"

Gretchen's fingers tapped against her thigh. "No," Gretchen said. "It's not that."

Both Josie and Noah looked up at her. With a grimace, she picked up a packet of pages and handed them to Josie. "It's the identity of the sperm donor."

"I thought those were anonymous," Noah said.

"Well, mostly they are, but a lot of sperm banks require photos of the donors as children. They don't release their names or address or anything, but the photos help prospective mothers choose the donor. Apparently, a lot of mothers like to have a donor who looks like them."

Josie looked up from the pages Gretchen had handed her which, so far, looked like the profile for a twenty-something blond Caucasian male. Donor number G8492. "How do you know all this?" she asked.

"I called the sperm bank while you were on your way. They wouldn't tell me much without a warrant, but they were able to give me 'general' information—and when I say general, I mean all of this is on their website, which I went onto after I hung up with them."

Josie read over the profile. Blood type: B-positive. Shoe size: 10. Right-handed. Athletic. College student with an interest in criminal justice. "What's so special about donor G8492?" she asked.

"Turn the page," said Gretchen.

A photo of the donor was centered on the next page. Josie stared at it for a long moment as the walls around her closed in. She felt like she was falling. Maybe she was, because the next thing she knew, Noah's hand was on the small of her back. "Boss?" he said. "You okay?"

She stared at the photo. She couldn't take her eyes off it. "I don't understand," she mumbled.

But she did understand. Josie couldn't bring herself to have children knowing that she carried her mother's genes, knowing that she had the potential to pass on that same evil to any child she and Ray might bear. What if Josie herself carried the same evil inside her that her mother had? Would becoming a mother bring it out? Josie couldn't risk that. Ray had always argued nurture over nature, but it was not a chance Josie had ever been willing to take. Ray had been fine with that, but he had joked that when they were old, they might end up with a child they never had to raise. It was then that, nervously, he admitted to Josie that he had donated sperm while he was in college. He'd done it to earn a few extra dollars. He'd done it on a whim. He'd done it because he'd always had an inflated sense of his own importance.

Now a photo of her dead husband as a ten-year-old boy stared back at her from the donor report. It was his nervous smile. The one where the corners of his mouth didn't quite go up all the way and there was the slightest furrow in the crease above his nose.

Josie knew it well. It was the same smile he'd given her right before he proposed and the same one he'd used the time he'd booked them a super-expensive trip to Disney World for their first wedding anniversary without discussing it with her first. It was the look he got whenever he wasn't quite sure if what he was doing was right, but he was going for it anyway.

"Oh, Ray," she murmured.

They'd been so stupid. She could have asked him to contact the sperm bank and have his samples destroyed, but she had only half believed him when he told her in the first place. But he hadn't been lying, hadn't made it up to get a rise out of her; he'd really done it. He'd donated his sperm, and somehow Misty had tracked it down. Little Victor Raymond Derossi was Ray's son.

"Holy shit," Noah said. His eyes, too, were glued to Ray's photograph. "Is this right?"

Josie tore her gaze from the photo and looked at Noah. His face had turned an alarming shade of gray. She looked to Gretchen. "How did you know this was my husband?"

"I didn't. I mean, I put that together. He looked so familiar. Then I realized it was the sergeant who died during the missing girls case. His photo was on the news a lot. There's a photo of him and some of the other officers in the break room. Plus, you have that photo in your office of the two of you as children. His name was Sergeant Quinn, you're Chief Quinn. Not hard to figure. He knew, right? He knew what was going on in this town, and he didn't say anything? That's what was reported. So, I was thinking if I was Misty, would I want people to know that that cop was the father of my baby? Even if we were engaged and in love? Don't you think she'd face backlash in a city this small? All those victims?"

Instinctively, Josie opened her mouth to defend Ray but clamped it shut again. There was no defending what he had done. Or not done. Gretchen was right. As much as Josie had tried to keep it out of the press, tried to keep her late, estranged husband's name from being dragged through the mud, people knew. People knew, and they talked. There were almost a hundred victims. A hundred families looking for justice and a place to direct their rage.

"A lot of people knew Ray," Noah agreed. "People remember. I can see the sense in her wanting to keep it under wraps."

"This doesn't explain why Kim Conway and Denny Twitch were here," Josie said. "So what? She used a sperm donor." *Never mind that it was my dead husband.* "That doesn't help us find her baby. What did Conway and Twitch want with her?"

"Maybe Conway was hiding here, and Twitch came for her," Noah suggested.

"Why would Misty hide Kim Conway?" Josie said. "They didn't know each other."

"Well, we know Misty had an affair with Brady, Kim's older brother," Noah said. "Also, they both knew Luke."

"How's that?" Gretchen asked.

Noah told her what they'd found at the Conway house as well as their theory that both Kim and Kavolis had been there the night of the shooting; that Kavolis had been killed there but moved to Luke's property to be buried; and also that Kim Conway might have been pregnant.

Gretchen raised a brow. "That's interesting stuff, but you're right, none of it helps us find the baby or Luke. Dunn is all over this."

"But what's Dunn's connection to Misty?" Josie asked.

Ray's photo continued to pull on her heartstrings. She moved to flip the page, but another page was caught on the back of it, held by a paper clip. Josie disentangled the sheet, tearing the corner of it as she did. The letterhead was from Atlantic East Cryobank. Its headquarters were in a town about an hour east of Denton—between Denton and Philadelphia.

It was dated six weeks earlier. *Dear Ms. Derossi,* it read. *We regret to inform you that it has come to our attention that the sample which was forwarded to Forest Hills Fertility Clinic in December of last year for your* in vitro *procedure may not have been the sample which you had originally chosen. Unfortunately, due to a clerical error, the incorrect sample may have been for-warded to the clinic on your behalf. As you know, you had chosen donor G8492. We believe that due to a series of computer and clerical issues in our storage facility, you were actually given samples for donor number G8491. We can provide a copy of donor G8491's profile upon request. Donor G8491's sample was significantly older than the sample you had chosen. It had been slated for destruction. Due to the age of this sample, there is a possibility that any child produced as a result of the use of this sample may have health issues or birth defects. Due to this risk, it was agreed we should immediately bring this potential error to your attention. We are also enclosing a check for a full refund of our fee. Please rest assured that we have launched an internal investigation into this matter. Once we have concluded the same, we will contact you immediately to let you know of our findings. We deeply apologize for any inconvenience which this may cause.*

"Sorry for the inconvenience?" Josie said incredulously. She handed the letter to Noah. Gretchen came to stand beside him so they could both read it.

"I didn't even see this," Gretchen said, her face pinched. "I looked through everything."

"It was stuck to the profile," Josie said. "I had a hard time getting it separated."

"Jesus," Noah said. He motioned toward the desk. "Is there anything else from the cryobank? Did they figure out which sample she got?"

Josie riffled through the remaining pages on the desk. She pulled out the drawers one by one and paged through every-thing in them. "I don't see anything," she said.

"I'll call them," Gretchen said.

"We need to know who donor G8491 is," Josie said. "They probably won't tell you anything without a warrant. Keep me posted. I still want to pay Eric Dunn a visit. This is all very enlightening, but I've still got three missing persons, and every-thing now leads back to Dunn."

CHAPTER 34

The Eudora Hotel was as old as Denton itself. It was one of the largest, most ornate buildings in the city, standing twelve stories high and taking up half a city block. Josie's feet sank into the emerald-green carpet as she and Noah walked into the lobby. The man behind the desk had fluffy blond hair and a toothy, painted-on smile that never seemed to falter. His "How can I help you?" sounded almost musical.

Josie and Noah flashed their credentials and said they wanted to speak to Eric Dunn.

"Just a moment," the man said evenly. He picked up a phone, pressed some buttons, and spoke in such a hushed tone that Josie could only make out a few words. When he hung up he said, "Mr. Dunn isn't taking visitors."

"I don't care what he is or isn't taking. We're here as part of an active investigation, and we need to speak with him," Josie said.

The smile remained in place. Again, the man picked up the phone, dialed, and had a conversation. This time he covered the receiver with one hand and said to Josie, "Mr. Dunn wants to know if you've got a warrant."

"We don't need a warrant to talk to him," Noah said. "Unless he's done something wrong."

Toothy kept on smiling. "I'll take that as a no," he said and spoke into the receiver again. He hung up and said, "Mr. Dunn said you can call his secretary and set up an appointment."

"And what's her number?" Josie asked.

"I'm sorry, that's private information. I can't give that out to you."

"We're here to serve a death notification," Josie said. "But if Mr. Dunn prefers to receive this information by watching the evening news like everyone else, that's fine with us."

For the first time, the receptionist's smile loosened just slightly. "A death notification? May I ask who died?"

Josie softened her tone, mocking him. "I'm sorry, that's private information. I can't give that out to you."

She didn't know it was possible to glare while still wearing a painted-on smile, but somehow he pulled it off as he got back on the phone. Ten minutes later, Josie and Noah were being ushered into Eric Dunn's penthouse suite. The main room was paneled in dark wood with ornate crown molding, the carpet was burgundy and every bit as plush as the floor of the lobby. Two matching burgundy couches flanked a large cherrywood, glass-topped desk that dominated the room. Dunn sat behind it, a panoramic view of the city of Denton spread out behind him. Josie counted four bodyguards—large, burly men in black cargo pants and fitted black polo shirts who stood like bulky sentries around the perimeter of the room. Josie couldn't help but wonder if they had been at Luke's house the night he went missing.

One of the bodyguards indicated the couches. "You can sit," he said gruffly.

Josie's cell phone chirped as she sat down. She pulled it out and looked quickly at the text message from Gretchen. "*Got Twitch's phone powered up. 5 calls to the Eudora in the last week.*" Of course. Calls to the hotel, but not specifically to Dunn. He could have been calling anyone at the Eudora, which is what Dunn would say. Josie slipped her phone back into her pocket and looked at Dunn.

He wore a tie over a silky gray button-down shirt. The sleeves of the shirt were rolled up, revealing thin, hairy fore-arms. His brown hair was slicked back. He was even less attractive in person than in his photos. His cheeks were pock-marked with acne scars. His eyes were set closely together over a long, straight nose that somehow seemed skewed on his face. He had a look of incompleteness about him, as though he only needed a slight genetic adjustment and he would have been quite handsome. His eyes were dark and flinty. Without making any introductions, he said, "You've got ten minutes."

Josie was thinking about how good it would feel to slap cuffs on his skinny little wrists. Noah said, "Mr. Dunn, one of your employees was killed in a car accident yesterday."

Dunn took a slow pan around the room, looking at his security guards. "That's interesting," he said. "Because all of my employees are accounted for."

"Denny Twitch," Josie said.

Dunn turned his penetrating gaze on her. "Denny doesn't work for me anymore."

"For what it's worth," Josie said, "he called you here at this hotel five times in the last week."

"Me? I didn't get any calls from him here. He must have been calling another guest."

Josie raised an eyebrow. "How many guests staying here in the last week do you think Mr. Twitch knew?"

"How should I know? I have no idea what he was doing. Like I said, he doesn't work for me anymore."

"When did he stop?" Noah asked.

Dunn leaned back in his chair and steepled his hands. "I don't know. It's been a while. A few months, maybe? I can have human resources get that information for you."

"How about Mickey Kavolis?" Josie asked. "He was found dead with a gunshot to the face."

Dunn looked to the man on Josie's right. "Kavolis?" he said, as though he didn't recognize the name. From the corner of her eye, Josie saw the man nod.

Dunn sighed. "Evidently he was on staff as well at some point. He doesn't work for me anymore either. If you're finished serving death notifications for people who no longer work for me, I've got meetings to get to."

"When is the last time you saw Twitch?" Josie asked.

"I don't know. Don't remember him that well. Like I said, I can have HR pull his file for you."

"How about Kavolis?"

"No idea. Again, I can have—"

Josie cut him off. "HR pull his file, yes, I know. Mr. Dunn, can you tell me why your former employees keep turning up murdered in my town?"

There was a split-second break in his bored façade—surprise—and then it was gone. "I'm sorry," he said. "Murdered?"

He wanted to know about Twitch, Josie realized. He must have realized months ago when Kavolis disappeared that he had been murdered, but as far as Twitch was concerned, Dunn had no idea that he'd been shot. All they had told him was that he had died in a car accident. Josie didn't speak. She and Noah let Dunn fill the silence. He said, "I thought you said there was a car accident."

"I said he was killed in a car accident," Noah said. "I didn't say how or what happened leading up to the accident. Now, I believe my chief asked you a question."

Dunn hesitated for a second. Then he said, "I see." He smoothed his tie. "I don't know why people are being murdered in your town."

"Not people," Josie said. "Your former employees."

"I don't know what these guys do after I let them go. It's not really my concern."

"Why were they let go?" Josie asked, although she knew what he was going to say.

"I can't tell you that off the top of my head. I'm sure it will be in the HR files."

Josie hadn't expected to get anything out of Dunn, so his denials and hedges behind his HR department were no surprise.

"When's the last time you talked to Kim?" Josie asked.

Dunn gave them a tight smile. "Kim who?"

"Your girlfriend, Kim Conway," Noah said.

"Oh, that Kim," he said. "I don't remember. We broke up months ago."

"How many months?" Josie asked.

Dunn looked at the heavy gold watch on his left wrist. "Your time is almost up," he said.

"When did you arrive here in Denton?" Josie asked, changing tactics.

Dunn shrugged. "A few days ago. I was asked by Tara—the mayor—to attend a charity benefit."

Josie held up her cell phone, the photo she had taken of Kim Conway on it. "Kim's face has been all over the local news for the last two days. We were asking for help identifying her. You didn't think it might be helpful to give us a call and let us know our Jane Doe was your ex-girlfriend?"

"I don't have time to watch your local news, Miss..."

"Quinn," Josie filled in.

"Chief Quinn," Noah added.

Dunn looked from Noah to Josie and back. "Chief, is it? As in the chief of police?"

Josie nodded. The smile that Dunn gave her then made her skin crawl. It was as though a mask had slipped from his face and beneath it was something ugly and unsettling, like a mass of insects scattering to reveal a picked-over carcass. "Denton does enjoy putting women in power, doesn't it?" he said.

"When is the last time you spoke to Kim Conway?" Josie repeated.

Ignoring her, he looked at Noah. "Are you her secretary?"

Noah bristled. "Lieutenant Fraley."

"Was Kim pregnant?" Josie asked.

Something in Dunn's dark eyes flared, but he tamped it back down, keeping his gaze on Noah. "Lieutenant Fraley, tell me. Do you like working beneath these women?"

"Chief Quinn asked you a question," Noah answered.

"I like powerful women," Dunn went on. "Especially when they're on their knees."

"What is your relationship with Misty Derossi?" Josie asked.

Dunn spared her a glance. "Never heard of her. What's her position? Deputy chief? Assistant mayor?"

"She's fighting for her life at Denton Memorial," Noah said. "She was attacked trying to defend her newborn child. He's missing. You wouldn't know anything about that, would you?"

"I've never heard of her, so no, I wouldn't."

"We have reason to believe Denny Twitch was involved," Noah said.

"What Denny did after he left my company doesn't concern me," Dunn said.

"Have you ever been to Foxy Tails?" Josie asked him. "The strip club here in Denton?"

Dunn laughed. "Do you think I need to visit strip clubs?"

Josie turned in her chair and took a slow pan of the room. Then she met his eyes again. "Yeah, I can see that you're over-whelmed by the number of women throwing themselves at you."

Without missing a beat, Dunn said, "You're here, aren't you?"

Josie said, "Have you ever donated to a sperm bank?"

Again, Dunn laughed. "Honey, I don't need to donate my sperm. There are plenty of women out there willing to take it. Just ask your mayor."

Josie strongly doubted that Tara Charleston would let this creep lay a finger on her, but she didn't say anything. Dunn was playing a game, and Josie wasn't about to rise to the bait. "You said Kavolis doesn't work for you anymore, but your company paid the charges on his rental car after it was impounded."

Dunn waved a hand. "So? I have people who tie up loose ends like that."

"Do you? What kind of people?" Josie asked.

Dunn looked at his watch again. "I believe your time is up."

"Why did you and Kim Conway break up?" Josie asked.

"Why don't you ask her?" Dunn said. "Isn't she in your custody?"

Josie didn't answer. Instead, she stood, and Noah stood with her. Together they walked to the door, where one of the bodyguards held it open. Before she left, Josie turned and said, "Since you arrived, we've had two murders and a couple of missing persons cases, and all of the cases involve people from your organization. If I were you, I wouldn't piss off the powers that be in a city where you're trying to build a casino."

Dunn's eyes blazed again. "Sage advice, Chief. It's never wise to piss off people who have what you want most, is it?"

CHAPTER 35

As Josie and Noah walked back to her vehicle, Noah clenched and unclenched his fists. His face flamed red with anger. "That guy needs a serious ass-beating," he grumbled as they got into Josie's Escape. He kept talking about Dunn, about all the things he'd like to do to the guy while Josie tried to get her keys into the ignition. Her hands were shaking. "He has Luke," she mumbled.

"I know you can't beat misogyny out of someone," Noah went on. "But I sure as shit would like to try."

"He has Luke," she said again.

Her keys fell to the floor. Awkwardly, she leaned around the steering wheel, stretching her arm to try to reach them.

"What did you say?" Noah asked.

Her fingers searched the rough fabric of her floor mat. "He has Luke," she said for the third time. "Didn't you hear him? He said it's not wise to piss off the people who have what you want most."

Noah said, "He didn't even know who you were. You think he even knows that you and Luke were together?"

Josie's hand closed around the keys. Finally, she found the ignition and fired up the engine. "Are together," she corrected. Maybe their relationship wouldn't survive this—especially if he had been sleeping with Kim Conway the last few months—but she would deal with that when she found Luke. Alive. Hopefully.

"I'm sorry, boss," Noah said.

"He knows plenty," Josie added. "But he's too smart to let on to the police that he knows anything at all. Even if we had him on tape doing something illegal, he'd deny it. It's easier for him to deny, deny, deny and then send in a team of lawyers if he gets charged with something. Eric Dunn is not the kind of man who has ever been held accountable for his actions."

"What do we do?" Noah asked.

"We need to put someone on him," Josie said. "Wherever he goes, they go. We can pull a couple of people from patrol to be on standby for backup. Maybe Gretchen. I can relieve her in a few hours."

"Boss, I don't think that's a good id—"

"He has Luke, and we have nothing. We follow him, we find Luke."

"Do you really think he is going to just lead us to Luke? Just like that? He'll be too careful for that. He's got people to do his dirty work. People he can later claim no longer work for him."

"Then we follow his people too," Josie said.

"We don't have the manpower for that," Noah pointed out. "We've still got a missing baby, a missing accident victim, and all the other usual shit that goes on in this city."

"Then we'll ask the state police for help. You know they'll give it. Call them, see what they can do. We have to find him. Dunn will kill him."

"We don't even know how many people he has with him," Noah pointed out.

"Gretchen might know. She interviewed the staff at the Eudora when she was checking out Kavolis. She's on her way now."

They sat in silence for a few moments. Then Noah asked, "Do you think he has Misty's baby?"

Josie closed her eyes for a moment. The thought of a tiny infant at the mercy of someone like Dunn was enough to make the hair on her arms stand up. Her mind's eye kept returning to the photo of Ray on the cryobank's donor sheet. She opened her eyes again and regarded Noah. "I don't know. I don't know why he would want Misty's baby. There's no connection between Misty and Dunn."

"Except for Conway and Twitch."

Those were the pieces that didn't fit. Josie was guessing that Dunn had sent Kavolis to get Kim from her brother's house and things had gone horribly wrong. Luke had gotten caught up in it. But none of that explained why Kim's or Twitch's prints had been found at Misty's house or why any of them—Kim, Twitch, or Dunn—would want Misty's baby.

"We need to find out who the other donor was," Josie said. "The one whose sample was mixed up with Ray's. When Gretchen gets here, we'll see if she got anywhere with the sperm bank."

CHAPTER 36

Gretchen arrived ten minutes later, sliding into the backseat of Josie's Escape along with a blast of cool air. Noah recounted their meeting with Eric Dunn, and Gretchen scoffed. "Charming," she said.

"Did you get anything else from the phone?" Josie asked.

"Not much. It's a burner. He called the hotel, like I told you, five times in the last week. Call history only goes back a week. The only other numbers he called were three other burner numbers. I can trace the cell providers but no names or other identifying information about their owners."

Noah turned his body toward Gretchen. "If we know the providers, we can get the phone companies to ping them and get their location within a few feet."

"Only if the GPS is turned on," Josie said. "Otherwise you'd have to use triangulation. If these guys are smart, they're not going to have the GPS activated."

"Triangulation would still give you their location within a couple of miles," Noah pointed out.

"So we'll find more of Dunn's men," Gretchen said. "How do we know he wasn't calling the goon squad in the penthouse with Dunn?"

"Because," Josie said, "as Dunn was so anxious to point out, Twitch was no longer working for him."

"Which is bullshit," Noah said.

"Twitch was on another team. The team that took the baby and attacked Luke. Think about it; if anything goes wrong,

Dunn can always claim he had no knowledge—that it's 'not his concern' what these guys do after they leave his company."

"Something must have gone wrong," Gretchen said. "Or else Twitch wouldn't need to call the hotel, right?"

A fluttery feeling began in Josie's stomach. "Maybe not. Maybe that's how he checked in. Dunn probably pays the concierge to lie if asked what room the calls went to. Even if we could prove the calls went to the penthouse, Dunn can just make something up: Twitch was begging for his job back, something like that. We can't prove the content of those conversations even if we can prove they took place. I think it's worth a try to locate the other phones."

"Text me the numbers," Noah told Gretchen. "I'll call dispatch and have them ping them. If that doesn't work, I'll write up the warrants to have the providers triangulate them."

Gretchen bent her head to her phone and began typing. Noah's phone buzzed three times in succession.

"How many people does Dunn have with him?" Josie asked.

"A team of four," Gretchen answered. "That's all the staff at the hotel has seen. If there's another team, they're off-site, like you said."

"How about the sperm bank?" Josie asked. "Get anywhere with them?"

Gretchen pocketed her phone and pulled her notebook out of her jacket pocket. She flipped a few pages. "No," she said.

Noah laughed and motioned toward her notepad. "You needed your notes to remember that? What's it say in there?"

Gretchen smiled good-naturedly. "It says that I talked to a woman named Diana Sweeney, a receptionist slash intake associate, and that she told me that she couldn't give me any information—either about the investigation into the mix-up or about the other donor. I told her I'd get some warrants written up, and she said it would take their legal department seven to ten business days to process them."

"Wait a minute," Josie said. "What did you say her name was?"

"Diana Sweeney," Gretchen repeated.

Noah said, "You know her?"

"I might," Josie answered. "Noah, go back to the station. Get on the phones. Then I want you to check on Misty—see if she's ready to talk to us. Then check if there's been any progress in the search for Conway, and get someone to take Twitch's photo around to the hotels and motels to see if anyone remembers him staying there while he was in town—in case we don't get anywhere with the phones. Gretchen, I want you to stay on Dunn until I get back."

Gretchen tucked her notebook back into her pocket and started to get out of the vehicle. "You got it, boss."

Noah looked at Josie. "Where are you going?"

"To have a talk with Diana Sweeney."

CHAPTER 37

Josie made it to the Atlantic East Cryobank just after lunchtime. It took up the second floor of a six-story square brick-and-glass office building. The door was solid and unwelcoming. Josie wondered momentarily if it was locked, but when she pushed, it opened to reveal a small reception area with black vinyl guest chairs lining the walls. A few end tables had been scattered throughout with magazines piled on top of them. *Field and Stream*, *Sports Illustrated*, and *Motorcycle Racing*. It was a waiting room tailored for men. Josie imagined they saved the porn magazines for when customers were giving samples.

A window had been cut into one of the walls. Josie walked up to it and peered inside. The area beyond it was filled with a series of cubicles. She rapped her knuckles against the glass, and a moment later a woman appeared and slid the window open. "Can I help you?"

Josie flashed her credentials. "I'm here to see Diana Sweeney."

The woman frowned. She looked as though she might ask questions but then decided against it, instead telling Josie to have a seat before closing the window. Josie had no sooner sat in one of the chairs when a door beside the window opened and a different woman stepped out. She was in her forties, heavyset, her brown hair tied back in a bun, gray strands just starting to show at her temples. A pair of glasses sat on her nose, and she looked over them at Josie, smiling.

"Josie Quinn?"

Josie stood and extended a hand but instead, the woman embraced her, pulling her tightly into a hug. "Miss Sweeney," Josie said when she released her.

Diana Sweeney smiled. "It's lovely to meet you finally. Come."

Josie followed her through the door and past a labyrinth of cubicles until they came to her tiny workstation. It was only big enough for Diana's desk and one guest chair. Diana cleared her purse and file folder from the chair and offered it to Josie. Around them rose the soft murmur of female voices and the steady click-clack of fingers typing away on keyboards. The inner walls of Diana's cubicle were filled with photos of Diana and various people who Josie assumed were family and friends. Josie recognized the photo of Diana and her sister. It was the same one that Diana had sent to Josie six months earlier.

Diana saw her staring at the photo, and she ran a finger over her sister's face. "She was missing for thirteen years before you found her."

Josie knew this from the letter Diana had sent along with the photo. "I didn't actually find her," Josie said. "It was a team of FBI personnel."

Diana turned toward Josie, a beatific smile on her face. Tears shone in her eyes. "Only because you told them where to look. Because of you, all those families finally have answers— just like us. They can finally lay their loved ones to rest."

It was familiar territory, and yet Josie still felt uncomfortable with the esteem that came with her having uncovered not one, but two, serial killers who had been operating in Denton for decades. She was happy that she had given so many families closure, but it was hard to feel heroic given that so many lives had been lost.

"Thank you for your letter," Josie said. "That meant a lot. I have that same photo pinned in my office."

A tear slid down Diana's cheek and she swiped it away. She took a moment to compose herself, taking in a deep breath and letting it out slowly. "What can I do for you?" she asked.

"My colleague called you earlier today," Josie said. "Detective Gretchen Palmer. It was about a donor mix-up."

Diana nodded. "I remember. She wanted to know the results of the internal investigation and more information about the other donor."

"Yes. Misty Derossi, the woman who received the, uh, donation, was attacked in her home. Her newborn baby was abducted."

Diana searched out a brochure from behind a stack of files on her desk. "That is truly terrible," she told Josie. "You know I am sympathetic—especially given the abduction—but do you really think that has anything to do with Ms. Derossi's donor situation?"

"We don't know," Josie replied. "But we have to explore every avenue. A baby's life is in danger."

Diana peeled a Post-it from the pad on her desk and pressed it into the folds of the brochure. She picked up a pen. "Well, Chief Quinn, as much as I would love to help you—and I would, believe me, I would—I can't breach confidentiality. I could lose my job."

She scribbled something on the Post-it, folded the brochure, and handed it to Josie. "But everything you need to know about our policies and procedures are in this pamphlet. As I suggested to Detective Palmer, if you submit some warrants to our legal department, I'm sure they can provide whatever information you need."

"That could take days," Josie said.

Diana reached over and tapped the brochure with one finger. She smiled conspiratorially at Josie. Her voice was sympathetic but firm. "I'm very sorry, Chief Quinn. This is the best I can do."

Josie said goodbye to Diana and left. Inside her vehicle, she opened the pamphlet and read the scrawled note. "*Give me a day or two. The files you're looking for are password protected and above my pay grade. I'll need to come up with a good excuse to access them. But I'll do what I can do.*" Beneath that was Diana Sweeney's cell phone number.

Josie punched the number into her phone and sent a text. "*The pamphlet was very helpful. Thank you.*"

The reply was almost instantaneous. "*My pleasure. Talk soon.*"

CHAPTER 38

WBAL-TV 11—Baltimore, Maryland

June 13, 2017

Teen Killed in Boating Accident

An eighteen-year-old woman was found dead after her fishing boat capsized in the Potomac River on Monday evening amid choppy waters. Police have identified her as Erin Appleby of Baltimore's Guilford neighborhood. A spokesman for the Maryland Natural Resources Police says the winds were as high as forty miles an hour that day. "We believe Miss Appleby was making her way back to the dock," the spokesman said. "But obviously she never got there." Appleby's body was pulled from the river after the owner of a power boat passing by spotted her capsized vessel.

Authorities say this is the eighth boating death of the year. Additional details surrounding the accident have not been made available.

CHAPTER 39

As Josie drove back to the station house, Dunn's words played again and again in her head. *It's never wise to piss off people who have what you want most, is it?* She couldn't help but hope that he had said that because Luke was still alive. She wondered what they wanted from him. She was working under the assumption that Dunn's men had gone to Luke's house looking for Kim—so why had they taken Luke, and what was the benefit in keeping him alive? Or had Dunn killed him already and dumped his body somewhere it would never be found? Was he just playing with Josie?

Josie's thoughts were still swirling as she made her way to the second floor of the station house, where her office was located. Before she even turned the corner into the main room, she could hear Trinity Payne's voice coming from the television on the wall. "Tomorrow, jurors will be presented with the weapons that police believe Aaron King used in the commission of his crimes, including the machete that he used to attack a state trooper the night of his arrest." Even Noah was perched on the edge of a desk, staring intently at the screen. Josie cleared her throat and everyone in the room scrambled, suddenly trying to look busy. Noah snatched the remote control from his desk and quickly turned the television off.

"Sorry, boss," he mumbled.

She pointed to her office and he followed her inside. "Misty was awake earlier, but very disoriented," he told her. "I went over there to see her. The doctors say she's in no condition to answer any questions yet, and they're right. She responded to her name but didn't have answers to any of my questions. The surgeon said it's not unusual in the case of head injuries for the patient to have poor recall at first. We can go back tomorrow. Try again. There are no new leads on the baby or on Conway. No one on the staff at the Eudora remembers seeing Denny Twitch there with Dunn earlier this year."

Josie plopped into her chair. "What about Gretchen?"

"Nothing. Dunn's gone to a couple of meetings. His four goons travel everywhere with him. They never leave his side."

"Did dispatch ping the phones?"

"Yeah, but they didn't get anything. I'm waiting for the results of triangulation now. As soon as it comes in, I'll let you know."

"As soon as we get the coordinates, I want to move on it. Luke might still be alive."

Noah opened his mouth to speak and hesitated. She knew what he was going to say—that she should prepare herself for the possibility that he wasn't. Why would Dunn keep Luke alive? Noah was probably thinking about the most tactful way of saying that to her. The phone on her desk rang, and she snatched it up. "Quinn," she barked.

It was Sergeant Lamay. "I've got the mayor down here. She's got some, uh, friends with her. Says she just wants to talk."

"Friends?" Josie asked.

"Gentleman friends. Three of them. Should I send them up?"

"No," Josie said. "Put them in the conference room down there. I'll be right down."

"What do they want?" Noah wondered as they took the steps down to the first floor.

"I have no idea," Josie answered.

Tara waited outside the conference room, looking every bit the mayor in her sharp black skirt suit with matching heels and perfectly applied makeup. Her hair hung to her shoulders, straight and shiny. From the scowl on her face, Josie could only guess that she had gathered some members of the city council to ask for Josie's resignation as chief.

"What the hell is this?" Noah said from the side of his mouth, quiet enough so only Josie heard. She didn't look at him.

"Mayor Charleston," Josie said stiffly, a sinking feeling in her stomach.

"Chief Quinn," Tara replied coldly.

Josie got straight to the point. "What is this about?"

Tara gave Noah an appraising look. Then she smiled tightly. "You know about my husband's . . . interest in Ms. Derossi's baby."

That's one way to put it, thought Josie. "Yes, I'm aware of it."

"Well, he suggested that we offer a reward for his safe return."

"That's a great idea," Josie said. "But as I am sure you're aware, we don't handle that here at the police department. Maybe one of the town watch groups could coordinate it."

"I realize that you don't handle it," Tara said, sounding irritated. "I'm not asking you to collect or hold the reward money. As a courtesy to you, I wanted to let you know what we intend to do. The hope is a reward will generate a lot of tips. Your department would have to handle that."

"I hope you're right," Josie said. "We'll be ready to handle any tips that come in. I appreciate your extending me the courtesy."

"Isn't that a conflict of interest?" Noah interjected. He ignored the dirty look Tara gave him and added, "I mean, you're the mayor. Would you then be expected to offer a reward for every person who goes missing in the city?"

Tara's icy façade warmed slightly. She folded her arms across her chest. "Well, yes, that's exactly what I said. My husband, however, suggested that we ask people in the community for help. People who would have an interest in helping Misty, or people who do a lot of charitable giving."

Josie suppressed her eye roll. Tara loved to turn everything into a meet-and-greet. She could have done all of this
behind the scenes over the phone or through email, but that
wouldn't garner her enough attention—or credit for saving the
day should the reward be fruitful. Even though it had been her
husband's idea because he had had an affair with Misty, if the
baby were returned safely as a result of a tip that came in from
a big reward, Tara would revel in it. Josie could see it now: Tara
at a press conference handing over a giant check to a happy,
heroic tipster while Misty bounced her baby boy on her knee
in the background. What better press for Tara's reelection bid?
Fucking politicians. "Who have you talked into giving reward
money?" Josie asked.

Like a game show hostess, Tara motioned toward the conference room door with a flourish. Noah brushed past both of
them and opened the door.

Josie immediately recognized Misty's boss, Butch. Beside
him was a man in his fifties with gray hair, wearing a suit with
no tie. Josie recognized him as Jack Coleman, the father of Isabelle Coleman, the teenager who had gone missing nearly two
years ago, sparking an investigation that ultimately tore apart
the town and got Josie's husband, Ray, killed. Misty was the one
who had found Isabelle, and Josie remembered how grateful the
Colemans had been to her for keeping their daughter safe. Tara
introduced the third man as Peter Rowland. He stood and shook
both their hands. For a town legend, Josie had expected someone
older, but Rowland looked to be only in his mid-forties, if that.
He had thick brown hair, brushed back neatly from his face, a
long, straight nose that hooked at the end, and closely set hazel
eyes. She had also expected him to be wearing a suit, but instead
he was dressed casually in jeans and a collared shirt.

Josie and Noah took seats at the table while Tara remained
standing, as if giving a presentation. "Thank you all for being
here," she said. "I think with the people in this room we have
gathered enough reward money to give this investigation a

much-needed jolt." She turned to Butch. "Mr. McConnell, you said you can offer $5,000, is that right?"

Butch's basset hound cheeks sagged. "Yeah, that's right," he muttered.

Josie raised a brow. "That's quite generous, Butch, putting that money toward an *ex*-employee. I didn't realize you cared that much."

"Yeah, well, my girls said it's the right thing to do."

Tara motioned toward Jack Coleman. "The Colemans have graciously agreed to give $10,000."

Coleman nodded.

Rowland spoke, "And I'll match both of those." He turned to Josie and Noah and smiled. "So you've got $30,000 to offer as a reward for the safe return of the Derossi infant."

Josie looked around the table. "That's very generous, and I'm sure that Ms. Derossi will appreciate this very much. We'll take any help we can get."

They spoke for a few minutes more, hashing out the specific language to be used in all press releases before Tara ushered the three men out of the room. She instructed them to wait for her in the lobby and suggested they have lunch with a member of the civic association who would be able to collect their portions of the reward from each of them. Josie tried not to laugh at the look of horror that crossed Butch's face. The civic association had never been a friend to the local strip club. Josie couldn't imagine a more awkward meal.

Once they were out of earshot, Tara turned to Josie. "Chief Quinn, I expect this reward money will generate a lot of tips. I would hate to see the generosity of these good citizens go to waste."

Beside Josie, Noah said, "We can't control the tips that come in."

"Noah," Josie admonished, but Tara didn't even look at him. Her gaze remained locked on Josie. She said, "I don't need to remind you what's at stake."

Lives were at stake, but Josie knew that wasn't what Tara was getting at. She was talking about Josie's job and how Josie's performance of that job reflected on her own reputation. "How did you get Rowland to contribute?" Josie asked.

Tara straightened her spine and folded her arms across her chest, looking at once defensive and smug. "I told him we could name the women's center the Polly Rowland Center for Women. You know, after his late daughter."

Josie and Noah nodded in unison. They knew the story. Rowland's wife and twelve-year-old daughter had been killed by a drunk driver in New York City a year earlier. Rowland had left the city and spent months at his secluded home in Denton afterward.

"So, you got your funding for the women's center," Josie said. "And reward money?"

"He was thrilled with the idea of opening the center in Polly's name. So much so that when I suggested he contribute to the reward for the Derossi infant, he readily agreed. As I said, I'd hate to see such generosity go to waste, especially when we are trying to do good things for this city."

Josie sensed Noah opening his mouth again to protest and nudged him with her elbow. Arguing with Tara would only incense her. Josie felt bad that these well-meaning people were giving their money for tips that would never come, but that wasn't a conversation she wanted to have with Tara at this juncture.

Assuming Eric Dunn had Misty's baby, he wasn't going to turn him in. She doubted anyone in his organization would rat him out and risk incurring his wrath for only $30,000. But it wasn't up to Josie to tell people what to do with their money. Reward money often led to important tips, she couldn't deny that. If there was even the slimmest chance of someone in Dunn's organization coming forward for the reward, then it was worth offering. She just prayed that the baby was still alive.

Forcing a smile for Tara's sake, Josie said, "We'll do our best."

CHAPTER 40

THURSDAY

Balancing a flimsy cup carrier with two steaming hot coffees in it, Josie walked briskly through the parking lot of the Eudora, searching the rows of cars for Gretchen's department-issue Chevy Cruze. It was just after six a.m. and the sun hadn't yet come up. She spotted the car and waved. She heard the click of the doors unlocking as she reached the passenger's side. Inside, she handed Gretchen a coffee, took the other one, and tossed the carrier into the backseat.

"Thank you," Gretchen said.

Josie sipped her own coffee. "You're welcome. When did you get here?"

"About an hour ago. Noah went home to get a few hours of shut-eye."

"Did you sleep?" Josie asked.

"A few hours. You?"

"Not really," Josie confessed. She had only gone home because she knew that Carrieann was there alone. They had discussed Eric Dunn some more. Carrieann had spent a great deal of her day online reading everything ever written about the young casino mogul. By the time Josie arrived, she was pacing the kitchen like a metronome. Neither one of them had been able to sleep, though they had tried.

"Did you check in at the station?" Gretchen asked. "Did the phone companies call yet about the triangulation?"

"No. Lamay is in. He's going to call me the moment the results come in."

"Any tips after the press caught wind of the reward money?"

Josie sighed. "No, and I don't think there will be any."

She didn't say what she was really thinking, which was that Dunn may have already killed Misty Derossi's baby. The thought caused a deep pain in Josie's stomach, like the coffee she had just swallowed was boiling inside her. She put her cup on the dashboard. They watched the main entrance of the Eudora in silence for a few minutes. Then Gretchen said, "Noah told me the mayor is really putting the pressure on."

Josie laughed. "You could say that. It doesn't change anything, though. We'll do our jobs the same with or without her pressure. Or the reward money. I still think our best bet to find the baby and Luke are either the phone numbers from Twitch's phone or staying on Eric Dunn."

Gretchen set her coffee in the cup holder and continued to stare at the entrance to the Eudora. "I agree. I'll let you know if he moves."

"Thanks. I'm headed to the hospital to see if Misty is ready to answer questions."

CHAPTER 41

Josie arrived at Denton Memorial well before visiting hours. Noah had told her Misty's room number on the fourth floor where Josie flashed her credentials at the nurses' station and was promptly taken to see Misty. She was propped up in bed, one of her arms in a sling, her head swathed in white gauze and her face badly bruised. Josie noticed that one side of her mouth drooped slightly.

"Not too long," the nurse whispered. "She's had a major head injury and a very invasive surgery. She's on a steady morphine drip. She needs her rest to heal."

A guest chair had been pulled up beside Misty's bed. A thin white hospital blanket was balled up on its seat. She knew Brittney had been keeping vigil at Misty's bedside. Her friend had probably gone home for some proper rest. Josie pushed the blanket aside and perched on the edge of the seat. For a few moments she watched Misty's steady breathing. Then she studied the monitor over her bed that kept track of her heart rate, blood pressure, respiration, and oxygen saturation.

Touching Misty's hand, Josie said her name a few times until Misty's eyes fluttered open. They were small slits in her swollen, purple face and they stared blankly at Josie. She opened her mouth to speak but only a scratchy sound came out.

Josie stood so she could get closer. "It's Josie Quinn."

"Jo…" Misty trailed off. A thin line of drool snaked from the side of her mouth. Josie could see the gap along her upper gum line where her tooth had been knocked out.

"Misty," Josie said. "I need to know what happened to you. What happened at your house? Can you tell me? Do you remember?"

Her eyes left Josie's face and searched the room, finally settling on her stomach. Her good hand pressed against it. Josie watched the terror blanket her face. "My baby," she said. "Where is—where is he?"

Josie squeezed her hand, wishing she had better news to give this poor, battered woman. "We're looking for him. I'm doing everything I can to find him, but I need your help. I need to know what happened after Victor was born. Who was with you?"

Misty's gaze found hers again. A tear slid from one of her eyes. "A man took him. I tried to…I tried to stop him. I tried…Is my baby okay? Where is he?"

Josie's stomach burned. "We're looking for him," Josie repeated. She took out her phone and pulled up a photo of Denny Twitch's driver's license. She held it close to Misty's face. "Is this the man?"

Misty gave a slow nod. More drool dripped down her chin. Josie searched out a box of tissues and used one to dab gently at Misty's face. "Do you know him?" Josie asked.

"No," Misty said. "He came in the…the back."

"There was no sign of damage to the back door. Was it unlocked?"

Another slow nod. More tears leaked from Misty's eyes. "My baby. Where is my baby?"

Josie didn't answer. Instead she pulled up a photo of Kim Conway and showed it to Misty. "How about her? Do you know her? Was she there?"

Misty's eyelids fluttered, and Josie knew she wouldn't be able to stay awake much longer. "Kim," said Misty. "Brady's sister. Luke's friend."

Josie felt a jolt go through her like a current of electricity. "She knew Luke? How did she know Luke?"

"She was there."

"Where? At your house?"

Misty's head bobbed in confirmation. "The baby came. She helped me..."

"She came to your house, said she was a friend of Luke's and—"

"Needed to stay."

"Needed a place to stay?"

"Yes."

"Then the baby came. Why didn't you go to the hospital?"

Misty's eyelids lowered.

"Misty," Josie said. "Stay with me. You were with Kim at your house when you went into labor. Why didn't she take you to the hospital? Why didn't you call 911? Where was Kim when the man took your baby? Misty!"

But her breathing started to even out, and Josie knew she had fallen back into a morphine-induced sleep. She watched Misty for a little longer, dabbing occasionally at the drool that leaked from her lips. When the nurse came in to check her IV, Josie left. She could always send Noah back later or return herself, but she doubted that Misty could tell them anything useful that they hadn't already pieced together. Except perhaps why she had delivered at home with Kim's help and where Kim was when Denny Twitch snuck into her home and took her baby. A thousand other questions raced through Josie's mind. Why had Kim gone to Misty's house in the first place? Had Luke sent her? What had Kim been after? Had she been there when Twitch attacked Misty, and if so, had she tried to stop the attack? Or had she run because she had known what he was capable of?

Back at the station, Josie spent her morning trying to catch up on the mound of paperwork she had to clear as chief. It did nothing to keep her mind off all the questions twisting round and round in her head. It also did nothing to quell the heavy ache in her chest which she was certain was a sob just waiting for an opportunity to erupt from her body. Every second brought new visions of what Dunn might have done to Luke. Her mind pictured his lifeless body in so many different scenarios that it started to make her feel sick. She put the paperwork aside and called the cell phone providers again, trying to impress upon them that lives were at stake. Twenty minutes later, Josie and Noah were behind her desk, shoulder to shoulder, looking at maps on Josie's laptop.

Noah pointed to the screen, tracing the triangle formed by the three cellular towers the cell phone companies had flagged as getting optimal signal strength from two of the phones Denny Twitch had been calling. "Here. This is our area."

It was a swath of land south of Denton, outside of Alcott County. She would have to get in touch with local police there if they were going to do any kind of search. "How big of an area are we talking?" Josie asked.

"It's about twelve miles."

Josie felt a sinking feeling in her stomach. "Twelve miles? I thought they could pin this down to within a mile or two."

"It's a rural area. The towers aren't as close together. But look, the fact that most of this is farmland or game land might actually help us."

"How do you figure?"

Nimbly, he ran his fingers over the flat square of the computer mouse, swiping and clicking until he had a Google map showing the overhead satellite images of the area. One half looked like a series of irregularly shaped green and brown squares threaded with the thin lines of roads. The other half was densely wooded and marked on the screen as state game land. Zooming in, Josie could see that he was right. Most of the green squares outside of the game land were cornfields and other crops. There were few manmade structures, and the ones that existed stood out white or gray in stark contrast to the earthy tones of the uninhabited land. Toward the bottom of the area was the northernmost point of a town called Fairfield.

Josie could see the roofs of various buildings grouped tightly together. "I don't think they'd be holding anyone in a populated area," she said. "We're looking for something out of the way. Where people aren't going to ask questions. Fairfield isn't that big. Thugs like Twitch coming and going in the town would draw a lot of attention."

"You don't think them coming and going from someplace remote would draw even more attention?" Noah asked.

"If it's remote enough, there won't be anyone around to see them coming and going, so no, I don't think that would draw more attention than if they were in town."

They stared at the screen. Josie reached forward and swiped the mouse, bringing the tiny arrow of the cursor over two buildings standing alone in the middle of several fields. One was quite large and L-shaped with a peaked roof. "This looks like a farm of some kind," she said. "There's the house and then, back here, that's a big barn."

"That looks like equipment," Noah said. "It's remote but if the farm is still operational then I doubt Dunn's men set up shop there."

"We'll need to call the county sheriff," Josie said. "We'll need to coordinate with them anyway. Maybe they can tell us whether the farm is still in business."

Noah marked down the names of the rural routes nearest to the farm. "Okay, let's keep looking. Zoom out."

Josie clicked on the zoom, and the screen panned out to a more expansive view of the area. They identified two more structures that seemed to be miles from any other buildings or populated areas. One was at the westernmost point of the area they were searching and looked like a factory of some kind. Given the state of good repair of the road leading up to it and the vehicles parked near it, they guessed it was still being used for something. Still, they put it on the list to check with local law enforcement. The second structure was north, closer to Denton, and appeared to be a church. The satellite images showed no vehicles near it, and the land immediately surrounding it was overgrown with grass and weeds. Beyond that it was bordered by trees on three sides.

"I think this is it," she said.

"A church?"

"It looks abandoned. Let's check it out."

CHAPTER 42

Whereas Alcott County had one major city and enough mid-size towns to keep law enforcement busy all year round, Lenore County was mostly rural. When Josie called the sheriff's office for assistance, they jumped at the chance to help. It took only minutes to find out that the farm and the factory that Josie and Noah had identified on the satellite map were indeed in operation. The sheriff's office promised to send officers to each location to have a look around, but Josie didn't think they'd find anything.

The church, however, had been abandoned for nearly a decade. It had been a Catholic church, and the land was still owned by the archdiocese, which had left it unattended for several years. The area was so remote, sheriff's deputy Phillips explained, that they had no need to worry about homeless people or junkies taking up residence in the old structure. "You're more likely to find a bear or a deer in there than people," he told them.

It was the perfect place to keep someone hostage, Josie thought. Her skin tingled with hope that Luke might still be alive.

An hour later, a team of Denton officers and Lenore sheriff's deputies had been assembled on the shoulder of a two-lane road about a mile from the old church. For the first time in a long time, Josie strapped on a bulletproof vest, feeling a surge of adrenaline. She missed this. This was the police work she had lived for from the moment she was sworn in. She checked her weapon, trying to keep her focus on preparing to raid the church so she wouldn't think about what they might find there. Or what they might not find. Her heart paused and then kicked back into motion, its beats suddenly too rapid. She willed her body to calm down.

"I've got eyes in the trees on all three sides," Deputy Phillips said. He was in his fifties with short, graying hair, a paunch, and serious brown eyes. He had taken up Josie's cause with gusto, putting together an eager and competent team in less than an hour. Josie pegged him for ex-military.

"Have you seen any movement?" she asked.

"Nothing. It's all quiet. There's one vehicle parked around the back of the church."

"How many entrances?" Noah asked.

"You got the three doors at the front, one at the back." Phillips pulled out a piece of printer paper where he'd drawn a rough diagram. He pointed to the rectangular layout on the page. "These three doors in front take you into a vestibule. We think there's a maintenance closet on one side and a bathroom on the other side. To get inside where the services were held, there's more doors. We assume the sanctuary still has pews and such." He had drawn two sets of lines to represent the pews and the aisles between. At the front of those he had drawn a square. "This is the altar," he said. "In front of it is a big open area—the transept. There are two doors on either side that lead into the sacristy. The back door is on the east side of the sacristy. There are confessional booths about halfway from the vestibule to the transept."

"Let's go in quiet," Josie said. "Clear the front first. Put teams here and here," she said, pointing to the back of the church. "They'll be on standby."

Phillips nodded. "Flush them out, yeah."

They assembled three-person teams for each entrance. Since it was out of their jurisdiction, Denton PD made up only one of the teams. They took the center door at the front of the church, Josie in front, Noah directly behind her and one of their most competent patrol officers in the back. They used hand signals and padded silently to the front of the church and up the steps.

Josie held her gun in one hand, pointed downward, and with the other she pushed the creaky church door open.

The front of the church was searched and cleared. As they moved through the second set of doors into the main worship area, the teams on either side of Josie's people moved more swiftly down the side aisles, clearing the confessional booths while Josie, Noah, and the other Denton officer kept eyes on the altar and the entrance to the sacristy. As they moved down the center aisle, Josie caught sight of a pair of jean-clad legs on the floor near the altar. Judging by the size and style of the sneakers, the legs belonged to a man. Her heart skipped ahead in rapid beats. Noah hollered something at her, but she was already running down the aisle toward the outstretched legs. *Not Luke*, a voice in her head said. *Please, don't let it be Luke*.

As she rounded the pews she saw that there were two crumpled figures. Adrenaline pumped so hard through her veins, her brain couldn't make sense of what she was seeing at first. As her hands touched the first body, she was transported back to the cold cell on top of the mountain where Ray died.

"No, no, no." It was her voice. She was saying it. "Not again."

There was shouting behind her as the rest of them caught up to her, but she couldn't hear what they were saying. Couldn't hear anything over the blood rushing in her ears and her own muttered voice. "No, no, no."

She rolled the man onto his back. Not Luke. Josie wheezed in a breath and held it. She was afraid to look at the second body, but knew she had to.

Not Luke.

She let out her breath. From behind her, a hand reached under her right arm and gently pulled her to her feet. "Boss," Noah said. She was aware of the pounding of feet all around them, the shouted commands, and the hollered word "Clear" each time a room was found to be empty and safe. Noah guided her to a nearby pew and she sat down. "Boss," he said again.

Josie's gaze drifted back to the dead men. Both wearing jeans and plain black T-shirts, boots and shoulder holsters. One of them still had his gun in place; the other guy's was a few feet away. Like someone had kicked it away from him after he was shot.

"He's not here," Josie said. "We were too late."

Noah frowned. He looked down at her, his expression filled with pity. "I'm sorry, boss."

One of the deputies stepped out from a room beside the altar. "Chief," he yelled. "There's no one else here, but we found something in the sacristy you should probably see."

Josie moved on numb legs with Noah at her back. She followed the deputy into the small room where the priest usually prepared for mass. There were no vestments left from the church's active days. Only an old vinyl chair and a couple of wooden benches lining one wall. That, and a baby's wooden cradle—white with zoo animals dancing across its bumpers. Josie stepped closer, feeling a dread so cloying she thought she might suffocate. But the bassinet was empty except for an unused yellow blanket sealed inside its store packaging in one corner. She looked around the room again.

"There's nothing else," she said.

Noah and the deputy stared at her. She looked once more at the cradle. "This doesn't even look like it was used."

Noah said, "They must have moved them. Luke and the baby."

"Why are Dunn's men dead, though?"

"Maybe Dunn didn't think they were doing a very good job?" Noah offered.

Josie shook her head and went back out to the altar. Nothing made sense. Why were the men dead? Who had killed them? Where was Luke? Had he ever been here? She panned the transept, noticing for the first time a folding chair in one corner, a vinyl chair turned on its side, bottles of water scattered around—most empty but one still full—a hamburger on the floor, and a hammer. Beneath the first row of pews were several fast food wrappers, foam coffee cups, and cigarette butts.

Phillips walked slowly around the perimeter of the transept, his eyes panning the floor. "Someone was being held here," he said, pointing. Josie stepped closer and noticed the severed zip ties on the floor, some crusted with blood.

She looked back toward the hammer, suppressing a shudder. She didn't want to think about what they'd been doing with it. Nudging an empty McDonald's French fry carton with her foot, Josie said, "Looks like they were here a few days."

"Look at that," Phillips said, pointing at the floor behind the overturned chair.

A white sneaker with a dark-blue Nike swoosh on it sat discarded on the floor. The top of it was splattered with brown-red spots that Josie recognized as blood. She sucked in a breath and turned away from Phillips so he wouldn't see the tears leaking from her eyes. Brushing them away, she croaked, "It's his. That's Luke's sneaker."

"How do you know?" Phillips said.

"It's a size eleven, isn't it?"

She heard him groan as he got onto all fours to get a closer look. He wouldn't move the shoe. The scene still had to be processed. Photos would have to be taken before anything was moved.

"Yeah, size eleven," Phillips confirmed, heaving himself back up.

"That's his sneaker," Josie whispered.

"I'm sure we can get DNA from it," Phillips said. "To confirm. Might take a while to get the results back."

She rubbed her temples, feeling a new headache forming. "I know. Labs move slowly. The state police might be able to expedite it since it might belong to one of their own. In the meantime, we need IDs on these guys. I'm guessing they're from Atlantic City or nearby."

Phillips nodded. "We've got an evidence response team. I'll get started. Let you know what we find."

CHAPTER 43

They stayed at the scene for a few hours, watching as the Lenore Sheriff's Office ERT processed the scene with an enthusiasm Josie normally only saw in rookies. Josie watched them closely, cataloging their movements in her mind to keep her thoughts away from Luke's bloody sneaker, the zip ties, and the hammer. The question *is he still alive* whispered over and over again in the back of her brain. Fear kept rising from deep within her like a heavy cloth trying to smother her, dragging her down and making it hard to breathe. She had to be strong, focused.

Phillips reported that the vehicle behind the church was registered to a New Jersey man named Buck Romeo. They found his body in the trunk, two stab wounds to his chest. Josie wondered if this was the man Luke had stabbed when they came for him.

When all the bodies had been photographed, assessed by the coroner, and loaded into ambulances, Josie, Noah, and their officers thanked the deputies and said their goodbyes. Noah and Josie drove together in a department-issued Ford Edge. Noah was silent. Josie knew he was angry; she could feel it coming off him like waves of heat, but her mind was too cluttered and exhausted to draw him out. There was no need to—after about twenty minutes, he spoke without being prompted.

"You broke protocol," he said. "You broke formation and ran ahead. You could have been killed."

She nearly said, *Who cares?*—her mind had gone to such a dark place. Then he said, "You could have gotten someone else killed."

She stared out the window, watching the rural roads turn to more populated areas as they approached Denton. "I'm sorry," she said.

"You're too close," he added. "No one benefits when you're out of control. Someone has to say it."

"What are you going to do?" she asked.

He made a noise of frustration deep in his throat. "The question is what are *you* going to do?"

He wouldn't go over her head. Noah would never rat her out and give the mayor what she wanted. He was too loyal, they had been through too much together. But Josie knew he was right, she was too close, and her connections to both cases were making her a liability. She'd had a handle on her emotions until the sight of those legs at the front of the church threw her. Josie shook her head, trying to rid herself of the memory and keep herself collected.

"I'm going to bring Misty's baby and Luke home," she said quietly.

"Boss—"

"I know, I know. With every hour that passes, the chances of them being alive when we find them get slimmer and slimmer. I can't control that, but I also can't stop looking. You know that."

"I know that you need to take a step back."

Josie stared at him. He drove with one hand on the wheel while the other tapped out a steady rhythm on his thigh. "And do what?" she asked. "Sit at home worrying and waiting? I can't. I physically can't."

"I know you can't," Noah replied. "I'm not suggesting that. I'm just saying that maybe next time you're not the first one through the door."

Josie didn't respond. Her phone chirped, as if on cue, and she pulled up a series of texts from Deputy Phillips. "*Found ID on your guys.*" Followed by photos of two New Jersey driver's licenses. One man was from Atlantic City and the other was from Absecon, which Josie knew from having studied a map of

New Jersey after Kavolis was found in Luke's yard, was near Atlantic City. Another photo followed, this time of a matchbook which read Oasis Grande Casino Resort, *"Guessing these guys worked for Dunn like you thought."*

Josie texted back, *"Thanks. We will confirm. Appreciate your help."*

She sent a text to Gretchen asking her where Dunn and his security detail were.

"What's up?" Noah asked.

"We're going to see Eric Dunn."

"Boss, I don't think that's—"

Gretchen's reply came back within seconds. "I didn't ask what you thought," Josie said. "He's at the Flats. Let's go."

CHAPTER 44

The Flats was an area at the southernmost point of Denton. It was a barren tract of land between the interstate and the nearby branch of the Susquehanna River with only one access road, which was flooded several times a year. For decades, developers had tried to build on the area, but their projects were almost always abandoned after the third or fourth time the access road flooded. A nightclub had lasted a few months, and then a few years later it was converted to a movie theater which lasted only a bit longer. Then someone had had the grand idea to build luxury apartments. The half-built six-story apartment building stood like a dresser with no drawers across from the old movie theater.

Although the casino was not a done deal, Eric Dunn had already received permits to start building a hotel on the site, and construction equipment and building supplies had been deposited alongside the apartment building. Josie saw a back-hoe and an excavator as well as a large flatbed truck with a cherrypicker in its bed to lift workers and equipment from the ground to the middle stories of the building. Some supplies had started being lifted by crane into the open top floors of the building. She could see from the ground that several pallets of timber, steel girders, metal HVAC piping, and a couple of air conditioning units had also been moved to the top floor. She didn't see any workers, however, and wondered if Dunn was having trouble securing contractors after the building collapse fiasco in Philadelphia. Or perhaps his track record of unsafe sites and not paying his workers was finally holding him back.

Dunn and his four men stood around the outside of a black Yukon that was parked next to the building. Dunn looked up, then pointed at various pieces of equipment, talking animatedly but out of earshot of Josie and Noah. They parked several yards away from the Yukon and got out. As they walked toward the men, Josie felt the hairs on the back of her neck stand to attention. For a moment, she wondered if one, or all of them, would pull weapons. There was something lawless about this unfinished place, and Dunn was a loose cannon. Josie had called in two patrol vehicles, together with Gretchen, to sit at the mouth of the access road, should they need backup, just to be safe.

Dunn stopped speaking and smirked at her as they drew closer, his gaze roving up and down her body, groping her with his eyes. He said, "What are you doing here? This is private property."

Josie flashed her badge. "I'm the chief of police. You're standing in my jurisdiction, and we need to talk."

Dunn folded his arms across his chest and tipped his chin in Noah's direction. "Tell you what, I'll have my secretary call your secretary, how's that?"

"Watch it," Noah said.

Dunn laughed. "How about if I watch the two of you turn around, get back in your car, and leave? If you have something to discuss with me, you can call my lawyers."

"Or you can cut the shit right now, stop hiding behind your lawyers, and tell us where Misty Derossi's baby and Luke Creighton are," Josie snapped.

Dunn narrowed his eyes at her. He appraised her for a few seconds before saying, "You're a spunky little thing, aren't you?" He turned to Noah. "I bet she's fun in the sack, huh?"

In her peripheral vision, Josie could see Noah's face turning fire engine red. She shook her head to keep him from speaking and addressed Dunn. "Stop wasting my time. You want to stand here all day seeing how many dumb things you can think of to say or do you want to get down to business?"

She thought she heard the beginnings of a muffled laugh from one of Dunn's men, but it was quickly cut off. Josie stared him down. He said, "What do you want?"

"You know goddamn well what I want. I've got two high-profile missing persons in this city right now—a baby and a state trooper—and all the evidence leads to you. So here I am. Now, how are we going to handle this?"

"All the evidence, huh? What evidence is that? A couple of my former employees turning up dead in your city?"

"More than a couple."

Josie pulled out her cell phone and swiped to the driver's license photos that Deputy Phillips had sent her of the men on the church floor. "These guys are dead too. Gunshot wounds. Found them holed up in an abandoned church outside of Fairfield. I'm guessing you don't know them either."

Something in his eyes changed. Josie swore she saw a flicker of surprise, or panic—or both? He collected himself quickly, swallowing and looking up from her cell phone to meet her eyes. "I don't know them. I'm not sure why you've become fixated on me, but I have nothing to do with your missing persons cases. I'm trying to get a casino built. That's it. Maybe I need to talk to Tara about you."

Josie ignored the threat. "What went wrong?"

He smiled to cover the look of puzzlement that came over his face. "It's your city council, some of them don't think it's a good idea to have a casino—"

"Not with your casino. What went wrong with the baby? The cradle wasn't used," Josie said. "Your three goons couldn't keep an infant alive for more than a few hours?"

"I don't know—"

"How about Luke? Your men are dead, and he's gone. So either you had him killed or someone else killed your men and then took him. Which is it? Who would want what's yours?"

Dunn clamped his mouth shut, a muscle in his cheek twitching. Josie pushed on. "Maybe it's one of your former employees.

There sure are a lot of them running around this area lately. Maybe one of them got pissed at you and decided to screw up your plans—whatever the hell those were. Or are we talking about something else? Maybe somebody who lost someone in the building collapse in Philadelphia? You know, the one that killed all those people?"

He pointed a finger at her. "You don't know what you're talking about."

"Don't I?" Josie pressed. "Isn't making people disappear your specialty? Are you getting a taste of your own medicine? Or is there something you want to tell me? Like, where I can find my missing persons."

He stabbed the air with his finger. "Now you listen to me, you bitch—"

His words were swallowed up by a loud groan from overhead, followed by noises Josie couldn't fully process—what sounded like a rumbling then a screech. Noah threw his body into hers, knocking her to the ground. Her left shoulder hit hard, and an involuntary cry ripped from her throat. From the dirt, Josie watched a series of pipes fall from the top floor of the building, like giant straws scattering haphazardly. One hit the roof of the Yukon with a clang, denting it nearly in half. One by one, Dunn's men went down, crushed or impaled by the falling pipes. There seemed no end to the number of them. Dunn himself stood frozen in place, his mouth wide open, staring up at the top floor of the building, watching them fall. Josie pushed Noah off her and scrambled to her feet. Noah's hands snagged her ankle just as she was about to sprint toward Dunn. She fell again, landing on top of Noah and rolling off him, away from the falling pipes. There was another sonic groan and then the flooring of the sixth story, where the piping had been, bowed, and off tumbled the heavy square of an air conditioning unit.

"No!" Josie screamed.

She kicked Noah away and started crawling toward Dunn, but it was too late. The air conditioning unit fell faster than the pipes but made almost no sound other than the crunching of bone as it landed on Dunn, knocking him over and crushing his lower body.

"No!" Josie screamed again. On her feet once more, she clambered over to him, kneeling beside him. He stared up at her, his eyes wide with shock. The behemoth air conditioning unit had pinned him from the pelvis down. Not just pinned him, Josie realized as she had a closer look, but driven his lower body into the ground. She fought back the vomit that rose in the back of her throat. Touching Dunn's shoulder, she hovered over his face. "Where are they?" she spat.

His shocked stare morphed into a look of fear and pleading. He blinked and opened his mouth as though to speak but nothing came out.

Josie heard sirens and was vaguely aware of flashing police lights approaching. Noah was behind her. "Boss!"

"Where are they?" Josie shouted at Dunn. "Goddamn it. What did you do with them? Victor Derossi and Luke Creighton. Where *are* they?"

Noah's hand grasped her shoulder. "Boss, get away from there."

She reached both hands down and pushed against the unit, but it was like trying to move a continent with her hands. "Help me," she said over her shoulder. "Help me!" Then to Dunn, "Where are Luke and the baby?"

"Boss," Noah said. "You can't help him. Come on. We don't know what else is up there. It looks like that whole floor might collapse."

"Where are Luke and the baby?" Josie shouted, leaning over Dunn's face again.

She saw him go, like the coil inside a lightbulb fades; the flicker of life in his eyes dimmed until there was nothing left but empty glass orbs. "No!" Josie shrieked. "Where are they?"

Noah scooped both hands under her arms and dragged her away. She struggled against him, legs kicking. A pallet of lumber slid into view on the top story of the building where the flooring had sagged to a V shape. It tumbled off the building, breaking apart in midair, boards flying everywhere. Josie's body stopped struggling. Noah took one final lunge, throwing both of them behind their vehicle as the boards started to ricochet in every direction. They heard several smacks as some of the boards landed on the hood of the car they had arrived in. Behind them, the two patrol cars and Gretchen in her Chevy Cruze pulled up. They raced out of their vehicles, positioning themselves behind open doors with their weapons drawn, as though they were in a standoff.

Noah stood up and waved toward them. "Stand down," he said. "There's no one left."

Josie let him help her up. She stared at the destruction from behind the vehicle, disbelieving. Her other officers holstered their weapons and walked over.

"What the hell just happened?" Gretchen asked.

"They're dead," Josie croaked. "They're all dead."

CHAPTER 45

CBS 3—Philadelphia

Bucks County

July 23, 2017

Teen Dies in Freak Camping Accident

Authorities say a large tree branch fell on a tent last night, killing a fifteen-year-old girl inside. Jessie Kanagie of Philadelphia had been camping with her family for the weekend. Emergency crews were called to Cherrydale Campground around 7:30 a.m. Sunday. The fire department cut the tree branch and removed it but found Kanagie inside the tent already deceased.

"It was just a freak accident," the fire chief said. "It's tragic."

There have not been any storms in the area recently, but authorities believe that a combination of erosion and wind may have caused the branch to snap off the tree and land on the girl's tent. Her brother and father were asleep in nearby tents but say they didn't hear anything and didn't know there had been an accident until they woke up and found Kanagie's tent crushed beneath the tree branch. "We're devastated," said her father. "We were here on a retreat. This was supposed to be a good thing." The teen had arson charges pending against her in juvenile court and was out on bail.

CHAPTER 46

Dr. Anya Feist shook her head as she surveyed the scene. The area where the bodies lay had been cordoned off. After composing herself, Josie had sprung into action, not wanting her officers to see her lose control, even though that was exactly what she felt like doing. She didn't have that luxury. She contacted a couple of local engineers and construction outfits to come out and assess the scene before her people could move in to process it and move the bodies. It had taken about an hour for them to determine that there was no more imminent danger. It would take longer for them to figure out what the hell had gone wrong.

Once Denton PD had the okay to start their work, Josie sent in her evidence response team and called the medical examiner. Dr. Feist now stood beside her, looking almost as perplexed as she was. "You just like seeing my face, or what?" Dr. Feist said.

"No," Josie deadpanned. "I really don't."

The doctor raised a brow. "I'm not that hard on the eyes."

Josie knew she should smile or make some joke back, but she couldn't bring herself to do it. She had gone on autopilot making calls and barking out commands, but all the while her eyes kept drifting back to the carnage. Her last lead to Luke and Misty's baby, gone.

Dr. Feist's fingers were warm on Josie's forearm. "Hey, Chief," she said. "You okay?"

Josie looked away from the scene, where some of the construction workers had begun using the crane to lift the piping and the air conditioning unit from the bodies. Dr. Feist's face was lined with concern. "I'm fine," Josie mumbled.

"Did you hit your head?" Dr. Feist asked.

"No. I'm fine."

The doctor put her fingers to the inside of Josie's wrist. "Your pulse is racing," she noted. When she pressed the back of her hand against Josie's forehead, Josie stepped away from her. "Doc, seriously, I'm fine."

Dr. Feist smiled wanly. "Physically, you mean."

"I need to make a phone call," Josie said abruptly. She walked away from Dr. Feist, weaving her way through vehicles and personnel until she found Noah looking over a rough drawing one of the engineers had made of the top floor of the building. "I'm taking Gretchen's car," she told him. "You stay on-scene here until everything is wrapped up, okay?"

She started walking away before he could ask any questions. Gretchen's keys were in the ignition. Josie backed up, turned the car around, and drove off. It was a short drive to the cemetery where Ray was buried. It was a small graveyard, one of the newer cemeteries in Denton. Josie liked it because it was well kept, but that hadn't stopped people from vandalizing Ray's headstone.

As she approached it in the twilight, she could see indiscernible graffiti across his name but at least she didn't smell urine this time. She couldn't blame the vandals—she still struggled herself with Ray's betrayal—but she didn't come to the cemetery to visit the man who had done nothing while innocent girls were violated and killed. She came to visit her childhood friend, her high school sweetheart, the man she had once loved and married. A man she thought was kind and decent. She wished he was alive. What would he say? What would he say if he knew the baby they were looking for might belong to him?

Had he ever really wanted children? The topic must have come up between him and Misty just as it had with Josie, otherwise Misty wouldn't have known to search out his donor sperm.

Josie hadn't had much time to think about what it meant for Misty to bring a baby into the world whose father was already dead, not to mention a pariah in his own city.

"I'm sorry, Ray," Josie whispered as she knelt in the grass in front of his headstone. She stared at his name, hating him for the thousandth time for what he did, and for leaving her alone to deal with it.

Night descended around her, and the air grew cold. Josie sat until she felt numb, the events of the last few days playing over and over again in her mind. She tried to find the place where everything had gone irreparably wrong, tried to figure out what she could have done differently. Should she have taken a more direct approach with Dunn? Should she have thrown him in jail and let his lawyers get him out in a day just to put a good scare into him? Even as she thought this, she realized it wouldn't have done any good. Dunn wasn't scared of anyone. Perhaps that had been his downfall.

The beam of a flashlight bobbed in the distance beyond Ray's grave. Josie quietly took her gun out of its holster and held it in her lap. She sat perfectly still, waiting. At first it didn't look as though it was heading for her, then the light jerked upward and Josie heard a mumbled "Shit." It was a woman. The voice was familiar.

"Boss?"

Josie let out a breath she didn't realize she was holding. She put her gun back and called, "Over here, Gretchen."

The beam of light turned in Josie's direction. She threw a hand up as it crossed her vision. Gretchen pointed the flashlight straight up in the air, illuminating her own face. "Sorry," she said. A bottle appeared before Josie's eyes. "Noah said you like this stuff."

It was Wild Turkey. Josie took it and Gretchen squatted down, setting the flashlight between them in the grass, pointed upward so they could see each other. "How did you know I was here?" Josie asked.

"Noah said you come here sometimes."

"Did he?" Josie was surprised; it wasn't something she told people about. Not even Luke knew that she came here—or how often.

As if reading her mind, Gretchen said, "He just worries about you. A lot of your staff do, you know."

"What do you mean?"

Gretchen shrugged. "I mean not in the way like they don't think you're fit. More in the way that they don't want anything to happen to you. They already lost one chief. They don't want to lose another. They respect you. You're a little bit of a hero around here after what you did up on that mountain."

Josie's index finger circled the cap of the Wild Turkey. She sighed. "I don't feel like a hero," she said. "I didn't then, and I don't today."

A moment of silence passed between them. Then Josie said, "Why are you here?"

"Thought you might want to know the engineers' preliminary assessment of Dunn's construction site was that it wasn't an accident."

Josie's throat tightened. "You mean someone was there?"

Gretchen nodded. "Looks like someone had cut into the beams to compromise the integrity of the floor, and then used a small forklift to push all that stuff to the weakest spot..."

"There was a forklift up there?" Josie said.

"Yes, and the straps holding the piping together were also cut. It wouldn't have taken much for someone to start the pipes falling by slicing the straps and giving a little push. Then once the floor started to bow... well, you know the rest."

Josie uncapped the Wild Turkey and sniffed it but didn't sip it. "So they think someone was up there while we were there?"

"Yeah."

Josie pictured the Flats in her mind. Technically, someone could get there on foot, and if they had come across the interstate and down the hill behind the buildings, they could even do it without being seen. They could easily have slipped away during the commotion they caused, and no one would be the wiser. There were no cameras anywhere in that area. It was the perfect place to stage an accident. It also meant that someone else besides Josie's people was following Dunn.

"You've been on Dunn for two days," Josie said. "Have you noticed anyone else keeping tabs on him?"

"No, but I wasn't really looking for someone else."

Josie was well aware of how many people might have their own reasons for wanting Dunn dead. But why then? And why there?

"It also didn't help that Dunn was already cutting corners everywhere he could on that site," Gretchen said. "The engineers will be at it for a while. They'll prepare a full report for you, but that's the bottom line."

"Which means absolutely nothing to me," Josie said flatly. "Because it doesn't help me find Luke or Misty's baby." She took a long swig of the Wild Turkey and then capped the bottle. It burned her throat and warmed her stomach. She held the bottle out to Gretchen, but she refused.

"I'm sorry, boss," she said.

Josie nodded and looked away from Gretchen. "Detective Palmer," she said. "I'd like to be alone now."

Gretchen waited a moment, but when Josie didn't say anything else, she stood up, shaking stiff legs. "You want to keep my flashlight?" she asked.

"No," Josie said. "Thank you."

Gretchen scooped up the light. "You know where to find me," she told Josie before walking off.

Josie listened to her picking her way through the headstones until there was only the silence of the night. She took another searing sip of Wild Turkey before curling up on her side. She closed her eyes, trying to stop her imagination from running wild with images of Luke's lifeless body, wondering what Dunn's goons had done to him—and to Misty's baby.

It didn't work. She was about to pour half the bottle of Wild Turkey down her throat when her phone buzzed several times. Fishing it out of her pocket, she squinted as the screen's bright light flooded her field of vision. It was Carrieann. She had probably seen a news report on Dunn's untimely demise. With a heavy sigh, Josie answered. She heard nothing but rustling. "Carrieann," she called a couple of times but got no response.

She was beginning to think Carrieann had called her by accident when her hushed voice finally came on the line. "Josie," she hissed. "Someone's here."

Josie's spine tingled. "In my house?"

"No, at Luke's. I came to straighten things up a little, and I think there's someone here. There are lights on on both floors."

"Where are you right now?"

"I just went back out to the road. I'm at the edge of the driveway in my truck."

Josie was already racing back to her vehicle. "Get into your truck and leave. I'm on my way. I'm going to call in some units."

CHAPTER 47

Carrieann was right. Less than a half hour later, Josie and Noah stood in the trees next to Luke's driveway, peering at his house. The living room windows glowed, and judging by the light that jumped along the swath of wall that Josie could see, the television was on as well. Upstairs, light shone from the windows of the master bedroom and bathroom.

"There are no cars in the driveway," Noah said. "Besides Luke's truck, which has been here all along."

"Yeah," Josie said. "But someone is definitely here."

"Who?"

"Don't know," she muttered. "But we're going to find out."

Behind them, three other officers waited in darkness, strapping on their bulletproof vests and checking their weapons. They couldn't risk driving up to the house because of the gravel driveway. Josie didn't want to alert whoever was in there too soon and risk them running out the back door or, worse, coming after Josie and her men. A fourth officer threaded his way toward them from the side of the property. "I looked around back," he reported. "There's no one there. Not that I can see. Barn is empty too."

"Great," Josie said. "Get your vest on. We're going in three teams of two. Your teams will clear the downstairs, and then Lieutenant Fraley and I will clear the upstairs."

Crouched low, they moved in tandem toward the house, their footsteps silent over the grass. As they reached the porch, sweat moistened Josie's palms as she gripped her gun. They took up position next to the front door. Once Josie gave the signal, the first team eased in through the front door, which was unlocked. The other team followed, with her and Noah bringing up the rear. The other officers moved quickly and quietly, finding no one on the first floor. But someone was obviously in the house—or had been very recently. The television in the living room played the local news. In the kitchen, on the table across from the bloodstains, was a plate with a half-eaten bagel on it. A cream-cheese-covered butter knife lay in the sink.

In the silence, Josie heard the sound of water running from upstairs. She motioned for Team One to take up position at the front door and for Team Two to follow her and Noah as they climbed the stairs. She pointed down the hallway, and the four of them moved together, checking rooms as they went. All of them were dark and empty. Even the master bedroom—though the light was on—was clear. The bathroom door was slightly ajar, steam billowing out around its edges.

Josie looked back momentarily and caught Noah's eye. He made a hand signal that she should proceed. A roar started in her ears. Even as she tried to stop it, hope soared inside her. Was it Luke? Had he escaped? Returned home to get cleaned up? She knew it was preposterous, but the part of her that desperately wanted a happy ending to this scenario couldn't help but wish she would find him on the other side of the door. Who the hell else could it be?

She felt Noah's hand on her shoulder and knew the time for hesitation was over. Best to surprise whoever it was while they were still in the shower. Pushing the door open, Josie moved inside. She felt Noah close at her back and her beating heart slowed somewhat.

Steam eddied and swirled around them. The only sound was the water running. For a split second, Josie wondered if there was really anyone in there. Was this some kind of trap? Who would set it? Dunn was dead. Unless he had put something in place before he died. But why set a trap at Luke's house, and for who? For Josie? The police? As retribution for the man Luke likely killed the day Dunn's goons took him? No, she decided. It couldn't be a trap. They'd checked every inch of the place. There was only Josie's squad and whoever was behind the shower curtain.

She reached out, pulled back the curtain and yelled, "Police!"

With a shriek, Kim Conway snatched the shower curtain, tearing it completely from the rod, and clutching it to her naked, soapy body. One hand flew to her chest. "Oh my God. You scared me. What the hell are you doing?"

Tension leeched from Josie's body. She was aware of a small wellspring of disappointment that it wasn't Luke. Raising a brow, she said, "The better question is what the hell are you doing? Kim Conway, you're under arrest for the murder of Denny Twitch."

CHAPTER 48

Josie had a female officer stay with Kim until she was dried off, dressed, and ready to be transported to the police station. The sight of her so comfortable at Luke's house was almost more than Josie could bear. A part of her still kept trying to give Luke the benefit of the doubt; he'd been protecting his best friend's little sister from a monster—she had to make herself believe that's all it was.

Patrol took Kim back to the Denton police station and booked her. Josie doubted that the charge in Denny Twitch's murder would stand; Kim could easily get off with self-defense given the circumstances, and knowing the district attorney, Josie didn't think she'd want to waste the county's time or valuable resources trying a woman who would be acquitted anyway. But Josie needed something to keep Kim in custody until she found out what she knew.

Once again, Josie found herself about to face Kim in the interrogation room, wearing yet another pair of Luke's sweatpants and a novelty T-shirt that Josie had given him for Christmas. She remembered the way she and Luke had laughed over it on Christmas morning. Above the outline of a large, openmouthed trout, the shirt read: *Men have feelings too...I mostly feel like fishing.* It had been perfect for him. Somehow, seeing Kim wearing it felt like more of a betrayal than seeing she had been sleeping in Luke's bed.

Josie jumped when Noah touched her shoulder. "You want me to talk to her?"

She managed a smile. "No. I'll do it."

As she pushed the door of the interrogation room open, she realized with a sudden pang that she really didn't want Noah anywhere near Kim Conway. Kim shot Josie a sullen look and crossed her arms over her chest. Josie noticed her hair was still damp; the smell of Irish Spring soap filled the air. Luke's soap. For a moment, Josie considered having Gretchen question Kim. But it would only help Gretchen agree with Noah that this had become too personal, that Josie was too close.

Kim said, "If you're here to question me about Denny Twitch, I want a lawyer."

Josie sighed and walked over to the table, taking a seat across from Kim. "I've already called the public defender's office. But I'm not here to talk about Twitch. I don't care about Twitch."

At this, Kim's gaze flitted up to Josie's face. "Then why are you here?"

"I want to talk about Luke."

Kim's posture softened. "I'm sorry about what happened to him," she murmured.

"What *did* happen to him?"

Kim looked away, her eyes traveling up and down the walls behind Josie. Josie imagined she was trying to figure out what she could safely tell her without implicating herself in more crimes.

Josie tapped her fingers on the tabletop, drawing Kim's attention. "Here's what I already know. You were in a relationship with Eric Dunn. He abused you. Maybe just once or twice, maybe a lot. He definitely put some burns on your back and punched you in the face hard enough to break your orbital bones."

Kim's eyes widened.

Josie forged ahead. "I know that at some point you left him. You came to Denton and stayed with your brother, Brady. You were pregnant. The night of the shooting, Eric sent Mickey Kavolis to Brady's house to get you. Kavolis shot Brady and Eva, and either you or Luke shot Kavolis in self-defense."

Josie gave Kim a meaningful look as she said the words "self-defense." She wanted her to understand she had no interest in stirring up old cases—it was out of her jurisdiction anyway. She just wanted to find out what Kim knew.

Josie continued, "You and Luke took Kavolis's body and buried it behind Luke's barn."

Kim let out a little gasp.

"I'm not done," Josie said. "Luke hid you at his house for a few months. Then you went to Misty Derossi's house. Misty says that for some reason, you helped her deliver her baby. To my knowledge, you're not a midwife or a doctor, and Misty was planning to give birth at the hospital, so I'm not sure why you did that—or why you were there at all."

Kim didn't offer an explanation, so Josie continued, "At some point, Denny Twitch was there. Once that baby was born, he beat Misty half to death and took her baby. I also know that after Misty's baby was abducted, you returned to Luke's house, and you were there when Dunn sent more goons to get you. Luke was there when they arrived, or maybe they were waiting for him when he got home. I know there was a struggle and that Luke wounded one of them. Then they took him."

Kim said nothing but chewed on her lower lip and hugged herself tighter.

"Here's what I *don't* know," Josie said. "I don't know what happened to *your* baby—if you were even pregnant to begin with. I don't know why you were at Misty Derossi's house or what you could possibly have wanted with her, or her baby. I don't know why Dunn sent Twitch there—was it to get you or to take Misty's baby, or both? I don't know what Dunn would have wanted with her baby or why Dunn's men took Luke and left you when they came to his house—unless you were hiding, and, most of all, I still *don't* know where Luke is."

One of Kim's hands reached up and tucked a strand of hair behind her ear. "How did you—?"

Josie said, "It's my job to find things out."

"Is . . . is Eric really dead? I saw it on the news this morning, but I—it's so hard to believe."

"Yes," Josie answered. "I watched him die. He is really gone."

The air seemed to go out of Kim, and her body slumped in the chair. She closed her eyes and whispered some words that Josie couldn't make out. A prayer? Words of gratitude? Her eyes sprang open again and she said, "There's a warehouse in Atlantic City. I've never been there, but I've heard the guys talk about it. They take people there. People that are never seen again. I'm not sure where it is exactly, but maybe someone on his staff could tell you now that he's dead. You should call the Atlantic City police. Maybe they took Luke there."

Josie shook her head. "They didn't take him there."

"But how do you know?"

"They were holding him somewhere nearby. By the time we got there, Luke was gone, and Dunn's men were dead."

"So, he's not . . . he's not—"

"We don't know where he is," Josie said. "Or if he's still alive. You were in a relationship with Eric Dunn for some time. I need to know if you have any idea who might have had it in for him. Who might have known where he was keeping Luke and been angry enough to kill his goons and possibly take Luke."

Kim shivered. "Oh, wow. I don't know. Eric made a lot of enemies. You don't understand how he was."

"I think I have a pretty good idea."

Kim's face crumpled. Tears leaked from her eyes as a wave of emotion rolled over her. "No," she said. "You really don't. Eric sent Mickey to Brady's house to teach me a lesson, not just to get me back. I was upstairs when he shot Brady and Eva. He was there to make it look like a murder-suicide and then take me. Eric wanted them killed so I would have no one left to run to—or so I wouldn't run to my mom, 'cause he'd kill her too. Luke showed up just as the whole thing was going down. I came downstairs, and I was screaming. Brady and Eva were dead. Then Luke wrestled Mickey's gun away from him and . . ."

"So, it was Luke who killed Kavolis," Josie said. She couldn't imagine what it had been like for him to carry that alone, especially after covering it up and, in doing so, making himself a criminal.

Kim nodded. "It all happened so fast. Eric didn't have to have my brother killed, but he did it anyway. Don't you see? He's evil. Pure evil."

"Was evil. He's gone now. Why were you with him in the first place?"

"I wanted out from almost the moment I started seeing him, but no one walks away from Eric Dunn. The burns on my back—they were from a curling iron, all because he thought I was taking too long to get ready for an opening we were going to. He burned me, and then he made me put on my dress and my heels and smile through the entire thing, all while I thought I was going to die from the pain. That was the first time he used the curling iron. The broken eye socket? That is just the tip of the iceberg."

"I'm sorry," Josie said.

"I lied about the pregnancy," Kim blurted out. "He was going to kill me. I'm trying to make you understand."

"I'm listening."

CHAPTER 49

Kim looked around the room again, eyes falling on the camera above the door. She leaned into the table and lowered her voice. "There was this building collapse in Philadelphia last year."

"I'm aware," Josie said and repeated what Trinity had told her.

"Jesus," Kim said. "You're thorough."

Josie didn't reply. "What does the building collapse have to do with you faking a pregnancy?"

"I had video of Eric bribing one of the municipal guys and video of one of his foremen telling him that one of the guys hired to do the demo was high on drugs and Eric saying he didn't care, to use the guy anyway. I was going to use them—take them to the police and see if they could put me into, like, the witness protection program or something. Anything to get away from him. I mean if he was in prison, he couldn't hurt me, right?"

"What happened to the videos?"

"Eric found them on my phone and deleted them. He was going to kill me. Torture me, then kill me. So, I told him I was pregnant. It was the only thing I could think of to buy myself some time. To make him stop. I knew how obsessed he was with having his own son one day. A real, blood-related child. Did you know he's a donor baby?"

"His parents used a surrogate," Josie said. "That's public record."

Kim shook her head. "Not just a surrogate. A sperm donor.

His dad couldn't have kids of his own. Eric's mom wanted to make sure he wouldn't divorce her like he did all his other wives. The best way to do that would be to have his kid. She convinced him he needed an heir."

"How do you know this?" Josie asked.

"Eric told me. He found out about it in high school, and it messed him up. He always had a chip on his shoulder about it. His mom wouldn't tell him shit about who his biological parents were. It was always a thorn in his side. So, when he said he was going to kill me—and I knew he really was this time, because I had really betrayed him—I said I was pregnant."

"He wanted the baby."

She nodded. "Yes. I think he probably still would have killed me, but the baby—a baby that was biologically his—it was important to him."

Josie raised a brow. "Dunn didn't seem like the caring type to me—or like he had any interest in being a parent."

"Oh, he wasn't. He wasn't going to be this fantastic dad or anything. You have to understand that Eric was all about acquiring things. He always got what he wanted, and he wanted the baby because it was his, and there was no way anyone else was going to have it."

"So, you went to your brother's house to hide."

Kim nodded. "Yes. His wife didn't like me very much, so I told them I was pregnant too. I told them and Eric that I was only a couple of months along, so I didn't have to worry about showing."

"But at some point, when your belly didn't get any bigger, they would have figured it out," Josie pointed out.

Kim shrugged. "Well, yeah. Brady and Eva would have, for sure. I think Eva started to when I was there for two months and didn't get any fatter. I planned to fake a miscarriage or something. I wasn't thinking clearly. I just wanted to get away. I thought I'd deal with the fake pregnancy thing later. Then Kavolis came and…" She closed her eyes, and a shudder ran through her body. "I never wanted Brady and Eva to get hurt. Problem is that Eric didn't know I was faking. He thought I was a couple of months along back when I ran away from him. I ran in March. When he sent Kavolis for me back in May, I should have been four months pregnant. But Kavolis didn't bring me back."

"So, in Dunn's mind, you would have given birth within the last couple of weeks."

"Yeah."

Josie's mind spun. She leaned back in her chair. "Dunn fully expected a baby. He sent Twitch this time. Twitch tracked you down at Misty Derossi's house."

"Denny was looking for me and the baby."

"But he didn't take you. He took Misty's baby. Did he know Victor Derossi wasn't your baby?"

Kim looked away. "I think so. I mean I tried to tell him that the baby wasn't mine, but he didn't believe me. Misty tried to tell him, too, but he hit her. She fought so hard, but he was too strong. I told him to take me and not the baby, but he said Eric would kill him if he didn't come back with a baby. Denny didn't care whose baby it was, as long as he delivered a baby. He said Eric wouldn't know the difference."

"He left you there."

Her eyes drifted to her lap. "Denny and I . . . we used to have a thing."

"What kind of a thing?"

Kim met Josie's eyes again, one eyebrow arched. "We used to sleep together, okay? Behind Eric's back."

"Did Eric ever find out?"

Kim gave a dry laugh. "Are you kidding? Eric would have had both of us tortured and killed. No, Eric never found out, and Denny was still loyal to Eric, but I kind of used our prior relationship to convince him to let me go. Denny said he would tell Eric he never saw me, but he told me he was going to have to track me down again. He was just as scared of Eric as I was.

He was giving me a couple of days. I was still trying to figure a way out of the whole thing—how I could get away from Eric and still get Misty's baby back. That's why I went to Luke."

"Why were you there? At Misty's house?" Josie asked.

Kim reached up again and tucked hair behind her other ear. "Can I have something to drink?"

Josie made a hand signal toward the camera and a moment later, Noah came in with a bottle of water. Kim eyed him as she took the bottle and gulped half of it down. She smiled sweetly at him and thanked him. Josie tapped her hand on the table to bring her back into focus.

"Why were you at Misty Derossi's house?" She tried again.

Kim took another sip of water. She was buying time, Josie realized.

"Luke wanted me gone," Kim said finally. "He said it was too stressful and that it couldn't go on forever. Like, I had to find a way out of the whole thing. Misty came to his house one day."

"She came to his house?" Josie said, more loudly than she intended, but Kim didn't seem to notice.

"Yeah, I mean I just saw her from the upstairs window. I don't know what they talked about, but I saw her come and go, and she was pregnant. So, I asked Luke if they were sleeping together, and if it was his baby, and he laughed and said no. He said he barely knew her."

This gave Josie a small modicum of relief. "Did he say why she was there?"

"He said that she wanted him to talk to his fiancée about something, something having to do with the baby."

That the baby was Ray's, Josie thought.

Kim added, "He said something like it would be easier for her to hear coming from him, whatever that meant."

Josie pursed her lips. For whatever reason, Misty had wanted Josie to know that she might be having Ray's baby. Luke had been the intermediary. She wondered if there was more to it, but soon Misty would be well enough for her to ask. "And so, what? You said hey, I can go stay with the pregnant lady?"

"I knew he wanted me gone, and I got the feeling this chick was alone. I mean, she looked pretty distressed. I told Luke that I was a midwife—"

"A lie," Josie interjected.

Kim looked down at her lap. "Yes," she admitted. "I lied. He never would have agreed to it otherwise. I said maybe you can ask her if I can stay with her for a few days till I figure something out."

"And he thought that this was a good idea? Knowing that Dunn's men were trying to kill you, he thought it would be okay to send you to the home of a single woman about to give birth?"

"Well, no, he thought it was a horrible idea," Kim said. "But there was no connection between me and Misty, so it was kind of perfect."

"Except it wasn't," Josie said. "Because Denny Twitch found you."

Something about Kim's story wasn't ringing true. Luke wasn't the kind of guy who would knowingly put a pregnant woman—or any woman for that matter—at risk, even Misty Derossi. Then again, Josie thought, taking another look at the fishing T-shirt draped over Kim's small body, did she really know Luke at all?

"I know," Kim said. "I don't know how. I really don't. The next thing I knew, the baby was gone and Misty—well, I thought she was dead."

"You didn't call 911."

"I couldn't. I didn't want Eric to find me. You don't understand—"

"I understand enough," Josie said coldly.

"No, you don't," Kim replied firmly.

"I understand that you put Misty in danger repeatedly. You lied about being a midwife, and you put her in Eric Dunn's crosshairs. Then when Twitch beat her, you left her there to die.

Instead of going with Twitch and leaving the baby, you let him take a tiny, defenseless infant so that you could remain free. You don't know the first thing about delivering a baby, but you convinced Misty to let you help her deliver at home. Did she ask to go to the hospital?"

Kim didn't answer.

"She did, didn't she?" Josie pressed.

Her voice was quiet. "I couldn't take her to the hospital. I couldn't risk being found. Anyway, she was fine. The baby was fine."

Josie's anger flared white hot, surging through her body. "Do you even know how to tell the truth?"

Kim's eyes widened. The childlike look of feigned innocence. Josie stood up. "Save it," she snapped. "It's not going to work on me. You manipulated people—your brother, Luke, Misty—you lied and said whatever you needed to say to get them to do what you wanted."

The innocent look slipped off Kim's face, and in its place was something hard and flinty. "Not what I wanted," she shot back. "What I needed them to do to help me survive. My life has been in danger from the moment Eric set his sights on me. I'm not proud of what I've done, but I'm still alive."

Josie glared at her. "You are but you may have sacrificed Luke and a baby. Tell me, was it your intention all along to pass Misty Derossi's baby off as your own?"

Kim remained silent, arms crossed over her chest, her eyes everywhere but on Josie. After a few moments, Josie asked, "What happened after Twitch took the baby?"

"I went back to Luke for help, and we were trying to decide what to do when Eric's guys showed up. Luke told me to hide and I did. The next thing I remember is coming to on his back porch with no memory of who I was or how I got there."

Josie laughed. "You're sticking to your amnesia story? Is that really necessary?"

Kim bristled. "It's not a story. I was traumatized. The

doctors said trauma caused my amnesia. I could have died twice that day—at Misty's and then again at Luke's. I mean Denny came here to this police station and told your people he was a marshal. Don't you see how ruthless Eric could be?"

What Josie saw was that by admitting that she had faked her amnesia, Kim would expose herself to more criminal charges—obstructing justice and interfering with a police investigation, just to name a couple. As she openly admitted, Kim did whatever she had to do to ensure her own survival. Continuing to stand by her amnesia story would ensure a measure of protection. Josie moved on. "You obviously knew you were in trouble when you saw Twitch in our lobby. Why did you go with him? You were in the police station. Why not tell someone then what was going on?"

"I didn't want anyone else to get hurt," Kim explained.

"In a police station? That's rich." Josie wondered if she had always been a pathological liar or if she really had just grown used to lying as a matter of survival during her relationship with Eric Dunn.

"When you fled the scene of the accident after you shot Twitch, where did you go?"

Kim said, "I think I need that lawyer now. If we're going to talk about the accident."

"Let me rephrase," Josie said. "After the crash, where did you go?"

Kim took a moment to answer, and again Josie wondered if she was making calculations about how much she could say without getting herself into even more trouble than she already was. Finally, she answered, "I ran until I found a backyard. There was a woman there. She helped me clean up and gave me something to eat, some clothes, and then she said the police were coming back and I had to leave."

"The woman with the treehouse in her yard?"

Kim looked up at her. "Yes, that woman. But look, please don't charge her with anything. She didn't know—"

Josie held up a hand. "I'm not interested in her. We didn't find you at Luke's until today. What else were you doing?"

Again, Kim's gaze drifted to the table. Josie had a feeling the truth was coming, but it seemed difficult for Kim to push it out. "There was this guy. He was following Denny. I mean, I didn't know that at first. I only found out later. I had seen him before, lurking around when I was at Luke's. That was why I had to leave there. I knew I had been found."

"One of Eric's men?"

"Well, I thought so at first, but he didn't work for Eric. He was weird anyway. Not like the kinds of guys Eric usually hired. Plus, he was older."

"How old?"

She shrugged. "I don't know, fifties, maybe? He was thin, average height, quiet as could be. I mean, I got a really strange vibe from him. I didn't realize that he was following Denny until I left that lady's house. A few blocks away, he caught up to me and took me."

"What was he driving?"

"I don't know. It was like a sedan or something. Black, four doors. I'm not good with cars. It looked like every other black car on the road."

Josie suppressed a noise of frustration. "Where did he take you?"

"Nowhere at first. Then I started talking to him. I told him all the stuff I told you about Eric wanting to kill me. I asked him if Eric had sent him to kill me, but he said no. He said he didn't work for Eric and that he was supposed to deliver me to his boss, but he wouldn't tell me who that was."

So, there was someone else in play. It made sense in light of Dunn's gruesome death. "What did he want from you?"

"He wanted to know about the building collapse in Philadelphia. He said the information was important to his boss and that his boss would protect me if I told everything I knew about the collapse. Anyway, I told him that no matter where he took me, no one was safe with Eric looking for me. So we made a deal. He said he would 'take care' of Eric and then I would go wherever he wanted me to go and get him the videos."

"The videos Eric destroyed?"

"Well, he didn't know that."

"Fair enough. What do you mean 'take care' of him?"

Kim shrugged. "I don't know. I thought he meant, you know, get rid of him."

"Kill him?"

"He didn't say that and neither did I. For all I know, he was just going to have a talk with Eric. Get him off my back."

Josie's eyes narrowed. "I see."

"Look, you wanted the truth, I'm telling you the truth."

"You were going to go with this man, but you had no idea who he was or who he worked for? You didn't ask who his boss was or how he knew to look for you?"

"He wouldn't tell me who his boss was. I just figured it was someone who got screwed in the building collapse. Anyway, I had no real intention of ever meeting him, I was just trying to get away from him in the moment."

Everything Kim did was in the moment. "Then what happened?"

"He dropped me off at Luke's. I was supposed to meet him about a mile away at this abandoned farm silo today. I walked there, but when I saw the car, I chickened out. I couldn't go through with it. I just didn't feel safe. So, I went back to Luke's."

"What was his name?"

"He told me to call him Leo. That's all I know."

"I'll have my people start looking for him," Josie said. "Did you have a conversation with Denny when he took you?"

"I can't talk to you about that. Not without a lawyer."

"I'm not asking you about anything that happened. I just want to know if the subject of the baby or Luke came up while you were with Denny Twitch."

Kim's fingers peeled away the label from the water bottle.

"He wouldn't talk about Luke. I asked about him, but Denny changed the subject. All he cared about was the baby. He thought I took the baby. He said he didn't have him."

A frisson of excitement shot up Josie's spine. "He thought you took the baby from him? When? How?"

"Yeah, he thought I followed him or whatever when he left Misty's with the baby and took the baby out of his car when he stopped for gas."

"Did you?"

"No," Kim said. "Like I told you, I went to Luke's."

"How did you get there?"

Looking almost sheepish, Kim said, "A cab. I used Misty's phone and then I threw it into the river. I had the guy pull over halfway across the bridge, and I threw it into the water."

Which meant she was covering her tracks not to avoid Eric Dunn but to avoid the police. Josie wondered if she was hiding something, but right now her only goal was to find Luke and Victor Derossi, dead or alive.

"All right, so if Denny didn't have the baby and you didn't have the baby, who has the baby?"

"I have no idea." For the first time that afternoon, Josie felt absolutely sure she was telling the truth.

"All right, well, who would have tried to take the baby? Who would have taken Luke from Eric? Who would have known where Eric was keeping them?"

Kim looked at her sadly. "Everybody he ever screwed over, which was a lot of people. But none of them would have had the balls to do it. If his men were dead, it's because Eric ordered them to be killed. Eric had a lot of guys on his payroll, and their only loyalty was to him. They went where he told them to go, and they did what he told them to do. If Luke and the baby weren't there, it's because Eric had them killed too."

CHAPTER 50

Josie closed the door to her office and leaned against it, taking a deep, long breath. She had to keep it together. She refused to believe that Luke and little Victor Derossi were dead; she wouldn't, she couldn't. Twitch had told Kim that he didn't have the baby, but *someone* had the baby. Josie didn't know if that was better or worse. At least Dunn's men had been prepared with a cradle and a blanket. She was certain they knew less than nothing about caring for an infant, but some effort had been made, which meant Dunn hadn't intended to simply kill the baby. But in the hands of someone else? A chill ran through Josie. She shook it off and went over to sit behind her desk. Kim was lying about a lot of things, but Josie didn't believe she had any information that would be useful in finding Victor or Luke.

There was a soft knock on the door and Noah let himself in. He looked at her with that half-pitying, half-pained look he'd been giving her since all of this started. Like he was watching her get a root canal.

"I'm fine," Josie snapped.

He stepped forward and put a paper fast food bag in the center of her desk. "We put Conway in holding for now. She'll go over to central booking after she's assigned a public defender."

Josie nodded. Her stomach clenched at the smell of the food. She peeked inside the bag. A burger and fries. Noah said, "You have to be hungry. Even if you're not, you need to eat."

She unwrapped the burger and took a bite. It turned out she was hungry; it took only seconds to devour it and, as a loud growl sounded from her abdomen, she reached for the fries. Noah sat across from her desk. "You think she's right?" he asked. "That Dunn had Luke and the baby killed?"

Around a mouthful of fries, Josie replied, "There's someone else. Has to be. The mysterious Leo in the black car? The baby taken from Twitch? The dead men at the church where they were holding Luke? And then someone killing Dunn and his men? Someone else is involved."

"I think so too. But who?"

"Someone with enough power and money to take Dunn down. Someone with big enough balls to take him down."

"Someone pissed about the building collapse?"

"Or someone planning to use the evidence Kim had to take him down. I want units out looking for this Leo guy. Start out by Luke's. Check the silo."

"You got it."

Sated, Josie leaned back in her chair and closed her eyes. She meant only to sit quietly long enough to still her swimming thoughts, but the next thing she knew Noah was shaking her awake. "Boss," he said. "You were snoring."

Josie sat up and wiped a line of drool from the corner of her mouth. "How long was I out?"

"Just a few minutes," Noah said. "Why don't you go home? Get some rest? I'll make sure you get a phone call if anything develops. You've been at this all day."

Everything in her wanted to object to his suggestion, but her limbs were tired and heavy. It was after nine o'clock at night. She could just go home and get two or three hours, she reasoned with herself, and then get right back to work. "Okay," she told Noah. "Just for a little while."

Josie weaved her way through the streets of Denton, both longing for her bed and desperately wanting to avoid facing Carrieann. She was only a few blocks from home when her phone buzzed. She pulled over and took out her phone; Diana Sweeney had sent her a series of texts and a PDF with the other donor profile and a photograph of the donor when he was a young man. Josie zoomed in on the photo. The fog of exhaustion she'd been feeling since she ate evaporated instantly.

"Holy shit."

Without thinking, she pulled back out onto the road and made a U-turn.

CHAPTER 51

In southeast Denton, a bridge extended over the Susquehanna River leading out of the city and into the mountains. About three quarters of a mile up the hill on the other side of the bridge was Peter Rowland's house. Everyone knew where Rowland lived both because he was a local legend and because he was the only person in the entire city with a helipad in his front yard. Josie missed his driveway twice as it was purposely unmarked. Finally, on her third pass, she found it. The driveway was paved, the blacktop pristine. It weaved through dense foliage on both sides. Occasionally, Josie's headlights illuminated a clearing with a sculpture in it. It had an *Alice in Wonderland* feeling to it. She knew Rowland was rich, but she hadn't pegged him for eccentric when they'd met the other day.

As she got closer to the house, LED lanterns sprouted from the ground on either side of the driveway, lighting the way. Finally, there was a large break in the trees. The helipad came into view, a small helicopter sitting unused in the center of it. Beyond that, Rowland's massive house seemed to pour from the sky onto the ground, each floor jutting out a little more than the last. The walls of the first floor were made almost entirely of glass. She could see into two of the rooms which were lit up, a library and a living room filled with white couches and a white chaise lounge. Peter Rowland sat in the corner of one of the couches, legs crossed, reading a book. He looked up as her headlights swept across the front of the house.

Josie parked and Rowland met her at the door. He smiled uncertainly. "Chief Quinn," he said. "Is everything okay?"

It was then that Josie realized how foolishly impulsive it had been to come to his home this late. But it was too late now. "Oh yes," she said. "I just . . . I needed a quick word with you."

He stepped out of her way to let her through the door. She moved up a small, open flight of steps and into the room he'd been sitting in. From inside the house, the floor-to-ceiling glass panels were inky-black except for her ghostly reflection. Rowland stepped up behind her and motioned to the windows. "It is glorious in the morning when you can see the trees. There's a small garden to the left as well." When Josie didn't comment he said, "Can I offer you anything?"

Josie turned and smiled at him. "No, thank you."

He gestured to one of the couches and Josie took a seat. As he sat down on the edge of the chaise lounge across from her, Josie got right to the point. "When Tara called you about putting up reward money for Misty Derossi's baby, did you know you might be his father?"

The polite smile Rowland had been wearing since she arrived froze in place, looking almost painful. "What's that?" he said.

"Did you already know that you might be Victor Derossi's father when you put up the reward money for his safe return? Is that why you offered to help?"

Now his expression morphed into one of confusion. He placed his elbows on his knees and leaned forward. "I'm sorry. I think you might have me confused with someone else. I'm not Victor Derossi's father."

"But you might be," Josie said. "There is a fifty-fifty chance you are. You must already know this."

"Know it? I've never met Misty Derossi. How could I have fathered her son?"

"I know about the sperm donation. I've got proof."

Rowland was silent for a long time. He sat back, straightening his spine and peering at her. He looked as if he were making a decision. Finally, he said, "When I was very young, I made a silly decision—a lot of silly decisions, actually—because I was poor and trying to get through college. I was even homeless for a while, did you know that?"

Josie did know it because almost every facet of Peter Rowland's journey from relative poverty to mega success was a part of Denton's city lore. "Yes," she answered. "I've heard that."

"Well, there was a time in my early twenties when I was looking for any way to make a quick buck. So yes, I donated some sperm—I found a place that would pay you to donate. But that was a very long time ago."

"Your sample still exists," Josie pointed out.

"Only because someone at the sperm bank screwed up. My sample was supposed to be destroyed many, many years ago. The sperm bank in question typically only keeps samples for seven to ten years. Twelve is almost unheard of."

"Yet your sample survived and was mixed up with Misty Derossi's chosen donor."

"I'm aware that it hadn't been destroyed. The sperm bank sent me a letter a month or two ago to let me know. My lawyer has been handling all of this. But we were assured that given the age of my sample, there was no way it would be viable."

"That's not what they told Ms. Derossi."

"I'm very sorry to hear that. I'm sure it was very upsetting to her, but I'm telling you, Victor Derossi is not my child."

"Then why would you put up $15,000 in reward money for his return?" Josie asked.

He smiled tightly. "I've told you. I wanted to give back to the community here."

"You're almost single-handedly funding the mayor's women's center."

Rowland sighed again. "Chief Quinn, do you have children?" Josie shook her head.

"I lost my daughter, Polly, last year."

"I'm sorry," Josie said.

"Thank you. You can't understand what that feels like unless it's happened to you. I wouldn't wish that on another parent. When Tara told me about Ms. Derossi's situation, I felt as though I should help. I happened to be in town. I have the funds. It's as simple as that."

Josie didn't believe him for a second but saw she would get nowhere with that line of questioning, so she changed the subject. "This is a lovely home you have here," she said.

If he was surprised by the sudden turn, he didn't let on. "Thank you."

"Can I use your restroom?"

"Of course," he said. He gave her directions to a first-floor bathroom. Josie found it, trying to take in as much of the house as she could as she negotiated the hallways. Every room was well furnished but looked as though it hadn't been used in years; although the house was clean and opulently decorated, it still felt cavernous and empty. Josie felt as though if she shouted, her echo would return to her. She saw no signs that anyone else was either residing there or staying there. She thought about sneaking up the stairs and having a look at the two upper floors but decided against it. When she returned to the living room, Rowland stood waiting. "Will that be all, Chief Quinn?"

"Yes. I'm sorry to have disturbed you so late." She waved a hand around them. "You don't have a security detail?"

He laughed. "No, do I need one?"

"I suppose not. Do you fly your own helicopter?"

"No, I hire a pilot for that."

"Do you know a man named Leo?"

He gave an impatient sigh. "I know a lot of men, Chief Quinn. No one named Leo springs to mind."

Behind her, Josie heard footsteps. She turned to look into the hallway but there was no one there. "You have pets?" she asked.

"No. That's probably my housekeeper, Marie."

"She works late, doesn't she?"

"I ask her to stay with me when I'm in town. I know it doesn't look like it, but I can make quite a mess."

He moved toward her, ushering her toward the front door. "Listen," he said as she stepped out into the night. "I'd appreciate if you could keep the information you've uncovered to yourself. Victor Derossi is still missing, correct?"

"Yes," Josie said.

"I wouldn't want the search for him to become...hampered in any way. If the press gets wind of this whole sperm donor thing, they'll turn it into a three-ring circus. Let's keep the focus on finding little Victor, shall we?"

"Of course," Josie said.

Then the door closed in her face.

CHAPTER 52

Josie had three missed calls from Carrieann and two text messages from her asking for updates. Josie replied that they had found Kim Conway at Luke's house and taken her into custody but that she hadn't had any pertinent information. Carrieann wanted to know what would happen now that Eric Dunn was dead and whether they could find Luke or not. Josie didn't have the heart to go home and face her knowing that the only thing she had to offer was more questions and no answers. She typed back to Carrieann saying she was still working on finding Luke, which was sort of a lie because she had no idea where to even restart. What she did know was that Peter Rowland was lying. It was too much of a coincidence that he was the mix-up donor and that he just happened to be in town and was willing to give reward money for Victor Derossi's safe return.

Josie had only been to Noah's house a few times before to pick him up or drop him off when they were juggling department-issued vehicles. She'd never been inside. Now she stood on his doorstep, shifting from one foot to the other to stay warm. He lived in a small, ranch-style house with absolutely no adornments. There wasn't even a welcome mat on the stoop. He definitely lived alone. Josie rang the doorbell for the third time. Finally, the light over the door blinked on. The door creaked open and Noah stood before her wearing nothing but boxer shorts. He'd obviously been sleeping. His thick brown hair was in disarray, his eyes heavy-lidded with fatigue. He blinked at her. "Boss?"

"I'm sorry for bothering you so late," Josie said. "Can I come in?"

He stepped aside and let her in. She stopped when she noticed the scar tissue on his right shoulder. Even though she was the one who had given him the scar during the missing girls case, she'd never seen it before. Noah looked down at it and rubbed his fingers over the top of it. "It doesn't hurt," he said.

"I . . . I'm—" Josie choked.

He laughed. "I know, I know. You're sorry. You don't have to say it again. Come on, come into the kitchen."

His home was furnished with what looked like secondhand furniture. Everything about it was utilitarian. He had what he needed, and only that: an old, two-seater couch that sagged in the middle; a scuffed coffee table with only a remote on top of it; a television on a small, three-shelf entertainment center that held only a DVD player and what looked like a game system. His kitchen looked like it hadn't been updated since the seventies. There was a small table in the center of it with two chairs. He pulled one out for her and walked over to the kitchen sink. From the cabinet above it, he pulled a can of coffee.

"I know this place isn't much," he said. "My mom's always after me to do something with it, but honestly, I'm hardly ever here."

Josie sat at the table and watched as he filled the coffeepot with water. The coffeemaker was about the only modern thing in the house. "I'm working you too hard," she said.

He threw a smile over his shoulder. "Nah, I'm fine." He poured water into the back of the coffeemaker and turned toward her, leaning his back against the counter. Again, Josie's eyes were drawn to the scar. It brought to mind the scars that dotted and zigzagged Luke's torso. Some from the gunshots themselves and some from where the doctors had opened him up. She wondered if she would ever trace her fingers over them again. Then she wondered if she would even want to—he had been lying to her and possibly cheating on her.

"What's going on?" Noah said.

She told him about the texts from Diana Sweeney and her meeting with Rowland. Noah gave a low whistle. "I didn't see that coming."

"Me neither."

"So, what are you thinking?"

"What if the reason we didn't find the baby at the church and the reason the cradle looked unused was because Rowland has the baby?"

"Boss—"

"Just hear me out. If Misty was notified of the mix-up, doesn't it stand to reason that Rowland was as well?"

"But they wouldn't have violated Misty's privacy by telling Rowland who she was, and you already said that he knew that his sperm hadn't been destroyed. Even if he knew, why would he take the baby? What would he do with a baby? I think you're reaching."

He got two mugs out of another cabinet and poured steaming coffee into each one. He prepared hers exactly the way she liked it and handed it to her.

Josie said, "It's too coincidental, though, don't you think?"

"What? That he put up reward money for a baby that might be his? Well, it's definitely a strange coincidence," Noah agreed.

"It's not a coincidence," Josie insisted.

"Boss, we have no evidence that connects Rowland to Misty other than the sperm mix-up, and we know that the sperm bank maintained confidentiality."

"But maybe they didn't. I got his information."

Noah set his own mug on the table and sat across from her. He gave her a lopsided smile. "You cheated."

"Only because going through official channels would take too long. Diana told me their legal department takes seven to ten days to process warrants. It's quite possible that all it would take for Rowland to get that information is a good lawyer—and I know he can afford one."

Noah pushed his hand through his hair. "I think this is a stretch. Why would Rowland put up reward money for a baby he actually has?"

"To make himself look like he doesn't have the baby," Josie replied.

"Okay, so what are you saying? That Rowland snatched the baby from under Denny Twitch's nose?"

"No," Josie said. "Someone who works for Rowland. Maybe this Leo person."

"Okay, in this scenario, Rowland finds out the baby could be his but instead of approaching Misty directly, he does what? Puts a man on her? To watch her? Then the baby comes, and Twitch shows up. Instead of saving Misty, he waits until Twitch beats the hell out of her and takes the baby. Then he follows Twitch and kidnaps the baby from him. Then he keeps the baby and puts up reward money for his safe return? For what? Why does Rowland want this baby so badly but is trying to hide him at the same time?"

"I don't know," Josie said. "That's the part I can't figure out. I mean he lost a child last year, maybe he sees an opportunity here."

"Then why do something illegal? Why all these behind-the-scenes moves using hired muscle? Why not just have his lawyers contact Misty and work the whole thing out that way?"

Josie gave a frustrated sigh. Noah was right. It didn't make sense.

"Boss, has it occurred to you that maybe you want Misty's baby to be alive so badly that you're latching on to Rowland as a suspect?"

She swallowed, looking away from him. Pulling her coffee closer, she cupped both hands around it. "Okay," she said. "That's fair. I couldn't save Luke, I couldn't find Misty's baby. The baby could be Ray's. Ray was my husband. I see what you're saying."

"Do you?"

She met his eyes again. "I do. I promise you, I understand where you're coming from."

Noah smiled, "But?"

"But my instincts are rarely wrong. I want to get into Rowland's house."

To his credit, Noah didn't miss a beat at all. He said, "Well, the only way to do that is to get a judge to sign a warrant based on the fact that Rowland's sperm donation was mixed up with Ray's—information you don't officially have, remember—and that's probably not going to do it."

"Noah, what if he has that baby?"

"A man like Peter Rowland wouldn't have any reason to kidnap a baby—especially if he thought it was his. Even if he didn't want the sperm donor thing getting out, he could have just approached Misty privately and worked something out with her. I'm sure he has enough money to keep her quiet."

"Maybe he was afraid she'd blackmail him. He doesn't know Misty well enough to know she wouldn't do that. I don't even know Misty well enough to know she wouldn't blackmail him."

Noah shook his head. "You're missing the point here. People like Peter Rowland don't need thug tactics. He's not Eric Dunn. Dunn wielded his wealth and power like a club, smashing everyone that got in his way. Rowland is a known philanthropist. A do-gooder. He sits on the boards of a bunch of corporations and charitable institutions. He downplays his wealth. The guy is a thousand times richer and more successful than Dunn ever would have been. You said yourself he doesn't even have a bodyguard. Rowland is not the type of guy who would handle things with a hired goon. He'd take care of things in a courtroom or with contracts and nondisclosure agreements and payouts."

Josie couldn't deny that Noah's assessment of Peter Rowland seemed spot-on, given what she knew about the man.

"Listen," Noah continued. "You're upset about what

happened at the Flats today. You're sleep-deprived. Everything is fucked right now. The best thing you can do is go home, get some sleep, and come back at this in the morning."

"Are you dismissing me?"

He laughed. "The last time I dismissed you, you shot me. What do you think?"

Josie blushed. She opened her mouth to say she was sorry again but clamped it shut instead. Noah leaned forward, reached across the table, and lightly touched her hand. "Boss," he said. "Just get a few hours of sleep, okay? That's all I'm asking. You can even stay here, sleep on my couch, and in the morning, we'll figure out where to go from here."

Josie took a long sip of coffee and pushed the mug back toward Noah. "Thank you," she said.

He walked her to the living room and watched her curl up on the couch. "I'll go get you a blanket," he told her.

She was drifting to sleep before he even returned with it. He laid the blanket over her. Without opening her eyes, she mumbled, "Noah. Rowland has a housekeeper. Maybe we can get to her?"

She heard his soft chuckle and felt his hand squeeze her shoulder. "Tomorrow, boss. We'll talk tomorrow."

CHAPTER 53

"This is a waste of time," Noah said.

"Shhh," Josie said, waving a hand in his direction. "I think I see something."

She peered through her windshield, staring down the road at the entrance to Rowland's driveway. After getting a few hours of sleep, Josie and Noah had returned to Rowland's house. They'd been sitting several yards down from Rowland's driveway in Josie's Escape all day, waiting for Rowland's housekeeper to leave the property.

"It's a deer," Noah said.

Sure enough, a doe poked its head out of the foliage surrounding the mouth of the driveway and then tentatively stepped into the road. Josie groaned. Initially, they had waited for Rowland to leave—he drove himself in a Mercedes-Benz— and gone to the house, knocking, ringing the doorbell, and circling the place to see if they could spot the housekeeper inside. Nothing. Then Noah had pointed out the various cameras that Rowland had posted all over the premises. They had pulled back, monitoring the driveway from afar. Josie was certain the housekeeper would leave at some point and then they could follow her and question her.

"Did you even see this woman?" Noah asked.

Josie tutted. "Of course I did. I—" But she hadn't seen the woman. She hadn't actually seen anyone. But why would

Rowland lie? "He said her name was Marie," Josie said. "Why would he tell me her name if she didn't exist?"

Noah sighed. "So that you would think he really had a housekeeper named Marie. It could be anyone. Maybe he has a secret lover he doesn't want people to know about. Or an illegal exotic pet."

Josie laughed. "An exotic pet? Like what?"

"I don't know. Like one of those little capuchin monkeys or something. Dude is rich and weird. Or maybe he is up to something and was just trying to throw you off, get rid of you."

"You think he's that diabolical?"

"I'm not the one who thinks he's got a baby in there."

Josie groaned. She, too, was beginning to think this was a tremendous waste of time. Maybe she was grasping at straws now that Dunn was gone, trying to force a miracle.

"Has it occurred to you that maybe if he does have the baby—and that's a big if—that he wouldn't keep him at his house? I mean, Dunn didn't keep Luke anywhere that could lead back to him."

"I know that," Josie said. "I had Gretchen check land records this morning, but this is Rowland's only property in the county. It's our only lead right now. Maybe the housekeeper can tell us something useful."

A ringing noise filled the vehicle. "Is that your phone?" Noah asked.

Josie fished her cell phone out of the cup holder between them and looked at the screen. "It's Gretchen," she said.

"Boss," Gretchen said when Josie answered. "I think we found the Leo that Kim Conway told you about."

CHAPTER 54

Josie and Noah waited for two other officers to relieve them at Rowland's and headed out to where Gretchen waited. A rutted dirt road led to the abandoned grain silo that stood a mile behind Luke's house. In Josie's Escape, she and Noah jerked from side to side as she maneuvered along the road. All around them weeds and overgrown grass encroached, as if reaching for Josie's vehicle. In the field to Josie's left, an old combine sat rusted out, its roof sagging. An air of desolation hung over the unused farmland and was heightened as they pulled up behind Gretchen's Chevy Cruze and glimpsed the crime scene beyond. Dr. Feist's truck sat beside Gretchen's car. Josie parked the Escape and she and Noah hopped out. Next to the silo, cordoned off with crime scene tape, was a black Ford Fusion. A four-door sedan, just as Kim Conway had described.

Gretchen appeared beside them, a roll of yellow tape in her hands. Dr. Feist circled the sedan, peering inside the passenger's side window.

"We're waiting for the evidence response team," Gretchen explained.

Josie took a few steps toward the vehicle and saw blood spatter on the driver's-side window. She felt a tightening in her chest. "Another body."

Gretchen nodded. Dr. Feist trotted over. "Looks just like your other guy. Gunshot wound to the front temporal lobe. Pistol left on the seat next to him."

Noah said, "Did he shoot himself?"

Feist shook her head. "I doubt it. Most people who shoot themselves put the gun into their mouths or under their chins. It would be pretty awkward to hold the barrel to the side of your head like that. I'll swab his hands for gunpowder residue when we get him to the morgue."

"Shit," Josie said.

Gretchen said, "The car is registered to Leonard Nance of Queens, New York. Once the scene is photographed and processed we'll see if he has any identification on him, but I think we can safely say that this is the Leo that Kim Conway was supposed to meet here."

Josie said, "We should have swabbed *her* hands for gunpowder residue. That's why she was in the shower at Luke's. Noah, call someone to come get you and head over to Luke's to look for her clothes. If she shot this guy at close range in a vehicle, she would have gotten blood on her."

He nodded and pulled out his phone, walking a few steps away to make the call.

"Gretchen," Josie said. "You'll stay here, wait for the ERT team, and call me if you find anything of interest. I'm going to go back to the station and run Nance's name. See what I can turn up. Queens isn't that far from Manhattan. I want to see if I can find a connection between him and Peter Rowland."

An hour later, Josie sat behind her desk, massaging the skin at her temples. Leonard Nance was a ghost; she'd been able to turn up his address in Queens and a date of birth that put him at fifty-four years old, but nothing else. No criminal record, no school or work history, no relatives—she couldn't even find any previous addresses for him. The one and only thing she was able to find was that he had served in the army for eight years as a young man. Other than that, he had no digital footprint whatsoever. Even after Gretchen texted her a photo of his driver's license, Josie turned up nothing useful. Nor did she find any connection between Nance and Peter Rowland. But she was convinced Nance had worked for Rowland.

Thinking of how she'd figured out Kim Conway's connection to Eric Dunn, she pulled up Google and typed in Peter Rowland's name. She clicked on Images and started scrolling through. There were thousands of photos of the man. Noah had been right—he gave very generously to many, many different charities. Most of the photos of him had been taken at charity benefits. In many he stood on a red carpet in a sharp suit, smiling for the cameras. In several of them, his wife and daughter stood beside him, smiling and radiant. His wife looked as though she had been a supermodel with her high, thin cheekbones and glossy blond hair. His daughter, Polly, was almost a carbon copy of her mother except for her nose, which she had clearly gotten from Peter with its telltale hook. Josie scrolled through thousands of photos of Rowland before she found what she was looking for on page twenty-eight of her Google search. It was a candid shot of Peter Rowland strolling through Central Park. He wore khaki pants, a yellow polo shirt, and loafers. Locks of his hair stood in the wind. Sunglasses obscured his eyes, which were focused on his cell phone. Next to him, far enough away that it looked like they weren't walking together, was Leonard Nance. Dressed all in black, eyes focused straight ahead, the camera had caught him in mid-stride.

"Jackpot," Josie mumbled.

Noah poked his head into the door.

"Hey," Josie said, beckoning him inside. The sight of him seemed to reduce the pounding in her head. "Did you find anything?"

He frowned as he sat across from her. "Clothes in the washer."

"Oh my God," Josie said.

"Boss, don't blame yourself."

"We weren't thorough enough," she said.

"People shower," Noah pointed out. "Kim Conway was a domestic violence victim. We thought she was in trouble. We didn't even know Leonard Nance existed until after we picked her up. I already called Gretchen. She's going to send the ERT over to Luke's house after they're done at the silo to process the house again. We'll gather everything and leave it to the district attorney to sort out."

"The DA won't want to prosecute. She's already admitted to being in his car and going to the silo, so even if her prints are all over the car, that's no smoking gun. She can easily claim self-defense, and it probably was self-defense. I think Leonard was a mercenary, someone paid to do the dirty work for someone richer and more powerful—like Peter Rowland. God knows what he intended to do with her."

"You found a connection between Leonard Nance and Peter Rowland?" Noah asked.

She motioned for him to come around the desk so he could see the photo she had found.

"That's it?" he said.

"That and they both live in New York City."

"Boss, I don't know..."

"Noah, this is all we've got right now. The baby and Luke are still missing. I've got to follow every lead."

He went back over to the chair in front of her desk and sat down. "I can see the connection between Rowland and the baby, but why would Rowland send someone after Kim?"

"Kim said Leo asked her about the building collapse," Josie said. "He wanted the videos she had."

"Why would Rowland be after incriminating evidence against Dunn? He was trying to cut a deal with him to put his security and surveillance systems into Dunn's hotels and casinos. Even if he wanted those videos to blackmail Dunn—to what end? Rowland didn't need to blackmail Dunn. Even if Rowland had a good reason for wanting those videos, a reason we're not aware of, what does any of that have to do with Luke?"

She didn't want to say it, didn't want to think it, but she already had, many times in the last few hours. "Probably nothing. I think it's more likely that Dunn had Luke killed." She couldn't keep her voice from cracking. She rubbed her eyes.

"Josie," Noah said softly.

She waved a hand, composing herself. "I'm fine. Listen, the chances of us finding that baby are still damn good, especially if Dunn never had him and Rowland thought Victor was his son. Can we try to focus on that?"

"Okay," Noah said. "But you should know that I haven't given up on finding Luke."

She gave him a wan smile. She hadn't given up either; she just understood that they were now looking for a dead body.

From the other side of her office door came the sounds of an argument. She stood but Noah was already at the door. "I'll take care of it," he said.

Outside, two of her officers were in a heated dispute over the remote control to the communal television. "She'll be pissed if she sees this on again. Turn it off," said one of them.

"They're showing an interview King did after he was first arrested. It's never-before-seen footage!" the other officer said, holding the remote control out of reach of his colleague.

On the television beyond them played more coverage of the Interstate Killer trial with Trinity Payne reporting from the Alcott County Courthouse. The text beneath her read: "*Juror Faints. Trial adjourned for afternoon*." "Today jurors were shown graphic crime scene photos of Aaron King's last known victim," Trinity reported. "The images were so grisly that one of the jurors, a man in his sixties, fainted, causing a commotion in the courtroom."

Feeling like a mother breaking up a fight between siblings, Josie walked over to them and held her hand out. "I *am* pissed. I have told you on more than one occasion to turn this shit off. You can stream this later, on your own time."

The officer with the remote handed it over immediately. "Sorry, boss," he mumbled.

"As promised," Trinity continued after describing the scene in the courtroom, "one of our affiliates has uncovered this interview King gave immediately after being charged with the interstate murders."

Josie held the remote up to turn off the television. The screen cut to a young man in an orange jumpsuit with short, neatly combed brown hair. His face was clean-shaven, and his eyes as penetrating as ever. He was being led in handcuffs from a sheriff's van into the Alcott County Courthouse. Reporters shouted questions at him. When he smiled, Josie felt a cold shock go through her. For a moment, she was so disoriented by what she was seeing, she couldn't speak. Clean-shaven, with his hair in perfect order, King didn't look like himself at all.

Noah and the two officers stared at her. Her arm ached from holding the remote aloft. She heard nothing King said. She was too busy looking at his face.

"Boss?" Noah said.

She handed him the remote. "Pick up Rowland. Now. I want you to do it. Take a uniformed officer with you."

She walked back to her office.

"Where are you going?" he called after her.

"I have to talk to Trinity."

She closed the door behind her. It took three tries to get Trinity on the phone. "What do you want? I was in the middle of a live spot," she said petulantly. "Not that I should help you. You didn't even call me when Eric Dunn died. Is it true you were there?"

Josie rolled her eyes. "Yes, I was there. Yes, I'll give you an interview if you want. I don't care. Right now, I need information from you."

"An on-camera interview," Trinity demanded. "An exclusive."

"Fine, whatever. Will you help me?"

A sigh. "This better be good. Is it good? Is it big?"

"I think so, yes."

"Fine. What do you want to know?"

"How much do you know about the Interstate Killer?"

Laughter. "Everything. I know everything."

CHAPTER 55

Josie's next call was to Diana Sweeney. She told her what she was looking for and waited for Diana to tell her to go to hell. Instead, Diana readily agreed to help and took down Trinity Payne's cell phone number. After hanging up, Josie checked the text notifications that had come in while she was talking with Sweeney. The messages were from Noah. *"Bringing Rowland in now, but you should know he was having lunch with the mayor when we picked him up."*

Josie groaned and the thumping in her head grew worse. A quick look through her desk drawer turned up some ibuprofen, which she swallowed dry before heading down to the conference room. Tension knotted her shoulder blades as she emerged from the stairwell and found Tara Charleston pacing in front of the conference room door, her four-inch black heels tapping a frenzied beat on the tile. Spotting Josie, she strode over and, for just a second, Josie thought she might slap her.

"Are you out of your mind?" Tara railed, color high on her cheeks. "What in the hell do you think you're doing?"

"I needed a word with Mr. Rowland," Josie said, folding her arms over her chest.

"So you had him picked up like a common criminal? You sent a uniformed officer?"

"They didn't cuff him, did they?" Josie asked.

Tara bristled. "Well, no, because Mr. Rowland is a gentleman, and he was gracious enough to go with your officers immediately. That's not the point. You are dangerously close to being removed as chief. Dangerously close."

"You're going to remove me for doing my job?"

Tara poked Josie's shoulder with one of her long fingernails. "Your job? This is how you do your job? First Eric Dunn is killed, and now you've had Peter Rowland dragged in here to answer questions—about what? What could you possibly need from him that you couldn't ask him in a more discreet manner? It's bad enough you've left me handling the Dunn nightmare on my own. Now this."

"Nightmare?" Josie said.

Tara made a sound of frustration. "You don't think having Eric Dunn killed in our city is a nightmare of *epic* proportions? His mother's lawyer has already contacted me about liability."

Josie laughed. "Liability? Please. He was on his own work site. He blatantly disregarded safety standards on the construction site, which made it easier for someone to walk onto the premises and compromise the integrity of the building. Let the city solicitor handle it."

"Oh, sure," Tara replied. "As though it's that easy. The press is all over this, and I'm not sure this is something I can spin."

"Don't you have a press liaison?" Josie asked, feeling more irritated by the second. Tara just wanted someone to complain to, and Josie really didn't have time to be her sounding board. "Look, I need to speak to Mr. Rowland."

"You speak to him, and you let him go, and you'd better hope that I can smooth things over with him. If I can't, you're finished in this town."

CHAPTER 56

NEWS 4 Gainesville

Gainesville, Florida

August 4, 2017

Pedestrian Killed by Hit-and-Run Driver

A nineteen-year-old Gainesville man identified as Joshua Johnson was struck and killed by a hit-and-run driver while walking on a sidewalk early Friday morning. Police believe the accident happened sometime between 4 and 5 a.m. along Southwest 34th Street near Windmeadows Boulevard. Johnson, who was on probation for a recent burglary conviction, was walking to a nearby diner where he had found employment as a short-order cook. A passing motorist saw his body on the sidewalk and called 911. He was pronounced dead at the scene. Anyone with information is asked to please call police.

CHAPTER 57

They waited an hour for a lawyer to show up on Rowland's behalf. Josie recognized him from the higher-profile criminal cases that took place in Alcott County. She didn't know if Rowland kept him on retainer to handle local matters or if he'd called the man after they brought him into the police station, but Josie knew he was an excellent criminal defense attorney. The moment she and Noah entered the interview room, he immediately launched into a tirade about their myriad violations of Rowland's rights.

"Excuse me," Noah interrupted the man. "We asked Mr. Rowland to come to the station to answer some questions and he agreed. We haven't read him his rights. He is free to leave at any time."

"We're just here to talk," Josie added.

The lawyer looked down his nose at them until Peter Rowland, who was seated beside him smiling politely, touched his arm. "It's fine," Rowland assured him. "Please. Let's see why they've asked us here."

Reluctantly, the lawyer sat beside Rowland. Noah sat down while Josie remained standing. "How long has Leonard Nance worked for you?" she asked.

Rowland's brow furrowed. "I'm sorry, who?"

Josie took out her phone and pulled up a photo of Nance with half his head blown off that Gretchen had sent from the crime scene. She turned it toward the two men. To their credit, neither showed any reaction. The lawyer said, "I think that's enough talking for today."

Rowland said, "I don't know that man."

The lawyer stood, straightening his suit jacket. "I don't know what you're trying to pull, but we're leaving now," he said. "If you've got something relevant that you'd like to ask my client, you can call my office."

Josie looked directly at Rowland, still sitting at the table. "I know about Aaron King," she said.

The room went eerily silent. She felt the lawyer and Noah staring at her, but her eyes were locked on Rowland's, a silent flood of communication roaring between them. Without tearing his eyes from Josie's, he used two fingers to signal his lawyer. The other man leaned down so Rowland could speak into his ear. There was a short but heated discussion that Josie couldn't make out. Then the lawyer stood up straight, glaring at Josie, and said, "I'll be outside."

Josie nodded at Noah and he too exited the room. Josie took a seat across from Rowland.

He leaned his elbows on the table and folded his hands, resting his chin on them. "Tell me, Chief, what is it that you think you know about Aaron King? We are talking about Aaron King, the Interstate Killer, are we not?"

"Yes," Josie said. "I know he's your son."

Rowland kept perfectly still. His gaze drifted away from her face, over her shoulder. For a moment she thought maybe he was looking for a camera, except that his face had taken on a blank, faraway expression. Josie waited a long moment. Finally, he said, "How did you come by this information?"

"I have my resources."

Now his eyes locked on hers, his gaze sharp again. "I'd like to know what resources you have that helped you come by such confidential information. You know, I have a number of highly sophisticated software programs created and implemented by a team of expert computer hackers who can't get their hands on information as sensitive as what you claim to have found in the last two days. Perhaps I should hire you."

There he was, turning on the charm. That was what he did, Josie realized. He was nice, polite, complimentary, but it was a distraction. Josie said, "Sometimes you just have to ask the right people the right questions. How long have you known that Aaron King was one of your donor children?"

"How exactly is this relevant to your investigation into Victor Derossi's abduction?" Rowland asked.

His lack of response told her that she was right. She would have proof within the next day or two. By then she might even have proof of more damning things. She still wasn't sure what all the coincidences meant. She needed a lot more information before she could properly use it as leverage against Rowland. But if there was even a chance that he had Victor or knew where the infant was, Josie had to make some kind of move now—especially while his lawyer was out of the room. "Why don't you tell me what the Interstate Killer has to do with Victor Derossi?" she asked. Two could play at his game of answering a question with a question.

"I wish I knew. What do you plan on doing with this information?"

"It's not what I'm planning to do with it that you need to worry about."

"What do you mean?"

"Trinity Payne knows."

His face paled. "The reporter?"

Josie nodded. "She's covering the Aaron King trial. She's very thorough. I used to think that was a bad thing, but in the last year and a half, I've found her skills to be quite useful."

"What does she plan to do with this information?"

"I don't know and I don't care. What I care about is getting Victor Derossi back safely. Now I know that Leonard Nance worked for you. I know that he took the baby out from under Eric Dunn's nose, and I know that he then approached Kim Conway because of her connection to Dunn, and he ended up dead."

"If you have proof of these assertions, I'm sure my attorney would be interested in that, as would I."

Josie ignored this. "Where is Victor Derossi?"

He managed a weak smile. "I wish I could help you, I do, but I don't know anything about Victor Derossi's abduction. Honestly, Chief Quinn, if I knew what happened to little Victor, I would have been in your office days ago. Now, I asked my attorney to leave because this information that you have come across...I have no desire to have my life turned into a circus. I'm sure you can guess that should I be connected in such a way to Aaron King, the publicity would be very damaging both to my personal life and my business."

"The same way your connection to Victor would hamper my investigation?" Josie said.

"Come now, Chief. You've had to bear the scrutiny of the mass media, haven't you?"

She had, but she wasn't about to agree with him. When she didn't answer, Rowland continued, "I'm sure you can understand why I would not want this information made public. True or not."

"Then we're at an impasse, because I can't help you with that. I'm only here for one reason and that's to find Victor Derossi."

"There are very few impasses that money can't bridge," Rowland said.

"What are you saying?"

"How much would it take for you to forget what you know and ask Trinity to do the same? Surely there are juicer stories out there."

"I don't take bribes, and I can't speak for Trinity."

"Not a bribe," Rowland said. "I'm asking you to perform a service."

"I serve the city of Denton," Josie reminded him.

"Yes, and I am one of its citizens. Need I remind you of my recent donation to the mayor's sorely needed women's center?"

Josie raised a brow. "Are you threatening to pull your funds?"

He spread his palms in a gesture of helplessness. "I'm not sure the mayor would want her women's center funded by the father of a serial killer."

"Then the impasse can't be broken. Thank you for your time."

CHAPTER 58

While Gretchen finished up with the Nance crime scene and Noah tailed Rowland, Josie had no choice but to spend some time catching up on her chiefly duties. The rest of the day was spent signing off on overtime, reviewing the staffing schedule, and responding to grievances both within her department and those made against her officers by citizens. It was mostly petty stuff that was easily resolved. She authorized some equipment requisitions and took a stab at some quarterly evaluations.

It was tough to stay seated at her desk when her mind was so consumed by anxiety. She kept checking her phone, but there was no news from either Trinity or Diana. In her mind, she replayed the scene with Rowland over and over again. He had been willing to bribe her to keep his connection to Aaron King private, but he wouldn't give up Victor Derossi. Because admitting that he had kidnapped a baby—or had a hand in doing it—would put him in prison, most likely.

There had to be someone else involved. Someone caring for the baby. Assuming Victor Derossi was still somewhere in Denton. Josie texted her team at Rowland's house, but they hadn't seen any sign of a housekeeper or anyone else coming or going from his property.

The day wore on. She checked incessantly with Gretchen, Noah, and her other officers but no one had anything of use to report. She tried to keep working through the mound of paperwork on her desk but her mind kept drifting, picturing Luke's lifeless body in various scenarios. How had Dunn's men done it? she wondered. A bullet to the head? A slit throat? Had they tortured him first? What had they done with his body? Would they ever find it?

Alone in her office, consumed with thoughts of Luke being tortured and killed, she finally let out the tears that had been fighting to burst forth. The tension and fear from the last few days raged through her, and she let them come. When it had run its course, she dried her face, patted some foundation on her skin, and headed home. She needed a drink. A very big drink. Carrieann waited at home, an uneaten pizza in front of her on the living room table. She was slumped in front of the television in almost exactly the same posture Luke had been the day that this all started. She glanced at Josie but was nice enough not to mention Josie's red-rimmed eyes.

"I guess if there was news, you would have called me," she said flatly as Josie took a seat beside her.

"We might have a lead on the baby," Josie said and told her about Rowland's connection to Victor Derossi. "We brought him in," Josie added. "He brought his lawyer. I got to talk to him privately, but it ended in a stalemate. Carrieann, you should know, we've now run out of leads on Luke's case."

Carrieann looked at her. "What about Rowland? He must have Victor. He has to—where else would that baby be? If he took Victor from Dunn, then he must have Luke."

"But there's no connection between Rowland and Luke, and no reason for Rowland to have taken Luke from Dunn. I think it's important—" Josie broke off, her voice cracking. Collecting herself, she tried again. "I think it's important that we be realistic."

Carrieann looked away, wiping tears from her eyes. She sat up and leaned her elbows on her knees, rocking back and forth. After a few minutes, she said, "I was never one for realism."

Josie laughed. "Really? I always had you pegged for a realist."

"A pragmatist," Carrieann clarified. "Not the same thing. I'm not giving up and neither should you. You said Dunn's men were dead when you got to that church. Their bodies were there but Luke's wasn't."

"We don't even know that Luke was still there when those men were killed. Carrieann, we don't know anything."

"What about a connection between Rowland and Dunn? What if Rowland's people caused the accident that killed Dunn and his crew?"

"I thought of that," Josie admitted. "Except I don't know why he would suddenly decide to eliminate him, and in a way that makes it obvious it really wasn't an accident. Although Rowland—or his people—did know where to find little Victor, that much is clear. Which means they were probably keeping tabs on Dunn and his men for some time. Maybe even for as long as Rowland's been trying to make the deal to get his surveillance systems into the casino Dunn wanted to build here." She shook her head. "I still feel like I'm missing something," Josie said. "Something important."

"Well," Carrieann said. "We're going to figure out what it is—one way or another."

*

Between the two of them they nearly finished the bottle of Wild Turkey that Gretchen had brought to the cemetery the night before. It didn't help them figure anything out, but it made Josie feel slightly less anxious and turned Carrieann into a weeping mess. Not their finest hour, Josie mused as she stumbled up the steps to her bedroom, collapsing fully clothed and face first into her king-size bed.

The sound of her cell phone ringing woke her at eight in the morning. She hadn't moved all night and had slept way later than she had intended. She rolled about on the bed, patting herself down until she found the phone in her back pocket. It had only a fourteen percent charge on it. She answered with a groggy "Hello?"

"Boss?" Gretchen said.

Josie sat up. "Yeah."

"Thought you'd want to know. Feist finished the autopsy on Nance. Same cause of death as Twitch. The pistol in his car was unregistered. The serial number was filed off. We found no prints on it."

"Which means someone wiped it down."

"Right."

Josie sighed. "Call Noah. I'll meet the two of you at the station in an hour, and we'll figure out where to go from here."

"You got it," Gretchen said and hung up.

On autopilot, Josie brushed her teeth, showered, and put on work clothes. Her mind was consumed with Carrieann's suggestion that Rowland had Luke as well as the baby. Was there any reason that Rowland would have taken Luke or was she just so desperate for any chance that Luke was alive that she was stretching the limits of plausibility? She tried to focus on Victor Derossi. She was certain Rowland had him.

In any other case, she would take Rowland's life apart piece by piece. Land records, companies, associates, friends. She would find out everything she could possibly find out about him and everyone he knew. She would have her people follow him and anyone associated with him she felt was likely to lead to little Victor. She had already started that process, but she couldn't shake the feeling she was running out of time. Rowland couldn't keep a kidnapped infant forever. Especially now, with law enforcement breathing down his neck.

In the kitchen, she put fresh coffee on and leaned against the counter, waiting for it to brew. From upstairs, the sounds of Carrieann's snoring drifted down the steps. Josie focused on it so she didn't have to think about how every single thing in her kitchen made her think of Luke. A sudden banging on her front door startled her out of her reverie. As Josie made her way to the foyer, she heard a woman's voice. "Quinn! Open up! I need to talk to you now."

Josie flung the door open to find Trinity Payne standing on

her doorstep. For the first time since Josie had known her, she wasn't camera ready. She wore an oversize New York Yankees T-shirt, a pair of gray sweatpants, and Uggs on her feet. No makeup. Her black hair was mussed, and in her arms she clutched a laptop and a stack of papers. She rushed past Josie and into the kitchen. "Oh, good," she said. "You made coffee."

Josie stood in the kitchen doorway, arms akimbo, watching as Trinity started spreading pages across Josie's table. "Have you been up all night?"

Trinity glanced up from the table and smiled. "Yeah, I have, and I could really use some coffee. Just give me a second. Trust me, this is going to be worth it."

Josie got two mugs from the cabinet and poured them both coffee. "How do you take your—"

"Two sugars and lots of half-and-half," Trinity interrupted. "You have half-and-half, right? Please tell me you have half-and-half."

Josie opened the fridge. "That's exactly how I take my coffee."

Hurriedly, she prepared their coffees and went back to the table. She handed Trinity a mug, and she gulped the liquid down. The table was covered with what looked like online news articles, donor profiles, and grainy photos that had been printed on computer paper using a black-and-white printer. "Was I right?" she asked Trinity. "About Eric Dunn?"

Trinity put her mug down, now half empty, and nodded. "Yes, you were right. Eric Dunn was Peter Rowland's son. I don't know how you made that connection, but yes. Aaron King is also Rowland's son. You were right about that as well."

"Cleaned up for court, Aaron King looks just like him," Josie said. "Eric Dunn's resemblance isn't as strong, but I Googled and found some photos of him as a teenager where you can see some resemblance to Rowland. Still, it was a shot in the dark. If I hadn't known that Dunn was a donor baby, it never would have occurred to me. Trinity, this is big."

"Oh no. It's not. Not compared to what else I found."

Josie raised a brow. Trinity rarely got this excited. "Tell me."

Trinity plucked a set of pages from the corner of the table. "This is Rowland's donor profile, the one you sent me. I did some digging. Your friend, Sweeney, was incredibly helpful. Talk about a source; I wouldn't have shit without her help. Anyway, as it turns out, Rowland's donation was used *nine* times."

Trinity gestured to the row of pages across the bottom of the table, all grainy photographs. "Nine kids ranging from fifteen to twenty-four. Eric Dunn was the oldest, followed closely by Aaron King. Some of them were born in the same year. Most of them were born in Pennsylvania, New York, and New Jersey. The rest were scattered up and down the East Coast and one in Ohio."

Josie looked at the faces. Most appeared to be from Facebook profiles.

"That was the easy part," Trinity continued. "Sweeney was able to provide me with the names of the couples. Tracking down the children took forever, but I did it, and here's where it gets interesting. With the exception of Aaron King, who is on trial for murder, *all* of Rowland's donor children have died in the last twelve months."

"Are you *serious*?"

"Dead serious," Trinity replied. "Every one of them, and get this: every one of them died in some kind of 'accident.'"

Josie had to sit down. Trinity reached for one of the news articles she had printed out and held it up for Josie to see. "This boy lived in Philadelphia. He was out for a jog along the Schuylkill River Trail. Two days later his body was found in the river. Accidental drowning." Josie took the article from Philly. com and skimmed it. Trinity scooped up four more articles and held them out to her. "Two hit-and-run accidents. Ohio and Florida. They never found the drivers. This girl," she said, picking up another page, "lived in Baltimore. Boating accident. Here's another girl, camping in Bucks County, crushed by a falling tree in her tent. This kid fell off a balcony. This one died of carbon monoxide poisoning."

"Oh my God," Josie said.

"And you know yourself what happened to Eric Dunn."

Josie paged through the articles in disbelief while Trinity stood by looking triumphant. "You're not serious—Rowland's killing off his donor children?" Josie said.

"Well, I have no proof of that precisely, but it's too much of a coincidence that *all* but one of his offspring have been killed in the last year—and the one that survived is either going to prison for life or getting the death penalty."

"And it wouldn't be that difficult to arrange an accident in prison, I'm sure," Josie said. She thought of little Victor Derossi and a chill ran through her. Rowland had been so certain that the baby wasn't his. Not because of the age of his sperm sample, but because he already knew. With Rowland's resources, he had probably had a DNA test run on the baby already. If he really was Ray's child, would he be allowed to live? "Why?" Josie asked aloud. "Why is he killing them?"

Trinity shrugged. "Who knows? Because he's über-rich, and he doesn't want any of this getting out? I mean, one of them is a serial killer."

"According to these articles a couple of his victims had criminal records," Josie said. "The kid in Philadelphia had felony charges pending."

"Right," Trinity said. "Not good PR for someone like Rowland. What I can't figure out is how the hell he found them all. I was only able to do this because of your source—and don't worry, I'm going to protect her. No one will ever know she helped me."

Josie thought back to her conversation with Rowland. "He's got hackers and unlimited funds," she told Trinity. "He probably had someone hack into the sperm bank's computer system."

"I'm going to my producer with this."

"Let me bring him in first," Josie said.

"What? Like, arrest him? How are you going to do that? All you can prove is that these are his donor children, and they all died in accidents. You have no proof whatsoever that he killed any of these people—or had them killed by someone else."

"Says the woman who plans to allege that very thing on television," Josie said.

Trinity raised a brow. "I don't have as high a standard as a court of law. All I have to do is release a story about these donor children being his and how they all died in the last year of mysterious accidents. The public draws its own conclusions. You, on the other hand, would need to provide definitive proof to a jury that he was behind all these accidents. You don't have that."

"Then I'll get it," Josie said.

"That could take months," Trinity pointed out. "You'd have to get all of these police departments to reopen their investigations and try to first find evidence of foul play and then find a connection to Rowland. If you bring him in for questioning, you tip your hand."

"If you run your story," Josie said, "then he knows what we're after. I have to try to talk to him first."

Trinity stared at her as if she'd just grown another head. "You really are out of your mind, aren't you? No way that man is talking to you without a lawyer. Plus, we're talking about multiple murders here. You think he's just going to admit to them?"

"I think I rattled his cage when I told him I knew about Aaron King," Josie replied. "I think he's holding Victor Derossi. I have to do something."

"Well," Trinity said. "Do it fast."

CHAPTER 59

SATURDAY

It took several calls to Rowland's attorney to set up another meeting. This time, Josie intended to put Rowland in the more intimidating interrogation room. But before that, she wanted to set the stage for what would look like a more friendly meeting between her and Rowland, assuming she could get him to dismiss his lawyer again. For this, Josie went to a small coffee shop on Denton's Main Street, Komorrah's Koffee. The inside was warm and redolent with the smells of coffee brewing and pastries baking. Two employees stood behind the counter to the right of the entrance, both staring at their phones. The walls were lined with black-and-white photos of various sites in and around Denton. She ordered several coffees and a dozen pastries.

While she waited, she perused the photos lining the walls. Many of them were of familiar rock formations found in the woods surrounding the city. They'd been taken by a local photographer who'd gone on to be quite successful and now traveled the world, freelancing for magazines and websites like *National Geographic* and the *Smithsonian*. Josie recognized a few formations that only residents intimate with the city's geography would know. She knew them well: Broken Heart, The Stacks, Turtle.

Her phone chirped. As she pulled up the text from Noah which simply read "*Rowland*," Peter Rowland stepped through the door to the coffee shop. He wore a light-gray suit and burgundy tie. For the first time since she'd met him, he looked like a businessman. He walked over and stood beside her. Motioning to the photos, he said, "They're beautiful, aren't they? I have several in my apartment in New York."

Josie stared at him. "I'm not sure we should be speaking without your attorney present," she said.

Rowland smiled but it didn't reach his eyes. "Some things can't be worked out with attorneys."

Josie turned her body toward his. "Is that right?"

"When my attorney called me to set up this meeting today he said you had uncovered information concerning what you and I discussed privately yesterday."

"Information about your other donor children," Josie said. "That's right."

She hadn't wanted to tell his attorney a damn thing about the reason for asking Rowland to come in for questioning, but the man refused to entertain her request without some kind of explanation. She'd been as cryptic as she could. She had told him that Rowland would know what she was talking about.

"Did you find them all?"

"You mean their graves?" Josie shot back.

A barely perceptible shadow crossed over his face. "How many do you know about?"

Josie's heart paused and then skipped ahead several beats. This was exactly the conversation she wanted to have in her interrogation room with a camera recording every word. This didn't count, not officially. There was a very distinct possibility that anything he told her in this context would be inadmissible should it ever make it to court. "I think we should discuss this at the police station," she said, turning toward the counter. "Like we planned. I'll see you there."

"You didn't have furniture for the first six months you lived in your house," Rowland blurted.

Josie's scalp tingled. She turned back to him. "What?"

Rowland stepped closer and lowered his voice. "When you

bought your house, you didn't have furniture for nearly six months. You had bedroom and kitchen furniture but that was it. You don't have doors on your closets even though there is a brand new door for your bedroom closet sitting in your garage, unused. Think about how I would know these things."

Her mind raced through the possibilities, but her heart knew there was only one way he would know that.

"You have Luke," she croaked.

He didn't answer or even nod his acknowledgment, but his gaze was laser-focused on her.

"Where?" she said.

"Not so fast."

"Why are you telling me this?"

"Because you won't accept my money."

"You mean your bribe." She knew she should leave. She should turn around and walk out and demand that they talk at the station, as planned. But she couldn't bring herself to do it. Her mind was flooded with thoughts of Luke. She didn't want to think about the possibility of getting him back alive—to be disappointed would be too devastating, but she couldn't stop the hope blooming inside her. She swallowed. "How do I know he's still alive?"

Again, he ignored her question. "I don't normally handle things this way—unofficially—but the information you've uncovered about me is . . . problematic, to say the least."

"You had eight people murdered. Problematic doesn't begin to describe it."

"I need your help."

"You want me to walk away from this?"

"I also need you to have a conversation with the reporter, Trinity Payne. Make sure all that you know doesn't fall into her hands."

"What if it already has?"

"You are close to her, are you not? Perhaps you can convince her to move on to more interesting stories," Rowland suggested.

Josie nearly laughed. Trinity would die before she walked away from a story this big. But Rowland didn't need to know that. "If I can convince her?"

"Then you'll have a wedding to plan."

Her breath caught in her throat. "What about Victor Derossi?"

"I might be able to help with your search, but I would need something else from you," he said.

Josie shook her head. "Something besides me pretending you didn't have eight people killed and convincing a reporter to do the same? You have some nerve."

"No," Rowland said. "I have things that you want. Think carefully, Chief, and choose wisely. Need I remind you that lives are at stake?"

Josie stepped closer to him. "What's to stop me from taking you into custody right now?"

"You're free to do that, obviously. But keep in mind, I've admitted nothing. Even if I had, you have no witnesses to this conversation. It would be my word against yours, and I need only make one phone call to the mayor to have you instantly removed from your position. In the time it will take to have my lawyer get me out of custody, you won't be able to find the things you're looking for, and by then it might be too late."

Her skin felt hot. He was right. Her mind worked furiously to make calculations, but even if she could hold him for twenty-four hours, she didn't know if that would be enough time to track down Luke and Victor, and she wasn't sure if she was willing to gamble with their lives. "What do you want?" she asked.

"I need a private meeting with Kimberly Conway."

"What?"

"Your Jane Doe, she—"

"I know who she is," Josie said. "Why do you need to talk to her?"

"I'm afraid I can't disclose that."

"She's in the custody of the sheriff. Surely you can pull some strings to visit her in the county jail," Josie said.

Rowland shook his head. "No, I need to speak to her in complete privacy."

"Well, Kim Conway is being charged with the murder of Denny Twitch and a bunch of other minor offenses. She will probably also be charged with the murder of Leonard Nance in the next day or so."

At this, Rowland winced. It happened in the blink of an eye. Josie nearly missed it. She went on, "The DA has already said they're going to ask that the judge deny bail because she's a flight risk. I can't just get her out of custody."

"Hmmm," Rowland said. "Well, she must need to be transferred from place to place, surely? What if we met in transit?"

"We can't just pull over at a Burger King with a prisoner in custody. That's not how it works."

"Have you ever stopped for a motorist stranded on the side of the road? Even with a prisoner in custody?"

There he went again, making suggestions and plans but doing it in such a way that should she ever be asked by an investigator or an attorney, she would have to concede that he never outright suggested anything criminal. But the problem was, everything they were discussing was criminal, particularly with respect to Kim. There was no legal scenario in which Josie could drive Kim Conway away from the county jail to meet with Rowland. There was no scenario in which Josie would ever have Kim in her custody again. Once she was transferred to the sheriff, she was out of Josie's control. If Rowland had asked yesterday, before Conway was moved to central booking, while she was still in Denton's holding area, Josie might have been able to pull off an off-site meeting between Kim and Rowland, but even that would have been problematic. She was certain that Rowland wasn't just proposing a meeting with Kim. He wanted to trade. Kim for Victor Derossi. But why?

What the hell was Josie missing? With Dunn dead, the

videos Kim had taken in connection with the building collapse meant nothing. Why did he want her?

"Chief?" Rowland said.

"I'm afraid I can't do it," she said. "Not without arousing a lot of suspicion."

"Well, have you ever stopped to assist a stranded motorist while transporting a prisoner?" he pressed.

Even if Josie had access to Kim, she couldn't trade her. Not even for the baby—or Luke. As much as she disliked her, Kim wasn't an object—a game piece—to be moved around. Josie hated men who treated people that way, particularly women.

"No," Josie said. "I haven't."

"Well," Rowland said, his polite smile back in place. "You think about it. We're due to meet at the police station in an hour. If you're able to work something out, perhaps you'll cancel today's meeting, and we can get in touch at another, more mutually convenient time."

One of the baristas slid a box of pastries across the counter. "Order for Quinn," she said loudly, as though Josie and Rowland weren't the only two people in the place.

"I'll see what I can do," Josie said, picking up the box.

With a nod, Rowland disappeared.

CHAPTER 60

"This is never going to work," Noah said.

"It will," Josie promised. She pushed the box of pastries from Komorrah's across her desk. Noah declined but Gretchen plucked out a gooey pecan-covered bun and bit into it. Josie pulled one of the coffees she'd bought from the cup carrier and took off the lid. The barista had given her a small paper bag of sugar, creamers, and stirrers. Josie dumped it onto her desk, put two sugars into her coffee and added half-and-half until the liquid took on a light caramel color. "I already talked to the district attorney and the sheriff. The sheriff was able to get me a phone call with Kim at the county jail," Josie explained. "She's in."

"Does she know Rowland?" Gretchen asked.

"She claims she doesn't, but who knows? Lying is the same as breathing for her."

"Did they show her a photo of Rowland?" Noah asked.

Josie sipped her coffee. "Yeah. She didn't recognize him."

"Then what the hell does he want with her?" Noah groused. "It can't be the videos she made of Dunn. They're meaningless now."

Josie picked at a cheese Danish. "Kim's fictional baby would have been Rowland's grandson."

Gretchen said, "But Kim only told Dunn she was having his baby to get away from him. I don't think it was common knowledge. Especially since she told him and then ran."

"Yeah, but Rowland had his own people keeping tabs on a lot of different players."

"You mean Nance," Noah said.

"Nance is the one we know about," Josie said. "Obviously, he was already watching Misty, waiting for her to give birth, because he snatched the baby from Denny Twitch. If Rowland has Luke that means Nance probably went to the church and killed Dunn's men. Rowland had eyes on a lot of different people—some of them from Dunn's organization. It's possible that word of Kim's pregnancy, false though it was, filtered back to him. I mean, we don't know how much surveillance he had on Dunn and his men or for how long. His donor children died within the last year. We don't know how long he was keeping tabs on them before causing their accidents."

"Still," Gretchen said. "This is a lot of trouble to go through to set up a trade for a woman who may or may not have given birth to your grandchild."

"This guy is all over the place," Noah said, picking up one of the other coffee cups. "I mean, he killed off his donor children, but he kept Luke alive. For what? Luke is no one to him."

"For leverage," Josie said. "He's kept him alive this long in case he needed him. When he outlives his usefulness, Rowland will find someone else just like Leonard Nance to dispose of him."

A heavy silence fell among them. Noah said, "We'll get Luke back, boss."

She could only hope. "Well, this is the best plan I could come up with between the coffee shop and here. Plus, the DA is willing to reduce the charges pending against Kim if she cooperates with us. Kim said she'll do whatever she can if it will help get Luke back."

"So now what?" Gretchen asked.

"I get in touch with Rowland and we set up the meet."

CHAPTER 61

The meet with Rowland was a logistical nightmare. Noah took every opportunity to remind her of this fact as they drove the route back and forth from the county jail to Denton Memorial Hospital. It had only taken one brief phone call to Rowland to set it up. Josie told him the only way she could move Kim was if she was sick—sick enough to have to be taken to the hospital. Josie assured him that she had already spoken with Kim, and that Kim believed she was coming down with something. Josie would transfer her from the county jail to the hospital within the next twenty-four hours. In his infuriatingly vague way, Rowland alluded to the fact that they might cross paths once Josie was on the way to Denton Memorial with Kim. He refused to agree to any specific meeting place. He poked around a bit more, wanting to make it clear that he expected Josie to come alone. "Well," she had told him, "with so many people searching for Victor Derossi and Trooper Creighton, I really don't have the personnel to have someone accompany me. I think I can handle getting one prisoner to the hospital by myself."

Rowland hung up happy. Josie had the worst case of butterflies in her stomach that she could ever remember.

"We have no idea where he's going to intercept you," Noah said, frustration hardening his tone.

"That's why we're doing a dry run," Josie said. "We'll pick the most likely spots and set up there. I've already asked the sheriff and the state police to assist so we've got bodies."

"And you don't think this guy is going to notice all these police personnel running around?"

"Once we mark the meeting sites, the crews will set up ahead of time, and a crew will go around making sure that nothing is too noticeable," Josie explained. "Noah, we have to do this. It's my only chance to get Luke and Victor back and hold Rowland accountable for what he's done."

"What if he doesn't admit to anything? You said yourself he wouldn't speak directly."

"He killed those people," Josie said with conviction. "I know he did, and he'll tell me what I want to know because I don't think he has any intention of letting me and Kim go. I think he intends for us to have an accident, just like his donor kids."

She felt Noah's eyes burning a hole in the side of her face. "Boss, I don't like this."

"Neither do I," she said. "But it's our best chance of stopping him and finding the baby and Luke."

"He won't bring them," Noah said. "If he wants Kim—for whatever reason—and he wants you dead, he's not going to bring them."

"I thought of that. If he doesn't bring them, maybe I can get him to tell us where they are. If we get him in custody, the DA is already willing to cut a deal with him if he gives up their location."

"He also wants to shut Trinity up," Noah pointed out. "Did you warn her?"

"I called her this morning. The sheriff is putting someone on her until we get Rowland in custody."

"*If* we get him in custody," Noah said.

Josie pulled off the road and onto a wide gravel lookout area. It was on top of one of the mountains that separated Bellewood from Denton. Red Hawk Lookout, a sign announced. She parked the car and they got out, walking to the edge of the lookout where a thigh-high aluminum barrier stood between them and the sharp drop-off to a tree-lined valley hundreds of feet below. Leaning over the barrier and looking into the vast canyon, Josie felt slightly dizzy.

"This is it," she said. "This is where he'll be."

CHAPTER 62

In the back of the Denton police cruiser that Josie had comman-deered, Kim Conway shifted in her seat. Josie heard the clink of her handcuffs and the rustle of her jumpsuit. Glancing in the rearview mirror, Josie could see her craning her neck to get a good look at the patch over her left breast where her inmate number was stitched. "Are you sure this thing is going to work? It's the smallest microphone I've ever seen."

Josie turned back to the road. "It works. The sheriff's guys tested it before we left. Don't mess with it, it's expensive."

"Where did you even get it?"

"We borrowed it from the FBI. I've still got a contact there. Apparently, it's the best small wireless communication system on the market. Rowland's own company developed it."

"Are you serious?"

"Ironic, isn't it?"

Both Kim and Josie had been fitted with wireless micro-phones that could fit on a pencil eraser. Kim's had been sewn in beneath her inmate number patch and Josie's was on the lapel of her jacket. Josie also had a small, clear receiver in her right ear, covered well by her hair, that allowed her to hear other members of the team. Noah was at a mobile command post, listening and recording their every move so he could give direc-tions to the teams on the ground at the three meeting sites Josie had chosen. She just hoped she was right about where Rowland would choose to intercept them.

"We're coming up on Red Hawk Lookout," Josie said, more for the benefit of the teams than for Kim. "It's around the next bend."

Noah's voice came back in her ear. "We've got eyes on," he said. "He's already there."

As she took the curve in the mountain road slowly, the lookout came into view. Josie saw Rowland's Mercedes-Benz and let out a long breath of relief. The butterflies in her stomach took flight as she saw Rowland leaning against the driver's-side door. The hood of the car was propped open. To anyone passing by, he would look like a man whose car had broken down. Josie panned the area but didn't see anyone with him. She pulled up behind his car and got out. His hair blew in the wind, and he took his sunglasses off and smiled tightly. As Josie got closer, she could see how stiffly he held himself. Gone was his signature poise; he was nervous, she realized. Because his muscle was missing? she wondered. Or because he had already disposed of Luke and the baby?

"Where are they?" Josie asked.

"Did you bring Miss Conway?"

"She's in the car. Where are Luke and Victor?"

Rowland didn't respond. *Shit*. She needed him talking. "You have them?" she asked, trying to get a verbal response. Nothing. Instead, he said, "Can I speak with Miss Conway first?"

Josie went back to the car and got Kim out. Although she didn't entirely trust Kim, she didn't want her hampered by handcuffs in case things went to hell, so she took them off. Grabbing her upper arm, Josie pulled Kim over toward Rowland. He extended a hand toward Kim. "I'm Peter Rowland," he said as she shook it.

"So I'm told," Kim said, shooting a sideways look at Josie. "What is it that you want from me?"

Rowland moved to the front of his car and closed the hood. He opened the passenger's-side door. "I'm hopeful we can discuss that in private."

"No," Josie said. "That wasn't the deal. You wanted a meeting, here she is. Whatever you need to discuss with her, do it here."

"I'm afraid I can't do that, Chief. It's a personal matter."

"I don't have any personal business with you," Kim said. "I don't even know you."

"She's a prisoner in police custody," Josie insisted. "I can't just let you take her."

This time, Rowland's smile looked almost menacing and, for the first time, Josie could see a definite resemblance between him and Eric Dunn. Kim must have seen it too because she shrunk away from him, pressing herself against Josie's side. "Did you really think this was just a meeting, Chief? This is a trade. That means I take her with me. I'm sure you'll think of something to tell your colleagues."

Josie didn't bother to address the absurdity of what he was asking. Instead she said, "If this is a trade, then where are Victor and Luke?"

"You'll have them once I take Miss Conway, and once I know that Trinity Payne has been convinced to keep quiet about what she's found."

Noah's voice sounded in her ear. "That's enough for a warrant. I'm sending a team over to Rowland's house now to search for them. Stand by."

"Well, we have a problem then, don't we?" Josie said to Rowland, trying to stay focused. "Because a trade isn't a trade if I get nothing in return for Kim, and I need time to talk to Trinity Payne. She found out a lot more, and it's going to be hard to convince her to walk away from a story this big."

A look of uncertainty flickered across his face. "What are you talking about?"

"She knows about all of your donor children and how they were murdered. She wants to air the story. It's going to take a lot for me to convince her not to, and I'm not sure I should bother if you're not going to hold up your end of the bargain."

"But we're already here. You said yourself it was extremely difficult to get Ms. Conway out of custody. There's no sense in your taking her back now," he said. He beckoned Kim toward him. "Come, Miss Conway, we have much to discuss."

"I'm not going anywhere with you," Kim said. "Chief Quinn is right. A trade is a trade. Why would I go anywhere with you when I already know you're a liar?"

"Because the alternative is prison, isn't it?"

"At least in prison I'll be alive," Kim said pointedly. "Leonard Nance—Leo—he worked for you, didn't he? You think I don't know what you hired him for? I've been around men like you before. I know how you operate."

"Men like me? Are you comparing me to Eric Dunn? I'm nothing like him," Rowland insisted.

"Sure you're not. Let's just forget about this. I'm not going with you if you're not going to hand over the baby and Luke to the chief."

Rowland motioned toward the open car door. "Fine, the chief can come too. I'll take you both to Luke and the baby."

Josie stared at him skeptically. "I'll take Miss Conway and we'll follow you."

"I'm afraid I can't agree to that," Rowland said. "Look." He took off his suit jacket and turned in front of them. "I'm not armed. I'm sure that you are, though—right, Chief? You've got the advantage. You both come in my car. I'll take you to Luke and the baby."

"Tell me where they are," Josie said. "I can call and have a team sent there while we wait."

"I'd rather not involve your team," Rowland said. "Please, let me take you to them. Then I'll take Miss Conway, you can talk to Trinity, and we can put this matter to rest."

"Hey, did you even hear me? What if I don't want to be part of this trade?" Kim asked, just as Josie had instructed her. She didn't want Kim to seem too eager. "I'm not going anywhere with you." To Josie she said, "Take me back to the jail."

She turned and walked back toward the cruiser. Rowland said, "You're my daughter."

Kim froze, then turned slowly and stared at him. "What?" she said.

Josie said, "She wasn't on the donor list. She's not a donor baby."

"No," Rowland said. "She's not a donor baby. But she *is* my child." He looked at Kim. "Your mother and I had an affair when we were very young. We met in New York and bonded over the fact that we had both come from Denton. Things progressed between us, but she loved her husband and wanted to make a go of it with him. I didn't find out until much later that she had had a baby—you."

"That's not—that's impossible," Kim blurted.

"No, not impossible," Rowland said. "I had deep feelings for Zora."

At the mention of her mother's name, Kim's eyes widened. "When I found out you might be mine, I had just started having some success in my business. I went to her. I wanted to get married and have a life together, but she refused. Her husband was dead by then, but she couldn't move on. She refused to give anyone in Denton the satisfaction of knowing they'd been right about her—that she had gone off and gotten pregnant by another man and tried to pass the baby off as her husband's. She clung to her secrets, my dear."

Revulsion stretched across Kim's face. "But Eric . . . the chief told me that he was your son as well."

Rowland grimaced. "I know. I'm sorry. That was an unfortunate coincidence."

Kim leaned over. "I'm going to be sick."

"I'm so sorry, my dear. Truly I am. But you couldn't have known."

"You're lying," Kim spat.

"No, I'm not. Kim, you are the only true heir to my fortune."

"You had all your donor children killed," Josie said. "Why

should we believe that your intentions toward Kim—assuming she really is your daughter—are good?"

"Because my donor children were not good people," Rowland blurted out.

"What?" Kim and Josie said in unison.

Josie hoped to God they were getting this on the wireless comm. As if reading her mind, Noah's voice crackled through. "We're hearing this. Keep going."

"What do you mean?" Josie coaxed.

Rowland sighed. "My donor children. They were . . . horrible, terrible people. Aaron King? That's when I first knew something was wrong. I hadn't given much thought to what happened to my donation until he was caught, and I saw footage of him on the national news going back and forth from court. He looked just like me. In fact, I got calls all day long from friends and work colleagues joking about the resemblance. 'Hey, Peter, did you know you had a serial-killer son in Pennsylvania.' It was all a big joke, except it wasn't. I knew he actually might be my son. So I had someone hack into the sperm bank records and then the records of various fertility clinics. I tracked down one after another to find that they were all bad, bad people. You've seen the news—you've probably heard it directly from Trinity. King is believed to be responsible for over thirty deaths in Pennsylvania."

Josie pointed a finger in his direction. "Are you telling me that you tracked down your donor children and had them all killed because they're bad people?"

"Not just bad people," Rowland explained. "Criminals. Murderers. Thieves. Liars. I had to set things straight."

Josie barely believed what she was hearing. "Set things straight? By *killing* them all?"

"It was my fault they were even in existence. Without my sperm donation, none of them would be here. Look at the havoc Dunn and King alone have wreaked on so many innocent people. I had a son in Newark who worked at a community center.

He had charges pending against him for physically abusing one of the children in his care. They had it on video. There was a boy in Philadelphia who was charged with armed robbery. A girl in Pennsylvania who routinely started fires and had charges pending for arson. She was not a good person and the path she was on...she wasn't going to reform. Don't you see, none of them reform. It's in their DNA."

"If it's in the DNA, why should we believe that you won't try to kill Kim?"

Kim stared at him, waiting for the answer. He looked from Josie to Kim and back again. He spread his hands in a pleading gesture. "She wasn't a donor child. She was born out of love. The right way. I loved her mother. Just like I loved my Polly's mother. Don't you see, she's like my Polly. Innocent. They are pure. Please. Kim is all I have left. That bastard took my Polly. Kim, please. You're all there is of my legacy. You're all that's left that's good."

Josie wished she could tell him that Kim wasn't pure at all. She would claim self-defense, but she still had no issues pulling the trigger. She also lied as easily as she breathed. But that wasn't important. They were getting what they needed from him to put him away.

"You knew about me my entire life," Kim said. "And you didn't care about contacting me until all your other kids were dead? Until your precious Polly was gone?"

"I'm sorry, but your mother made me promise. You can ask her. She made me swear that I would never approach you."

"Why did you have that Leo guy tell me you were interested in what I knew about the building collapse?"

"He thought it was the only way you would feel safe going with him," Rowland explained. "Kimberly, please, I'm sorry for all the subterfuge, but we're here now. Please come with me."

Kim stood up straight, her dry heaves having subsided. She gave Rowland a calculating stare—and it was in that expression that Josie could see the resemblance between the two. "Fine," she relented. "I'll go with you, but you have to tell the chief where Luke and the baby are."

"Okay," Rowland replied.

"And we will call my mother to confirm all this," Kim added.

"Of course."

"And I want it out in the public. I'm your heir. You're going to put me in your will and everything."

"Done," Rowland said.

"What is the official story?" Josie asked. "If I let you take her from my custody?"

"As I suggested, she got so ill that you pulled over. She overpowered you and ran away. I found her wandering around in the woods and turned her back in. I'll arrange for her to have the best lawyer money can buy. She won't spend any time in prison."

At this, Kim nodded.

Noah's voice came through again in Josie's ear. "Rowland's house is clear. No sign of Luke or the baby."

"Where are they?" Josie asked for what felt like the hundredth time.

Rowland gestured toward the open door to his Mercedes once more and, with a look at Josie, Kim walked over and folded herself inside. Josie knew they wouldn't get very far. The moment they pulled away, one of her teams would be in pursuit.

"Behind my home, in the woods, is a cottage. You can't get there by car but there is a walking path. It's a half mile back. They're there."

Noah's voice crackled. "We're on it."

"Once I have eyes on them," Josie told Rowland, "I will speak with Trinity. Maybe I can convince her that a better story is you being reunited with your long-lost daughter."

"This town needs some good news," Rowland agreed. "Thank you, Chief."

"See you soon," Josie said. She watched them pull away.

Noah said, "We've got eyes on Rowland and Conway. We're in pursuit. Stand by."

"What about the cottage?" Josie said, feeling a little strange talking into the open air.

"The team is almost there."

Josie got into her car. As she turned the keys in the ignition, her hands shook. She had to remind herself to breathe. She was trying to figure out how long it would take for her to get to Rowland's house when Noah's voice came back. "Boss, they're not here. The cottage is empty. Team one is already in pursuit of Rowland."

Josie gunned her engine. "I'm going after him," she said.

CHAPTER 63

Spraying gravel from beneath her back tires, Josie flew out of the lookout, her foot pressed against the gas pedal. The winding road went on for several miles and she was confident that Rowland would still be on it. Her speedometer jumped upward and she white-knuckled the steering wheel, taking the curves as fast as she could without losing control of the vehicle. She spoke into the silence of the car. "Noah, do you have eyes on Rowland?"

"They're following him. He's driving erratically."

She flew past a mile marker and read it off to him. "How close am I?"

"You should come up on them around the next bend. A half mile."

Josie's Escape tore around the next curve in the road, coming up fast on the unmarked car her officers were in. She slowed behind them and looked ahead. Rowland's Mercedes-Benz jerked violently from side to side.

"What the hell is going on?" she said.

"They're arguing," Noah said. "Boss, Rowland lied. It's not good. He—"

But Josie stopped listening as Rowland's vehicle jerked once more to the left, the wheels on the passenger's side lifting from the ground. In an instant, the small car flipped over onto its roof, crashing through the guardrail and rolling down the steep embankment, out of sight. The sound of metal crunching and glass shattering split the morning silence of the lonely road.

"Oh my God," Josie said.

In front of her, her officers pulled over and hopped out. Josie followed suit. They ran to the edge of the road, standing amidst what was left of the guardrail. It wasn't a sheer drop-off like Red Hawk Lookout, but it was steep, and Josie estimated the car had rolled the length of a football field. It looked tiny crumpled below them, thin wisps of smoke escaping from its mangled hood. It had, at least, landed upright, the driver's side crushed against three tree trunks.

"Let's go," Josie said. "We have to get them out of there in case the car catches on fire."

They started picking their way down toward the car. The smoke thickened as they approached. The smell of burning metal, rubber, and chemicals clung to the back of Josie's throat. Suddenly, one of her feet slid in the grass and she fell, tumbling the rest of the way down, her body scraping over rocks, twigs, and glass from Rowland's Mercedes-Benz. She landed a few feet from the car, her breath coming in labored gasps. From above, her officers shouted. She waved toward them to indicate she was okay and rose to her feet. Blood streamed from a gash on the back of her right hand. She swiped it on her jeans. Her whole body felt bruised and shaken, but aside from the gash she didn't think she was injured. She moved to the car. Peter Rowland's side was crushed against the tree trunks, so Josie tried the passenger's-side door. It opened with a groan and Kim Conway tumbled out. Her blond hair glittered with pieces of glass, and thin streams of blood leaked from her scalp down her face. Josie laid her out flat on the ground and felt for a pulse. It was strong.

"Kim," Josie said. "Can you hear me?"

Her eyes opened. She tried to take a deep breath and moaned in pain. "Stay still," Josie told her. "Just keep still, okay? We're getting you help."

Kim lifted an arm toward the car. Josie had to put her ear to Kim's lips to hear her words. "He lied."

"I know," Josie said.

As her officers reached the scene, Josie climbed into Rowland's car. Glass crunched under her kneecaps as she maneuvered across the passenger's seat. Rowland was slumped over the steering wheel, his arms slack at his sides. Josie pressed two fingers to the side of his neck. "Thank God," she mumbled when she felt his faint pulse. She turned her head and yelled to her officers, "We need two ambulances!"

"On their way, boss," one of them hollered back.

Josie nudged Rowland's shoulder. "Wake up," she said. "Mr. Rowland."

The smoke from the hood now formed a thick, black column. Heat radiated from the front of the car. The smell was unbearable. Josie tried to unlatch his seat belt, but the mechanism was stuck. "Son of a bitch," she said. "Mr. Rowland, I need to get you out of this car."

No response. She pulled at his shoulders. His head lifted. Blood trickled from his ear. An ugly bruise was already darkening his temple. She turned and yelled for one of her officers. "I need a knife!"

One of them poked their heads into the car. "We don't have one, boss," he said.

"Then help me," Josie yelled. "Help me get him out of here before this car goes up."

He squeezed inside with her and together they tried to pull Rowland out of his seat. The strap that went over his chest was easy enough to extricate him from, but his lower body was stuck under the taut lap belt. Both Josie and her officer were covered in sweat and coughing. "Boss, we can't stay in here. This car is going to explode. It's not safe."

Josie clutched Rowland's shoulder. "I can't leave him here."

They tried pulling him again, but he was stuck. In the distance, sirens blared. "I'll see if one of the EMTs has a knife," her officer said, scrambling out of the car.

Josie shook Rowland. His head lolled. Lightly, she slapped

his cheek. They couldn't wait for the EMTs. There was no time. Fire engulfed the hood, leaping toward the windshield, flames licking the inside of the car where the glass had broken. "Rowland," Josie shouted. "Where are they? Where are Luke and Victor?"

She slapped him again. His eyes opened to narrow slits. She cupped his cheeks with both hands, turning his head toward her, keeping it still. She shouted into his face. "Where are they? Where are Luke and the baby?"

His eyes glanced to the windshield. Fear enlivened them for a split second. He looked back at her. "This is your last chance," she told him. "Do the right thing. Where are Luke and the baby?"

"P—Puh—Patio . . . Mo—"

Something beneath the hood of the car exploded, shooting flames and engine parts upward. Josie felt an arm circle her waist and pull her back, out of the car. Then she was being dragged back up the rocky, debris-strewn hill. She heard shouting and sirens and the roar of the fire as it engulfed Peter Rowland's vehicle. As her body bounced along the uneven terrain, she craned her neck, twisting her body to watch as Rowland was swallowed up in the flames and smoke.

CHAPTER 64

Gravel bit into her back. She stared upward at the blue sky, watching billows of black smoke roll across her field of vision. Noah's face swam into view. He pressed something cold over her forehead. She closed her eyes, just for a moment, focusing on his touch. Next, he reached for her hand. She felt something cold and stinging flow over the gash and then something warm and dry pressed into it. She cried out in pain.

"So you are still with us," Noah said.

Her body erupted into a coughing fit. Noah helped her turn onto her side as sooty saliva and vomit gushed out of her. He rubbed her back as her body spasmed. When she finished, he slipped an arm around her waist and lifted her to standing. She leaned against him. The smell of burning was so strong, she didn't think she'd ever get it out of her skin or hair. "Did you pull me out?" she asked.

"Someone had to." He gave her a pained smile, and she realized she must be in pretty bad shape because he didn't even bother to scold her for nearly dying in the car.

"Did Kim survive?" she asked.

"She's in bad shape, but yeah, she's on her way to the hospital. Gretchen's going with her. The sheriff's team will process this scene."

She already knew that Rowland perished in the fire. "He said the word patio," Josie said. "Before you pulled me out of the car. I was trying to get him to tell me where Luke and the baby were. He said patio."

Noah frowned. "Patio?"

"Patio Mo—that's all I heard."

"Mo?"

One of the EMTs walking past said, "The Patio Motel, maybe? We get calls for that place twice a week."

Josie and Noah exchanged a look. She knew the place. They'd busted more prostitutes and drug addicts there than anywhere else in the city.

"Let's go," Josie said.

CHAPTER 65

The Patio Motel lay just off the interstate on a weed-infested asphalt slab. The motel's two floors boasted sixteen rooms in total—eight on each floor. Some of the doors still had their metal silver numbers nailed in the center of the bad green paint job. Others had long ago lost their numbers. It looked like the motel staff had simply scribbled the numbers onto the doors with a thick black Sharpie. Parking spaces lined up in front of the two-story eyesore. A few older-model cars filled in about half the spaces. An empty in-ground pool sat between the parking lot and the motel office. Half of it was filled with trash. In the other half, someone had started a garden—dropping in some dirt and planting a few scraggly looking flowers.

Josie and Noah arrived with both state troopers and sheriff's deputies in tow. Josie waited at the car as Noah jogged over to the office. The place was like a ghost town, but Josie knew that no one who frequented the Patio would show their faces to a parking lot full of cops. While she waited for Noah, she popped her trunk and pulled out her bulletproof vest, strapping it on. Her body felt sore from her tumble down the embankment and then her bumpy ride back up. She had no doubt when she finally got a shower, her body would be covered in bruises. The troopers and deputies followed suit. Soon they were armed and amassed in the parking lot, ready to breach some doors.

Noah emerged from the office, holding up four fingers as he trotted over. "Manager recognized Leonard Nance from his driver's license photo. Says a few days ago, Nance rented a room for the week, paid cash, double the rate for privacy."

"How'd you get the manager to talk?" Josie asked.

"I told him the faster he told me what I needed to know, the faster we'd get out of his hair. He doesn't like the police presence." Noah grinned, and in his hand a key appeared.

Josie smiled. Her first genuine smile of the day. "Let's go," she said.

In front of Room 4, Josie and Noah lined up with two state troopers across from them, guns drawn, prepared to breach the door. The sheriff's deputies were covering the back of the building. Ignoring the frenzied beat of her heart and the tightness in her shoulders, Josie used her bandaged hand to slide the key into the lock and turn the doorknob. Once the lock disengaged, the four of them moved through the door, sweeping the room and shouting "Police!"

It was empty.

The room was small and stunk of sweat, vomit, and excrement. A full-size bed took up most of it, sitting across from a small dresser with a television on top of it. Images from a sitcom played on mute. The bed had been stripped down to its sheets, the gaudy green-and-pink comforter bunched up at the foot of it. There were drops of blood scattered over the sheet and what looked like a vomit stain on one side. On the nightstand next to a lamp was a brown prescription bottle and three empty baby bottles with what looked like remnants of formula congealing in their bases. Wedged between the window and the bed was a threadbare mustard-yellow armchair. A sheet was bunched up on its seat. On the floor in front of it was a rectangular blue laundry basket. In the bottom of it someone had stuffed a pillow.

"That's where they were keeping the baby," Josie said.

"Jesus," Noah said. He held a hand over his nose.

"Dirty diapers in the bathroom," called out one of the troopers.

As Josie maneuvered around the bed, her foot caught on

something sticking out from beneath. She dropped to her knees and peered underneath. A lump formed in her throat. There sat a white sneaker with a blue Nike swoosh on its side. Luke's other sneaker. She stood back up, feeling dizzy and fighting tears. "They were here," she said. "Dammit. They were here."

Noah had put on a pair of latex gloves. He held up the prescription bottle. "It's from a pharmacy in New York City. Oxycodone for a Marie Muir."

"Marie," Josie said. "Rowland's housekeeper."

"Not a housekeeper," Noah said. "A babysitter."

"Chief Quinn," came a shout from outside. One of the sheriff's deputies.

Josie ran outside to see one of the deputies several doors down where a small alley led to the rear of the hotel. He waved her over and she followed him behind the motel. It was more cracked asphalt littered with trash, weeds, broken glass, and needles. A grime-covered green dumpster sat along a chain-link fence. Beyond that was a barren strip of land that stretched a quarter mile before it terminated at the concrete barrier blocks that separated the land behind the motel from the eastbound lanes of the interstate. Beyond those were the westbound lanes. Tractor trailers and cars zoomed past in both directions. The wind whipped Josie's hair.

"There's someone out there," the deputy said. He pointed beyond the fence to the highway. "Westbound." Sure enough, in the center of the lanes of the westbound interstate, a figure loped along, half-limping, half-running. He held his hands to his chest as he moved. Horns blared as car after car narrowly avoided him. He was too far away to see clearly, and his back was to them, but Josie would know the shape of his body anywhere. For a second, she couldn't catch her breath. She tried to say "Luke," but her throat didn't work.

"He probably climbed through that hole in the fence right there," the deputy was saying. "Gonna get himself killed." On his shoulder, a police radio squawked.

"Call in some units," Josie said. "And get Lieutenant Fraley out here."

She was through the hole in the fence in seconds, her feet pounding through the dirt as she ran alongside the concrete barriers. "Luke!" she screamed, but her voice was swallowed up by the noise of the vehicles thundering down the highway. He had maybe a half mile on her, and her lungs still ached from the fire. She stopped momentarily, chest heaving, and shed her bulletproof vest. Without it, she was able to move much faster. The moment there was a break in the eastbound traffic, she hopped the concrete barriers and raced across the lanes to the shoulder of the westbound lanes. As she gained on him, she saw he was running barefoot. He must have stepped in glass on his way out to the interstate because bloody footsteps trailed behind him along the white line dividing the lanes.

"Luke!" she screamed again but he didn't hear her. He kept lurching along, oblivious to the vehicles swerving around him, their horns screeching.

Where the hell was he going?

They were coming up on an overpass that crossed the Susquehanna River. An eighteen-wheeler roared past, and the highway shook beneath her feet. Opposite Josie, Luke stumbled toward the edge of the overpass. He reached the barrier and leaned against it. She was close. She just had to cross the lanes without getting crushed by a car or truck. Josie glanced behind her and saw Noah in the distance, running along the shoulder of the eastbound lanes. When she turned back toward Luke, he was climbing onto the barrier.

"No!" she screamed. "Luke!"

He stood, wobbling, trying to balance on the edge, and glanced back at her. There was something wrong with his hands, she realized. They were both badly swollen, the skin taut, shiny and pink. Bloody welts circled his wrists. His face was bruised in various shades of blue and purple, one eye swollen nearly shut. Blood crusted along his bottom lip. Their eyes met across the highway.

Josie yelled, "Don't!"

He said something, but the sound was drowned out by the traffic passing between them. Then he turned his head back toward the river, crossed his arms over his chest and stepped off the barrier.

CHAPTER 66

Josie sprinted across the highway, narrowly missing being crushed by a pickup truck. Her chest was so tight, she wheezed as she braced herself against the concrete barrier and looked over it into the river. Below her, the current carried Luke away, downriver. He was paddling awkwardly, but it was clear that he was struggling. Again, she wondered what the hell he was doing, and then a flash of bright color farther down the river caught her eye. Several yards downriver from Luke, another person bobbed. Josie squinted and made out long, dark hair. A woman. She floated face up and on her chest was the brightly colored object that caught Josie's eye.

"Oh God."

It was a bright-blue baby carrier. Nausea rocked Josie's stomach. Had the woman jumped off the overpass with the baby strapped to her, like Luke? She looked down, trying to measure the drop. It was mid-hurricane season and the river was high. An adult would easily survive a dive from the height of the overpass, but a newborn? Josie panned the shoreline, hoping the woman had run down the embankment instead of jumping with the infant. What looked like a small white blanket or perhaps a pillowcase fluttered from the low branch of a tree. Her eyes found Luke again. His head disappeared under the water. Josie counted off the seconds. After five, she saw the top of his head again. His arms flopped around. He was going to drown.

Josie pulled off her holster and shoes, mounted the barrier, and jumped.

Her body sliced into the water, a cold jolt to her senses. Her legs kicked until she broke the surface. Legs working, she spun around in the water, getting her bearings, until she spotted Luke's floundering form ahead. Luckily, the current was moving fast. In smooth, even strokes, she swam toward him. Her lungs burned. A cough threatened to erupt from her. She slowed momentarily, willing her body not to dissolve into a coughing fit. She was almost there. Finally, her fingers brushed his T-shirt. Another powerful kick beneath the water brought her within reach, and she clutched the fabric at the nape of his neck, pulling him toward her. His body thrashed.

"Luke," she rasped. "It's me. Josie. You're okay. I've got you."

She hooked her arms under his armpits, holding him close as his body stilled. For a few seconds they floated together in the water. Luke said, "The baby."

"I know," Josie told him.

"You have to get the baby."

"I will."

"Go now."

"I can't. I can't leave you, you'll drown. I'm taking you back to shore."

"There's no time for that."

Josie looked downriver, but the woman and Victor were just a small dot bobbing toward the horizon. Rapidly moving out of her reach. Denton PD, the Alcott County sheriff, and the state police were en route, but none of them knew that Marie Muir had gone into the river with the baby. The overpass wasn't even visible anymore. They wouldn't know to try to head the woman off farther down the river. Josie was a good swimmer and, with the current carrying her along, there was more than a good chance she could catch up to the woman. But she couldn't get Luke to shore and pursue the woman. There wasn't enough time for both. If she lost the woman, she lost Victor Derossi. If he was even still alive.

"You have to," Luke said, as if reading her mind. "Josie. You have to. It's Ray's son. I should have told you. I'm sorry. That baby is Ray's son. You have to go after him."

Tears stung the backs of her eyes. She moved out from behind him so that they were face to face. The shoreline tore past as the current whipped them along. She paddled with her feet as she clutched the sides of his face. "Noah was behind me. I'm sure he saw me jump in. He'll come after me. He'll find you."

"Go," Luke said.

Josie pressed a kiss against his mouth and, before she could change her mind, she pushed away from him, turning onto her stomach and swimming as fast as she could toward Marie Muir and Victor Derossi.

CHAPTER 67

Josie kept her eyes on Marie Muir's head as it bounced along with the current. She had to keep going. The summer had just ended and, although the temperatures had been cooler, the water was not yet freezing. Still, the river was cold, and it couldn't be good for a newborn to be in it for very long. That was assuming he didn't drown. Josie pushed her body, but her limbs felt loose and jelly-like. Her lungs were on fire. It got harder and harder to take in air. She felt like someone was squeezing her, crushing her torso. Her vision grayed.

Then she heard it. A faint wail.

Adrenaline coursed through her, propelling her arms and legs through the water with renewed vigor. As she drew closer, Victor's angry wails grew louder. Unfortunately, there was no sneaking up on the woman. Marie, who was floating along on her back with the baby in his carrier on her chest, spotted Josie. Panic crossed her pale face. Her hands shot out and started paddling, putting more distance between her and Josie.

"Stop!" Josie yelled. As soon as the word was out of her mouth, she realized how ridiculous she sounded. There was no stopping in the middle of a river.

"Get out of the river," Josie hollered instead. "Swim to the shore."

Marie's arms splashed harder. Josie's legs scissored through the water, catching up to her. Without a baby strapped to her chest, Josie had the advantage. She was almost within reach.

"Marie," Josie spluttered. "Swim to the shore."

She grunted and slapped Josie's hands as Josie reached for the baby carrier. "Get away from me."

Josie stopped clawing at the carrier. "Fine," she said. "Give me the baby. Just give me the baby. I don't care who you are or where you came from, and I don't care what you've done. Just give me the baby."

Marie labored to breathe as her arms flapped, trying to get away from Josie. Up close, Josie estimated her to be in her sixties. Floating was easy, but if she had to swim Josie didn't think she would get very far. Her lined face was already an alarming shade of white.

"Stop paddling," Josie said. "Conserve your energy or you'll drown. I'm not here for you. Just give me the baby."

Marie slowed her efforts and resumed floating. Bundled on her chest, the baby heaved in time with her breath. He let out a few more healthy wails for good measure.

"Please," Josie said. "He's freezing to death out here. Let me get him out of the river."

After what seemed like an eternity, Marie slid one of the straps down her arm, then the other, pulling the carrier away from her torso. She turned it over so Victor was faceup, floating on his back in the carrier. Relief coursed through Josie.

Then Marie pushed Victor away from both of them and started swimming for the shore.

"Son of a bitch," Josie cried.

She lunged toward the carrier, her fingers brushing one of its straps. Victor's high-pitched howls spurred her on. She couldn't get this close and lose him. Not now. Not like this. With a final kick, she snatched one of the straps. She pulled the carrier to her and swam like hell for the shore.

It took several tries to get her footing on dry land. Exhaustion weakened every limb. Little Victor was screaming now. There were no houses or docks along this stretch of river. Only trees. Her sense of disorientation was overwhelming. She had no idea how far they had traveled or where she was—were they even still in Denton? Josie got her footing and placed the carrier on the ground so she could extricate Victor. He squirmed as she lifted him out of it. His tiny face was purple—Josie didn't know if the color was from his crying or from cold, or both, but she clasped him close to her chest and ran.

Her wet socks slid down her ankles, catching on twigs and rocks as she ran. The sound of Victor's shrieks was drowned out by her own gasping breaths and her blood rushing in her ears. When she finally reached a two-lane road, she fell to her knees. She panned her surroundings but saw no homes or buildings of any kind. She was trying to decide which way to go when the sound of a vehicle approaching drew her attention. From her right side, an old red pickup truck lumbered along the road. Josie stumbled to her feet, clutching Victor to her chest with one hand and waving the truck down with the other.

The brakes squealed as the truck stopped a few feet from her. A man in his fifties with thinning brown hair and glasses looked out the driver's window, his mouth forming a perfect O. Josie could only imagine what she must look like. She scurried over to the passenger's side and climbed into the truck. The man's head swiveled in her direction. "I just rescued this baby from the river. He's wet and freezing. We need to get to the hospital."

Wordlessly, the man took off his jacket and handed it to her. He reached up and twisted the dial to turn up the heat. Then he made a U-turn and sped down the road. Josie was vaguely aware of him shooting her repeated glances as she placed Victor in her lap and stripped down to her bra. Next, she peeled off Victor's wet onesie and dropped both their wet clothes onto the seat beside her. She picked the baby up and held him against her chest, skin to skin, then she pulled the man's jacket over both of them. Hot air blasted from the dashboard vents. Beneath the jacket, Josie stroked Victor's tiny back. Eventually, exhausted, his cries subsided, and he fell asleep cocooned against her.

CHAPTER 68

At Denton Memorial's ER, Josie pulled the Good Samaritan's jacket around her shoulders and paced outside of a glass-walled room while a doctor and three nurses checked out Victor Derossi. His screams pierced the air, making passersby pause in front of the room and stare inside. One nurse smiled at Josie as she passed and said, "That sounds like a hungry cry." What it sounded like was that someone was torturing the poor infant, but Josie realized the nurse was probably right. They had no idea when he last ate.

"Boss." Noah appeared beside her, soaked and covered in mud and leaves.

Without thinking, Josie grabbed him in a tight hug. She released him in time to see a flush color his cheeks. "Did you get him? Did you find Luke?"

He smiled. "I got him. He's fine. They're working on him now down the hall. He's in bad shape but he's alive."

Josie sagged against him and he slid an arm around her waist, guiding her down the hall a few paces to a chair. She tried to hold back her tears but a couple of them leaked out. Noah walked away and reappeared seconds later with a wad of tissues in his hand. Josie took them, mumbling a thank-you, and concentrated on pulling herself together. Both Luke and Victor Derossi were alive and safe. She took a few deep breaths and dabbed at her eyes.

Noah asked, "How is the baby?"

"Pissed."

Noah walked up to the glass and peeked inside. Josie followed, looking over his shoulder. Mercifully, one of the nurses was shaking a bottle full of formula. The other nurse swaddled the baby and scooped him off the stretcher, holding him expertly in the crook of one arm. She took the bottle from her colleague and rubbed the nipple across Victor's lips. He took it into his mouth greedily, quieting finally. Glorious silence descended on the ER. The doctor emerged from the room. "He's fine," he told Josie. "Remarkably. There don't appear to be any injuries, no signs of illness or even dehydration. No hypothermia. No fever. He's... perfect. Whoever had him took good care of him. No ill effects from his swim."

Josie's shoulders slumped with relief. "Thank you," she said.

"We'll keep him overnight just to monitor him. Does he have a parent or guardian who can come stay with him or do we need to call child services?"

"No," Josie said quickly. "You don't need to call child services. We'll find a family member." Once the doctor left, she told Noah, "See if Misty's friend can come. If she can't do it, I'll call Ray's mom."

"Ray's mom? Boss, you don't even know for sure if that's Ray's baby."

Josie stared at the bundle in the nurse's arms. They had put a little blue hat on his head. Josie could just make out the pink of his forehead from where she stood. "That's Ray's son all right," she said. She didn't know how she knew, but she did. Confronted with him, she thought she would feel sad or betrayed in some way. Misty had a piece of Ray that Josie would never know. She had done something that Josie had never been willing to do—that Ray had never wanted her to do. Josie had been certain she'd feel somehow inadequate seeing Ray's son, but all she felt was a sense of protectiveness and relief like she had never known. She had no idea what kind of mother Misty would make, and still she questioned the wisdom of bringing a child into the world whose father was both already dead and a social pariah, but none of that mattered. Not just then. What mattered was that she had found the baby, and he was alive.

She waited for Noah to argue with her about possibly calling Kay's mother. Instead he made a phone call to Brittney. Josie could hear her squeals of joy from five feet away. "I guess she can come stay with him," Josie said when they hung up.

Noah smiled.

"Did you get Muir?" Josie asked.

He nodded. "Sheriff picked her up. She started talking as soon as she found out Rowland and Nance were dead. Apparently, Nance put a pretty good scare into her. Told her he'd kill her and everyone she knew if the police found the baby. That's why she ran when she saw all the police vehicles outside."

"And Luke followed her. Tell me, did she say if she jumped off the overpass?"

"Nah, she went down the embankment. I think Luke jumped because it was faster."

"He was right. So Muir was taking care of the baby and Luke."

"She's a retired nurse from Brooklyn. Rowland paid her quite a large sum of money to look after a baby for a couple of days. They actually were at Rowland's house until a few days ago. She says a man named Leo came and took some kind of cheek swab from the baby. Then Leo came and took the baby, dumped her at the Patio Motel, and later brought Luke. She felt bad for Luke so she gave him some of her pain meds that she gets for chronic back pain from a car accident. She says she didn't know who the baby or Luke were."

"Bullshit," Josie said. "I'm sure she had a television in the motel room."

"Well, we'll let the DA deal with her," Noah said. "Gretchen's over there overseeing everything while the evidence response team processes the motel scene."

"How's Kim?"

"She has some fractures and a bruised sternum. She had

pretty good lacerations to her scalp and leg, lost a lot of blood. Concussion."

"She survived." As little as Josie cared for Kim Conway, she was glad that Conway had survived the accident. "Do we know what caused the accident?"

Noah took out his phone. "Yeah. Kim and Rowland were arguing when they went over the embankment. Things got heated. I had the sheriff's office email me the segment from the comms from inside the car, after Rowland pulled away. It's best if you just listen."

They had no headphones so they found a unisex bathroom and locked themselves inside. They stood nearly forehead to forehead with the phone between them as Noah queued up an audio file. It started out as dead air. Then they heard Kim's voice. "All of those things you promised me back there—you could make those arrangements through an attorney. I mean you're rich, right?"

Rowland replied, "Quite rich, yes, and I could certainly make all the arrangements to legitimize you as my heir without ever seeing you in person."

"So you could have sent me back to the prison with Chief Quinn."

"Indeed. I should have sent you back with her. This is going to cause a bit of trouble for her, I'm afraid."

Kim said, "Then why am I here? It's a little late for you to swoop in and play daddy dearest."

Rowland laughed. "Oh, Kimberly, I'm not interested in being your father."

Kim's voice sounded slightly anxious. "What do you mean?"

"Did you really believe all that nonsense back there about you and Polly being pure because you were products of love?"

"What are you saying?"

"I'm saying I lied, my dear. You're quite familiar with the practice."

"Wh-what about Polly? Your other daughter?"

Rowland made a *hmmph* sound. "Polly was a born psychopath. From a very early age she was incorrigible. My wife refused to see it. Even after she pushed one of her schoolmates down a flight of steps. That girl will never walk again thanks to my Polly. I know she did it on purpose. She told me so. Took millions to keep that quiet. She had no remorse, and her mother stood by her."

"Did you—did you kill them? Polly and her mother?"

"The driver who hit them had some very serious gambling debts. The kind that were causing his family members to be killed. I paid off his debts, sent him off to tie enough of a load on to be over the legal limit, and then told him which corner to be on and when. He's been well compensated. He'll be out of prison in a few years with good behavior and have quite the tidy sum set aside to live out the rest of his life. His family is safe, and he can't rack up gambling debts while he's incarcerated."

"My God."

"And you—you think I don't know what kind of person you are? I went to your mother again when you were twelve. This was before I married my wife. I wanted to give it a chance. She told me all about the lying and the stealing."

"But I—"

"Save it. Please. I know you spent a year in juvenile detention."

"You knew about me my whole life. Why am I the last one?" Kim asked.

"It wasn't until I found out about Aaron King that I realized the scope of what I'd done—what I had allowed to be brought into the world. It was only after he was caught, and I knew he was my son, that I knew I needed to rid the world of my bad seed. I saved you and Eric for last. You were always visible, easy to find. The others were harder to track down. I wanted to lock down the casino contracts before I got rid of Eric, but Leonard screwed that up. He killed Eric too soon. But I had him keeping watch over you and Eric long enough to find out that you had pretty much whored your way through every male in Eric's organization. Chief Quinn believes you killed Denny Twitch and Leonard, which makes you a murdering whore."

Kim's voice shook. "I was Eric's prisoner. I did what I had to do to stay alive. No, I'm not proud of every choice I made, but I'm still here."

Rowland laughed again. "Not for long, my dear."

"What will you tell the chief? What about Trinity Payne?"

"I need only make arrangements to silence them."

"You're going to kill them?" Kim asked.

"Only if they do not accept my very generous offers."

"You mean bribes."

"Call it what you will. I don't like slaughter, but I'll do what I have to do to protect myself."

"You don't like slaughter? How many people have you killed?"

"None," Rowland said.

"Oh, right, you don't get your hands dirty. 'Cause you're such a good person, right?"

"I saved Trooper Creighton, didn't I? I could have left him to die at that church, but he was innocent in all this, and Victor Derossi—he'll be returned to his mother eventually."

"Eventually?" Kim asked. "They're not where you said they were, are they? You lied. You're a liar and a killer, and you think I'm a bad person? You think all your children were terrible people? Did you ever wonder where they got it from?"

Rowland's voice was raw with either anger or passion, Josie wasn't sure. "I am taking responsibility for what I've created! Unlike any of you little assholes, I am trying to make the world a better place."

"Well, this is a pretty fucked-up way of doing that, *Dad*," Kim snapped. "I don't think you give a shit about the world. I think you only care that none of us get our grubby hands on your empire. I think you care about your own legacy more than you care about anything."

"It doesn't matter what you think," Rowland said. "No one will ever suffer at the hands of one of my children again, and if my legacy remains intact, it's an added bonus."

There was silence. Josie watched the seconds on the audio file tick off. Thirty seconds, forty seconds, forty-three seconds. Then came the sound of rustling, what sounded like slapping and some grunts. "Stop!" Rowland shouted. "What are you doing? Stop that!"

More sounds of a struggle. Rowland yelled, "Let go! Let go of the wheel! You'll kill us both. Goddamn—"

The recording went dead. Josie and Noah looked at one another for a long moment.

Josie said, "Make sure the DA gets this, okay?"

"Sure thing."

"You know where to find me," Josie told him, and left him in the bathroom to call Carrieann.

CHAPTER 69

Carrieann met Josie at Denton Memorial's Emergency Department. Standing side by side, they waited outside a glass partition as a nurse hooked Luke up to an IV. He was passed out cold, exhausted from his ordeal and the pain meds they were pumping into him. Josie had had a chance to speak to the doctor but not Luke.

"He's badly dehydrated," Josie said. "Almost all of his fingers are broken. A few bones in each hand. Apparently, Dunn's goons used a hammer on him. Because he was hiding Kim, they thought he knew where the baby was and tried to beat it out of him. Anyway, the ER staff is waiting for the hand surgeon. He's finishing up an operation now, and then they'll get Luke up there. Try to fix what they can."

Carrieann shook her head. Tears streamed down her face. "Bones'll heal," she said. "He's still alive." She reached out a hand and Josie squeezed it. Carrieann met her eyes. "But let's not do this again, what do you say?"

Josie laughed. "I'm on board with that."

CHAPTER 70

Luke sat propped up in his hospital bed, a tray table full of food in front of him. Both his hands were heavily bandaged. He stared longingly at the tray. With his right hand, he nudged his fork. Josie watched from the door for a few seconds before she walked over and picked it up, stabbing at the turkey breast and bringing it to his lips. She fed him in silence for several minutes. Finally, he shook his head to indicate he'd had enough. "Thank you," he said.

She nodded and sat in the chair beside his bed. It was going to be a long recovery for him. For them both. He would need a lot of care. Possibly a visiting nurse. As if reading her mind, Luke said, "Carrieann said I can come stay with her for a while. She has enough people to work the farm that she can look after me pretty much twenty-four seven. I'm thinking of taking her up on it."

Josie was surprised at the disappointment that flooded through her. Especially since the truth was that deep down, she hadn't expected their relationship to survive. Not something like this. Too many lies had been told. And she knew that when she found out the truth of what happened between him and Kim Conway, it would deal the death blow to whatever remained between them. Tears welled in her eyes. She looked down at her lap. "Are you sure you want to leave?" she said.

"Josie, there's something you should know."

She looked up. "You slept with Kim."

He turned his head away. "I'm sorry," he said. "I am truly, deeply sorry. I never meant for things to get this...out of control."

"You should have come to me," Josie said. "After all we went through together? You didn't think you could come to me?"

His brow furrowed. "I've never been put in a situation like that before. I know I made some bad choices, and then it was one bad choice on top of another, until I was in so deep I knew I couldn't get out of it without ruining my life—and maybe even yours."

"I was going to be your wife," she said. "You should have trusted me. Instead, you shut me out."

"I'm sorry. I truly am."

"Why?" Josie asked. "Why didn't you come to me? You were so cold, so distant. It was like I couldn't reach you."

"I'm not the only one who's closed-off, Josie."

She narrowed her eyes. "What's that supposed to mean?"

He gave her a wan smile. His tone wasn't accusatory. Just sad. "You think I don't know about all those dark memories you've buried? About all the things you keep bottled up in that crazy head of yours? You don't let me in either."

Josie stood, feeling her stomach drop to her ankles. "You don't know what you're talking about."

He shook his head, laughing softly. "There you go, getting defensive. Josie, I'm trying to talk to you. I'm sorry I wasn't open with you, but you're not completely honest with me either. You don't tell me things. You come off just fine, and you handle all your shit, but whatever happened to you when you were a kid—it did some damage. But you never trusted me enough to let me in, to let me help you."

A single tear slid down her cheek and she swiped at it furiously, hating herself. She pointed a finger at her chest. "Because I don't need help. There is nothing wrong with me."

"Why don't any of your closets have doors, Josie? Huh? What is the scar on the side of your face really from?"

"None of your goddamn business."

He nodded, as if in agreement with something. "Right. It's none of my business. We're supposed to get married, and you won't tell me anything about you."

"Stop making this about me," Josie snapped. "I'm not the one who lied, who covered up a triple homicide, who hid a murderer and a liar in my home for months. I'm not the one who cheated. I've done nothing wrong."

"You've never lied to me?"

"No, I haven't."

"How many times have you been to Ray's grave? Ballpark? How many times just in the last month?"

"Don't you talk about Ray."

"Oh, right, I can't talk about Ray. I can't bring Ray up. Ray knew all your secrets. Ray is dead, and you still love him more than me."

Josie felt something inside her soften. Another tear slid down her cheek. Her voice cracked when she spoke. "That's not true."

Luke held up his bandaged hands as if in surrender. "It doesn't matter. I don't think we would have worked—not in the long run. I'm sorry." As he spoke, Josie could see small beads of sweat forming along his hairline. His face turned ashen. "Do you—do you need pain meds?" she asked. He nodded, his breath coming harder. Josie fled to the hallway to find his nurse. When they returned, he was vomiting on his tray.

"Oh dear," the nurse said. She pumped some meds into his IV while Josie got him cleaned up. "I gave him something for the nausea, too," the nurse said before leaving them alone again. Josie sat back in the chair, watching him doze and trying not to cry. Once he was snoring, Josie left to get some air and a cup of coffee. She returned an hour later, and he was awake, staring sightlessly at the television on the wall. He gave her a weak smile when she came in.

"Sorry," he said. "The pain...it's..."

"I understand," Josie said. She didn't sit down.

"I'm sorry," Luke said again. "For the way things turned out. I love you, you know. I really do."

"I believe you," Josie answered. She leaned in and planted one long, final kiss on his mouth. She was almost through the door when she stopped and turned back. "Luke, did you send Kim to Misty Derossi's house?"

"No," he said. "I didn't know where the hell she went until she came back and told me that she had been there and that one of Eric's guys took the baby."

"Thought so."

"Kim said she told Misty that I sent her there and that if Misty helped her, I would be more inclined to do what she wanted, which was to talk to you about the baby being Ray's. You have to understand, Kim is very manipulative and can be very convincing when she puts her mind to it. I wouldn't put it past her to have talked Misty into a home birth."

"Oh, I'm aware of how manipulative she is," Josie said. "What did Misty want to talk to you about? When you met with her at Foxy Tails and she came to your house?"

"Mostly about Ray's baby, but I'll let her tell you. That's what I should have done in the first place."

CHAPTER 71

Misty was two floors up from Luke. Josie knocked softly on the door before stepping inside. "You came back," Misty said, smiling. One side of her face still drooped. With her free hand, Misty reached up and touched her cheek. "Temporary paralysis," she explained. "They said it should come back. It will take a lot of therapy, but they think I'll get full function back."

Josie took a step closer. "That's good."

"Never thought I'd be happy to see you," Misty commented.

Josie nodded. "Same here." She looked around the room. "Where's the baby?"

"Oh, he's home with Brittney. She's going to bring him back in a few hours. My neighbor, God bless her, is going to watch him while Brittney gets some sleep."

"That's great," Josie said.

"I know we haven't always been . . . the best of friends," Misty said. "But thank you for what you did."

"It's my job," Josie replied.

Misty laughed. A thin stream of drool leaked from the drooping side of her mouth. "That's what Ray always used to say. 'It's just my job.'"

"You miss him," Josie said. Her own heart ached for him nearly every day, and she was still furious with him. She wondered if those feelings would ever go away, or at least quiet.

"Yeah," Misty said. "Like crazy. Listen . . . about Victor."

"I know," Josie said. "He's Ray's son."

"Luke told you?"

"No. I found out while I was trying to find him. Listen, Misty, it's okay. I'm okay with it, all right?"

"Are you just saying that because I look...like this?" She laughed again, and more drool spilled from the corner of her mouth. Josie plucked a tissue from the box on her night table and handed it to her. Misty dabbed at her face.

"No," Josie said. A war still waged inside her—the sense of unreality she had at having been the love of Ray's life yet not being the one to bear his child, set against the instant feeling of connection she had had with the baby from the moment she held him in her arms. "Look, it doesn't matter. Ray would want me to be okay with it. You understand?"

"Thank you."

Josie nodded, feeling awkward. "Luke said there was something else you wanted to talk to me about, but he said he would let you tell me."

Misty squeezed the tissue in her hand, squeezing and releasing over and over again. "Please don't take this the wrong way," she said, and Josie felt a groan rise up inside her. She kept silent, though. Misty continued, "The thing is I used up all my savings on the *in vitro*. I know that Ray had life insurance. I was wondering if there was anything left or if there was anything left from his estate to help with...Victor. I hate to ask, but...well, I definitely can't go back to dancing after this."

A small ember of anger flared inside Josie, but she reminded herself that, for whatever reason, Ray had fallen in love with this woman. His dying wish was that Josie respect that—and her—however much Josie detested her. "Ray did have a small life insurance policy," Josie said. "I used some of it to pay for his funeral after his mother made the arrangements, and the rest I gave to her. That's what Ray would have wanted. As far as the estate goes, there was no estate. We were still married, so everything automatically went to me. When I say everything, I basically mean our house. That was all we had, and it was heavily mortgaged. I didn't get much from the sale of it."

"Oh," Misty said, slumping against her pillows.

Josie felt acid rise in her throat. A voice in her head told her to turn around and leave the room and never come back. This was not her problem. But she could hear Ray, as clearly as if he were standing beside her. *Come on, Jo.*

Josie squeezed her eyes closed, counted to five, and opened them again. "But listen," she said, the words uncomfortable in her mouth. "I'll help however I can, okay? On two conditions."

Misty's eyes brightened with hope. "What are they?"

"You have to tell Ray's mom. She's had a hard life, okay? That's her grandson. She deserves to know him—and she'll help you. I know she will. Let her be a part of this."

Misty nodded. "Okay. I promise. What's the other condition?"

"You can't name that baby Victor."

"What?"

"Victor. You named him after Ray's dad, right?"

"Yes, that's right."

Josie took a deep breath. "Ray's dad used to beat Mrs. Quinn. Badly. He wasn't all that nice to Ray either. I can tell you one hundred percent that Ray would not want his son named after his dad."

Misty's good hand flew to her chest. "Oh my God. Oh no. I didn't know. I'm sorry. I—"

Josie reached out and touched Misty's arm. "It's fine. You didn't know. Not a big deal. But you haven't filled out his birth certificate yet, right?"

"No, I haven't."

"Then you'll choose another name."

Misty was silent for a long moment. "How about Harris?" she asked finally. "After the chief? Harris Raymond Derossi."

Josie smiled. "Or Harris Raymond Quinn."

"Really?"

Josie gave a half shrug. "He's Ray's son."

"Thank you," Misty said.

Josie patted her arm again before leaving and said words she never thought she would say to Misty Derossi. "Keep in touch."

CHAPTER 72

Kim Conway was discharged from the hospital after two weeks and was being held at the Alcott County Jail pending the reduced charges against her in the death of Denny Twitch. The DA was investigating what had really happened at Brady and Eva Conway's house as well as the murder of Leonard Nance. Josie heard that they were planning to charge both Kim and Luke with obstruction and abuse of a corpse for the business with Kavolis. Carrieann told Josie that Luke was resigned to whatever happened and was ready to be held accountable. Josie hoped for his sake that he would be able to make some kind of plea deal and avoid actual jail time. For certain his law enforcement career was over. Kim would most definitely avoid jail time once she got her hands on Peter Rowland's assets. Word was that a high-powered lawyer had already been retained to make sure she was named Rowland's sole heir. Josie still had mixed feelings about Kim, but there was little she could do but give the DA all the evidence and let the prosecutor do his or her job.

Trinity Payne ran with the entire story, which turned out to be bigger than the Interstate Killer, and her face was now on every news program on every channel that Josie could find. Only HBO gave Josie some relief from Trinity's face.

She spent almost two days in bed after the donor children story broke, finishing off a bottle of bourbon. Everything wedding-related she could find in her house was searched out and disposed of. Her engagement ring was hidden deep in the recesses of her jewelry box where she couldn't possibly get a passing glimpse of it—right next to her old wedding ring. Once the need to booze and cry wore off, she started cleaning. She scrubbed every surface in her house, vacuumed every square inch of carpet, even the corners, the steps, and beneath furniture. She rearranged everything so that each room looked different. She changed her kitchen cabinets around. Then for the next day she kept going to the wrong cabinet for her coffee mugs and banging her shins on furniture that wasn't where it had always been.

She had just cracked her knee on the corner of her coffee table two evenings after her major house overhaul when there was a knock on the door. Limping to open it, she snapped on the overhead light to her front stoop to see Lisette, Noah, Gretchen, and Dr. Feist packed closely together on her porch. "Surprise!" they yelled in unison. It was then that Josie noticed a bottle of champagne in Gretchen's hands, balloons tied to Lisette's walker, a sheet cake in Dr. Feist's arms, and flowers bunched against Noah's chest.

"What is this?" Josie asked. She suddenly wished she wasn't wearing sweats and three days of unwashed hair.

Lisette pushed her way through the door, the balloons smacking against Josie's face on the way past. As Josie batted them away, everyone else stepped inside. Noah handed her the bouquet of flowers. "Those are from Trinity," he said. "She wanted to be here, but she's on CNN tonight."

Josie followed them into the kitchen and watched in stunned silence as they went to work setting her table, ferreting out wineglasses, and putting candles pulled from Dr. Feist's jacket pocket into the cake.

Lisette glanced over her shoulder and smiled at Josie. "You forgot, didn't you?"

Josie stepped forward and looked at the cake. Blue icing spelled out "Happy Birthday, Boss!"

"It's your thirtieth birthday," Lisette reminded her.

Noah said, "We ordered food. Should be here any minute."

Josie looked around at them all, for the first time since Ray's death feeling something, ever so small, fill the void that he had left in her life and her heart. "Thank you," she said huskily.

A LETTER FROM LISA

Thank you so much for choosing to read *The Girl With No Name*. If you enjoyed it, and want to keep up to date with all my latest releases, just sign up at the following website. Your email address will never be shared, and you can unsubscribe at any time.

LisaRegan.com

If you've returned for this second installment of Josie Quinn's adventures, I want to thank you from the bottom of my heart for sticking with her. I know there are so many amazing books out there to read, so I really appreciate your spending your time with Josie. If you're new to the Josie Quinn series, thank you for giving it a try. I hope you enjoyed it! I hope you'll stick around for Book 3 when we get to find out much more about Josie's past.

I love hearing from readers. You can get in touch with me through any of the social media outlets below, including my website and Goodreads page. Also, if you are up for it, I'd really appreciate it if you'd leave a review and perhaps recommend *The Girl With No Name* to another reader. Reviews and word-of-mouth recommendations go a long way to helping readers discover one of my books for the first time. As always, thank you so much for your support! It means the world to me! I can't wait to hear from you and I hope to see you next time!

Thanks,
Lisa Regan

LisaRegan.com

@LisaRegan

Lisa-Regan

ACKNOWLEDGMENTS

As always, I must first thank my wonderful readers. Thank you for reading, reviewing, and recommending my books to others. Thank you for your relentless enthusiasm, which keeps me going.

Thank you to my husband, Fred, and daughter, Morgan, for keeping me motivated to finish this book and for knowing exactly what to say whenever I got frustrated. Thank you to my parents: William Regan, Donna House, Rusty House, Joyce Regan, and Julie House, my constant and ardent companions on this amazing journey. Thank you to my most trusted friends and first readers, all of whom are incredible writers: Nancy S. Thompson, Dana Mason, and Katie Mettner. You ladies are my lifeline, and I could not do this without you! Thank you so much to Torese Hummel for your passion, honesty, and willingness to help me become a better writer! Thank you to Susan Sole for so many words of encouragement and support—always coming when I needed it most. Thank you as well to the following friends and family members who cheer me on and spread the word without fail: Melissia McKittrick, Ava McKittrick, Andy Brock, Kevin and Christine Brock, Michael J. Infinito Jr., Carrie A. Butler, Helen Conlen, Marilyn House, Dennis and Jean Regan, Laura Aiello, Tracy Dauphin, and the Tralies, Conlen, Funk, and Regan families.

Thank you so very much to Sergeant Jason Jay for once again answering so many of my police work questions in such great detail. I am in your debt!

Thank you to the incomparable Jessie Botterill for always pulling the best out of me and being such a staunch advocate for my work. I am so grateful to the entire team at Bookouture, including Oliver Rhodes, Kim Nash, and Noelle Holten for working so hard on my behalf. Major thanks to Alex Logan, Kirsiah McNamara, Alli Rosenthal, and the entire team at Grand Central Publishing for continuing to make my dreams come true! I am so humbled to be working with two such fabulous publishing teams.

ABOUT THE AUTHOR

Lisa Regan is the *USA Today* and *Wall Street Journal* best-selling author of the Detective Josie Quinn series as well as several other crime fiction titles. She has a bachelor's degree in English and a master of education degree from Bloomsburg University. She is a member of Sisters in Crime, International Thriller Writers, and Mystery Writers of America. She lives in Philadelphia with her husband, daughter, and Boston terrier named Mr. Phillip.

For more information you can visit:
LisaRegan.com
Facebook.com/LisaReganCrimeAuthor
Twitter @LisaLRegan

THE
POWER
OF
Praying™
Together

STORMIE OMARTIAN
WITH JACK HAYFORD

HARVEST HOUSE™ PUBLISHERS
EUGENE, OREGON

Scripture quotations are taken from the New King James Version. Copyright
©1982 by Thomas Nelson, Inc. Used by permission. All rights reserved.

Cover by Koechel Peterson & Associates, Inc., Minneapolis, Minnesota

Harvest House Publishers, Inc., is the exclusive licensee of the trademark THE
POWER OF PRAYING.

THE POWER OF PRAYING™ TOGETHER
Copyright © 2003 by Stormie Omartian with Jack Hayford
Published by Harvest House Publishers
Eugene, Oregon 97402
www.harvesthousepublishers.com

Library of Congress Cataloging-in-Publication Data
  Omartian, Stormie.
      The power of praying together / Stormie Omartian and Jack Hayford.
        p. cm.
      ISBN 0-7369-1003-4 (pbk.)
    1. Prayer groups. 2. Prayer—Christianity. I. Hayford, Jack W. II. Title.
BV287.O43 2003
248.3'2—dc21   2003006807

  03 04 05 06 07 08 09 10 / BP-KB / 10 9 8 7 6 5 4 3 2 1